PRAISE

THE ACCIDEN

"A fast-paced, amusing tale starring an engaging lead couple and the return of the previous stars. Lighthearted, fans will laugh at the scenarios that the OOPS squad confronts due to Jeannie's out-of-control wishes."

—*Midwest Book Review*

"The OOPS team faces a peculiar problem in the newest wisecracking and wacky novel from the always delightful Cassidy. The dialogue is fast and furious, the characters are offbeat, and the situations bizarre, but Cassidy pulls it all together for another laugh-filled adventure."

—*RT Book Reviews*

ACCIDENTALLY DEAD, AGAIN

"The dialogue in this book is fast and furious. Cassidy's quirky and offbeat series continues to be outlandish fun laced with a hint of poignancy. There's never a dull moment with this bunch!"

—*RT Book Reviews*

"I really loved this book from beginning to end. From the start I fell into a daze with the characters' quips and quirks . . . This book is great at intertwining a great plot with quirky characters espousing wonderful dialogue, which just happens to be funny."

—*Night Owl Reviews*

"Do yourself a favor and go buy everything that Dakota Cassidy has ever written . . . This book is not only well written, with a twisty plot and great characters, it is hysterical. HYSTERICAL! . . . The characters are over-the-top but hilarious, and you really do care about them and their situations, which makes this paranormal romantic romp even more wonderful."

—*Fresh Fiction*

continued . . .

ACCIDENTALLY CATTY

"This light, comedic paranormal romance delivers simple, unencumbered entertainment. A lively pace, the bonds of friendship, and bright humor aided by vampiric sarcasm make for a breezy read with charming characters and no shortage of drama. Cassidy's fans are sure to enjoy this, while newcomers will be reminded of MaryJanice Davidson's or Kimberly Frost's work." —*Monsters and Critics*

"I have been a fan of Dakota's since *The Accidental Werewolf*, book one of this series. I loved all of the books in the series, but I think this book is my favorite . . . *Accidentally Catty* is very funny, cute, and sexy." —*Night Owl Reviews*

"A fun read with some meat to it that will have people looking at you, wondering why you're laughing, if you're out in public." —*Fresh Fiction*

ACCIDENTALLY DEMONIC

"The Accidental series by Ms. Cassidy gets better and better with each book. The snark, the HAWT, the characters, it's all a winning combination." —*Bitten by Books*

"An outstanding paranormal romance . . . Dakota Cassidy delivers snappy dialogue, hot sex scenes, and secondary characters that are just too funny . . . *Accidentally Demonic* is a hold-your-sides, laugh-out-loud book. With vampires, werewolves, and demons running around, paranormal romance will never be the same." —*The Romance Readers Connection*

"Dakota Cassidy's books make me laugh and laugh. They are such great fun that I always look forward to the next one with gusto . . . I totally loved this book with a capital 'L.'" —*Fresh Fiction*

The Accidental Human

"I highly enjoyed every moment of Dakota Cassidy's *The Accidental Human* . . . A paranormal romance with a strong dose of humor."

—*Errant Dreams*

"A delightful, at times droll, contemporary tale starring a decidedly human heroine . . . Dakota Cassidy provides a fitting twisted ending to this amusingly warm urban romantic fantasy."

—*Genre Go Round Reviews*

"The final member of Cassidy's trio of decidedly offbeat friends faces her toughest challenge, but that doesn't mean there isn't humor to spare! With emotion, laughter, and some pathos, Cassidy serves up another winner!" —*RT Book Reviews*

Accidentally Dead

"A laugh-out-loud follow-up to *The Accidental Werewolf*, and it's a winner . . . Ms. Cassidy is an up-and-comer in the world of paranormal romance." —*Fresh Fiction*

"An enjoyable, humorous satire that takes a bite out of the vampire romance subgenre . . . Fans will appreciate the nonstop hilarity."

—*Genre Go Round Reviews*

The Accidental Werewolf

"Cassidy, a prolific author of erotica, has ventured into MaryJanice Davidson territory with a humorous, sexy tale." —*Booklist*

continued . . .

"If Bridget Jones became a lycanthrope, she might be Marty. Fun and flirty humor is cleverly interspersed with dramatic mystery and action. It's hard to know which character to love best, though—Keegan, or Muffin, the toy poodle that steals more than one scene."

—*The Eternal Night*

"A riot! Marty's internal dialogue will have you howling, and her antics will keep the laughs coming. If you love paranormal with a comedic twist, you'll love this book." —*Romance Junkies*

"A lighthearted romp . . . [An] entertaining tale with an alpha twist."

—*Midwest Book Review*

More Praise for the Novels of Dakota Cassidy

"The fictional equivalent of the little black dress—every reader should have one!"

—Michele Bardsley, national bestselling author of *Only Lycans Need Apply*

"Serious, laugh-out-loud humor with heart, the kind of love story that leaves you rooting for the heroine, sighing for the hero, and looking for your own significant other at the same time."

—Kate Douglas, author of *Dark Wolf*

"Expect great things from Cassidy." —*RT Book Reviews*

"Very fun, sexy. Five stars!" —*Affaire de Coeur*

"Dakota Cassidy is going on my must-read list!" —*Joyfully Reviewed*

"If you're looking for some steamy romance with something that will have you smiling, you have to read [Dakota Cassidy]."

—*The Best Reviews*

Berkley Sensation titles by Dakota Cassidy

YOU DROPPED A BLONDE ON ME
BURNING DOWN THE SPOUSE
WALTZ THIS WAY

KISS & HELL
MY WAY TO HELL

THE ACCIDENTAL WEREWOLF
ACCIDENTALLY DEAD
THE ACCIDENTAL HUMAN
ACCIDENTALLY DEMONIC
ACCIDENTALLY CATTY
ACCIDENTALLY DEAD, AGAIN
THE ACCIDENTAL GENIE
THE ACCIDENTAL WEREWOLF 2: SOMETHING ABOUT HARRY
THE ACCIDENTAL DRAGON

THE ACCIDENTAL DRAGON

DAKOTA CASSIDY

BERKLEY SENSATION, NEW YORK

THE BERKLEY PUBLISHING GROUP
Published by the Penguin Group
Penguin Group (USA) LLC
375 Hudson Street, New York, New York 10014

USA • Canada • UK • Ireland • Australia • New Zealand • India • South Africa • China

penguin.com

A Penguin Random House Company

This book is an original publication of The Berkley Publishing Group.

Library of Congress Cataloging-in-Publication Data

Cassidy, Dakota.
The accidental dragon / Dakota Cassidy.—Berkley Sensation trade paperback edition.
p. cm.
ISBN 978-0-425-26863-6 (softcover)
1. Paranormal romance stories. I. Title.
PS3603.A8685A625 2015
813'.6—dc23
2014040085

PUBLISHING HISTORY
Berkley Sensation trade paperback edition / February 2015

PRINTED IN THE UNITED STATES OF AMERICA

10 9 8 7 6 5 4 3 2 1

Cover illustration by Katie Wood.
Cover design by Diana Kolsky.
Interior text design by Kristin del Rosario.

Acknowledgments

To anyone who's ever picked up one of the Accidentals, thank you. Thank you for the amazing journey they've taken me on. Thank you for the love you've shown my girls over these last seven years. Thank you for the laughter. Thank you for the indescribable joy I've experienced when a fan asks me the infamous Accidental question, "Is this in my color wheel?"

Thank you to the fans for the many hours you've allowed me to spend holed up in my writing cave, creating utterly implausible, foul-mouthed paranormal accidents. Thank you for the emails, good and, yes, even bad.

Thank you to everyone involved behind the scenes in the making of an Accidental: my editor, Leis Pederson; my agent, Elaine Spencer; and the incredible Accidental cover artist, Katie Wood.

Thank you to all my friends who plotted with me over the years. Thank you to my sons, my mother, my dad, my amazing husband for so many years of support while I wrote each new edition.

Thank you, readers, for giving this real-life "accidental author" the chance of a lifetime.

And always, thank you, Nina, Marty, and Wanda.

You're forever my girls.

Forever and ever amen.

CHAPTER 1

"Did you hear me, Tessa?" McAllister Malone asked, tamping out a pile of embers with his foot in his best friend's sister's store, Auntie Q's.

"Oh, you were heard," Tessa Preston replied, her full lips compressing, then thinning into a sharp slash of a line on her soot-covered, water-streaked face.

"I said I was sorry." *Sorry I set the store you work your ass off for on fire*. On. Fire.

"Three times in the last three or so minutes. Noted and appreciated."

Mick gazed down at her in concern, lifting what was left of one of his eyebrows. "You counted?"

Tessa waved a hand under her nose to ward off the stench of burnt electrical wiring. "I like numbers. They soothe me when I'm stressed. It's a hyper-focus thing."

"Understood."

"More appreciation." Her response, still filled with rational words, held only a twinge of sarcasm.

That worried him. "Tessa," he coaxed, looking for the usual signs her crank had officially been yanked. He knew she was angry. But right now, maybe due to her shock, her behavior seemed practically catatonic as she floated in and out of the clear need to give him hell and the inability to do so for the magnitude of what he'd done.

So he tried to get a rise out of her again. "C'mon—say something. Call me a slug—or what was that thing you screamed at me the other day? You said I was a—a—"

"An overbearing penis wielder," Tessa provided with a scowl, clenching her fingers together in a fist. Then the haze she'd been nursing seconds ago clouded her bright eyes again, and her hands relaxed.

Mick nodded his head and gave her a thumbs-up with an encouraging grin. "Yeah. That was it. As always, clever comeback, T. So go ahead. Let's get your scream on." He rolled up the charred remains of his sleeves, almost the only bit of material left of his now backless shirt, and mimicked a boxer's stance to try to get the kind of rise out of her he was accustomed to. His feet stuck to the sopping-wet floor as he got into position. "I'm ready. Let's do this, Sugar Ray."

Instead of reacting, Tessa took a shuddering breath. With her fingertips just resting on her bottom lip, she spoke in a hushed whisper. "Fire . . ." Her eyes, darting and wide-eyed, scanned her trashed antiques store, Auntie Q's.

"Biiig fire," Mick agreed, spreading his arms wide, still waiting for her to explode. "Like, bonfire. Five-alarm, maybe."

She gave him a dazed, glassy-eyed glance instead. "Flames . . . so . . . many. Soooo . . ."

"Bet that pissed ya off, huh?" He poked at her verbally, hoping she'd respond like the crouching tiger she was.

But hidden dragon she remained. Though her feet did shift in the puddle of water she stood rooted in, as though she wanted to summon the wherewithal to clock him but couldn't due to shock. "Die," Tessa stated, dull and monotone, spitting out more water dribbling down her face.

"As in, once you catch your breath and get past the shock, I'm going to?" Mick inquired sweetly, letting a subtle taunt grace his words.

Tessa gulped, then breathed in and out. "Bloody. Very bloody. Entrails and organs everywhere. Promise."

Mick chucked her under the chin and winked. "Excellent, my fine she-warrior. I wait with the kind of girlish anticipation only organ-riddled battles can bring. Until we don our swords, got any more full sentences in you?"

Tessa let her cheeks puff outward. When she gazed up at him, her eyes were wild with an unspoken rage, which meant she was warming to the idea of killing him.

Yet her words were still stilted and eerily wooden. "McAllister Malone. No. Words."

Mick pondered that momentarily. Tessa out of words? Nah. She was just catching her breath before she spewed a mouthful of rude name-calling. Or maybe her lack of lung power had something to do with the coughing fit that had wracked her body just moments ago.

Undoubtedly induced by smoke inhalation.

At this stage of the fiery hell he'd created, he should be gearing up to argue a Tessa rant—loud and proud while he chuckled to goad her on. He hated to admit it, but he got a kick out of arguing with his best friend's sister.

They'd been doing it for over twenty-five years. But today . . . well, today, if—or better yet, *when*—she blew her top, he'd have to get on board with "Team Tessa." He deserved every rude comment about his genitalia and his big doofy feet she could creatively put together. Until then, Mick just didn't know what to do with her freakish composure.

"You think you can put a time frame on when exactly I should prepare for your big windup? I'd feel much better if I at least knew it was actually coming," Mick goaded her through a thin veil of smoke. "This rational, verbally challenged Tessa is like an extra in *Invasion of the Body Snatchers*."

Tessa spread her arms wide, making small black clouds appear from under her armpits. For a second or two, Mick thought she'd come out swinging, guns loaded. Her throat worked, taking in gulps of air, and her mouth opened with a squeak.

However, rather than let fly all those heinous pet names she'd given Mick over the years, she bit the tip of her fingernail. That meant she was trying to keep from crying. Tessa would rather die than cry in front of him.

In what Mick knew was an effort of sheer will, Tessa managed to hold up her finger to indicate he should wait for it.

Mick winced, waiting.

She cleared her throat and smiled up at him. The phony smile she used when she was going to sink his battleship. "After this, I think I should be allowed an unlimited amount of time to build up my rage, Mick. I want to be sure it's hot and fresh out of the kitchen when I finally let you have it. Until then, I have customers." She tilted her head in the direction of the ladies who'd entered at the exact moment of his fiery impact.

The three stunned women who'd happened upon Tessa's antiques store, Auntie Q's—while on a road trip, if he'd overheard right—stood rooted to the floor, their mouths wide open with surprise on their soot-blackened faces. They'd remained silent until now.

But the pretty brunette with the singed wavy long hair who was dressed like a man in work boots, a red hoodie, and a sweatshirt that read I KNOW VIOLENCE ISN'T THE ANSWER. I GOT IT WRONG ON PURPOSE didn't stay that way for long.

She slapped the arm of her jacket to put out a lingering flame. When she spoke, she, too, articulated with an eerie calm. "Goddamn it, Wanda. We can't even go on an all-girls, no-damn-rugrats flippin' vacation anymore. Would you just look at this shit?" She swung around, her finger taking an accusatory position when she thrust it under a pretty blonde's nose. "Marty? I blame you. I don't know how many times I said I didn't want to look for shit that has not just a fat-ass price tag but cobwebs, too, in stupid Vermont, while we sat by a roaring fire and drank hot chocolate with those mini-marshmallows I can't even goddamned eat. We could have been snowboarding by moonlight, but nooo. Instead you have me picking through used crap from the Stone Age in a state that should have been named the Ice Age."

The blonde shifted positions, taking a defensive stance that made her heeled brown boots with the still-smoking fur rub together. Her hair stood up on end as though she'd stuck her finger in a live socket, and her presumably once-white tie-waist jacket was what some would call well-done.

Yet she lifted her chin defiantly, her blue eyes blazing, the clink of her multiple gold bracelets making a racket as she shook her finger right back at her friend. "They're antiques, heathen. If you had an ounce of culture in all that pissed off, you'd recognize their beauty." She followed her statement up with an angry poke to the brunette's shoulder.

The brunette grabbed her finger and twisted it, snapping her teeth together with a menacing crack. "*This* is fucking beautiful?" she crowed, stomping on a reprint of a melted Grandma Moses painting with her stained, soot-covered work boot.

In response, a puff of smoldering ashes in orange and blue rose and fell in fluttering flecks of color.

The third woman, chestnut-haired and elegantly dressed in a knit dress and dark shawl, pushed her way between the two women. She reminded Mick of Grace Kelly, her stature long and tall, her carriage willowy and reeking class.

Mick noted that somehow, in all the rubble surrounding her, and even with a burnt patch in her shawl the size of the black hole, this woman managed to look collected. "Ladies!" Then she hacked a cough—because, well, Mick conceded, the smoke had been thick.

She cleared her throat and straightened, cocking her chin upward. "We're in a public place. Granted, that public place is experiencing some disharmony, but we're still in public. Behave as such. And excuse me, but OMG, it's almost like the universe sent us an engraved invitation, girls. Clearly," she whispered, partially covering her mouth with her gloved hand and leaning into her friends, "I believe, after what we just saw go down, we have a *paranormal crisis* here."

Mick wiped his mouth on his forearm to rid himself of the horrible aftertaste lingering on his tongue. It tasted like he'd eaten a fireplace whole. And apparently, he was "in" some kind of crisis. Whether it was whatever she'd labeled it was debatable. "You have a what?"

She dug inside her melted black purse and pulled out a gold business card while giving him a genuine smile. "You, sir, are in paranormal crisis. That's what we specialize in. We're sort of paranormal counselors, if you will. And aren't you a lucky duck that we just happened to be here?"

The brunette snorted, tightening her tattered hoodie around her lean face. "Yeah. Lucky, lucky, lucky. I'm never fucking going on vacation with you two crazies again."

The elegant woman slipped the twisted remnants of her mangled purse back over her forearm, where it dangled precariously, the balance of it now gone due to its untimely death by blowtorch.

Holding her hand out to Mick, she ignored the brunette completely, tripped on a broken stool, then righted herself. "I'm Wanda Schwartz-Jefferson. This mouthy abomination to your ears is Nina Blackman-Statleon, and this over here is her sparring partner, Marty Flaherty." She waved a dismissive hand in the direction of the other women like she'd done this introduction a hundred times before.

Mick wiped the soot off his hands onto his jeans before shaking hers. "Mick Malone, and the store's owner, Tessa Preston." A black cloud of smoke followed his words, shooting from his mouth without warning. He frowned.

So curious.

While Tessa shook Wanda's and her friend's hands with stiff fingers, Mick held up the card Wanda had given him, and by the glow of the one pile of burning antique armoire still not completely tamped out, read, "OOPS—an Out in the Open Paranormal Support group, serving all your paranormal crisis needs." "Paranormal crisis?" His eyes shifted to Tessa, wary.

Hers returned a vacant stare in response, and she remained silent. But her puckered goldfish lips began forming. The same lips she'd used when he'd pulled her pigtails as a kid or, later in life, when she'd disapproved of his prom date, Francine Lewbowski.

Nina bumped his arm with her shoulder, making him, at almost six feet six and 234 pounds, jolt forward. "Yeah. You read that right. Now, here's the short of it, and believe me, it's gonna be short because I'm sick and fucking tired of repeating the same bullshit over and over. But first, you're a dude, so do me a solid?"

Mick stared down at her, frowning, still stuck on the words *crisis* and *paranormal*. "A solid?"

"Yeah. A solid. Figures someone from the Ice Age—er, I mean, *Vermont*—wouldn't know what that is. It's like a favor. Here's the favor. Shut the fuck up and don't whine. Being a dude, you're supposed to keep all your girly crap on the inside. I like it when you keep it on the inside. In fact, I like it so damn much, it would bring tears to my eyes if I could still cry."

Mick crossed his finger over his chest, bewildered but still willing to adhere to the man code. "I'm not sure why you anticipate girly crap, but the girly crap stays on the inside. Swear it. But if you don't mind my asking, why am I hiding my feminine side?"

Because a really small part of him wanted to whine as he surveyed the damage in Tessa's store. From the blackened curtains now hanging in crispy clumps to the burned-clear-through-to-the-wiring walls, Mick figured whining would be a forgivable act after today's events. You know, if he were to let his man guard down.

"Oh, you'll see, Optimus Prime. Jesus, you're big. Anyway, just remember you swore," Nina warned with a cluck of her tongue, placing an elbow on what was left of Tessa's glass checkout counter to lean back, clearly assuming a more comfortable position. "Okay. So here goes the spiel." She swung her head in Tessa's direction and wagged her finger. "You might wanna hear this, too."

"Nina . . ." Wanda let out a warning growl, which struck Mick as odd.

The Nina woman rolled her eyes. "Just shut it, Suzy Sunshine. I've been streamlining this stupid speech so we can avoid all the minutia. It's dragging us down, and to be honest, it's as old and boring as Marty is. Plus, if you'll fucking remember, we're on vacation. So we don't have the damned pamphlets to give him." She turned back to Mick. "Anyway, no hand-holding, no bullshit poor babies. He's a man. For the love of peaches, he'll take this like one."

Now, that statement brought cause for concern. He raised his hand. "Being the man here, what exactly am I taking?"

Tessa sucked in her cheeks, using an impatient hand to brush at her soggy hair. Hair he himself had dumped a vase of water on. So he could keep his knight-in-shining-armor status and save the distressed damsel's hair.

Mick knew what that look meant. Her patience was dwindling. He should know. It did that all the time when he was around. Their love-hate relationship was an enduring one.

He brought out the worst in her, and she brought out the ten-year-old in him. His instinct to protect and look out for her had become fierce since her brother, Noah, his lifelong best friend, had died three years ago—and she didn't like it. Which was what had led to their screaming match and then to the mess now surrounding them.

Tucking her burned turtleneck around her chin, Tessa spoke with a caution she reserved for difficult customers. "I'm not sure what minutia we'd be avoiding, and rude is the absolute last thing I want to be, but I think you can see from this mess, I have to go look on Craigslist under the heading *bulldozer.*" She gritted out the last word and finally shot the old glare of death at Mick.

Yep, from the way she was kicking at the slushy pile of blackened receipts she'd thrown the bucket of mop water on, Tessa was preparing for liftoff.

But goddamn it all. He'd lost his focus now. He couldn't take pleasure in the potential verbal battle with Tessa, deserved or not, if he could only focus on things like the fact that he wasn't supposed to need "bullshit poor babies," whatever that was.

Nina squinted at Tessa, giving her an almost thoughtful glance. "Bulldozers. Okay, that's as good a starting point as any. So *why* is it you have to rent heavy machinery, lady?"

Tessa blinked for a moment, as though saying out loud what had occurred would sound as ludicrous as it really was. Though, as Mick scanned her face while she mentally formulated her words, he saw the first sparks of anger.

He straightened, his shield of armor at the ready. But scratch that. While Tessa had much more practice being pissed at him, she wasn't quite ready to throw down. "Because—of—*him*," she mumbled in Mick's direction.

"Bingo, lady," Nina agreed, slapping the countertop for emphasis. "And what did *he* do?" she prompted, with what Mick would swear was a whiff of demonic pleasure.

Tessa waffled then, a clear indication that her disbelief had returned full force. She clamped her teeth on her lower lip, her hazel eyes grazing the littered floor. "He . . ."

"He *what?*"

Marty pinched Nina's arm with French-manicured nails. Mick knew they were French manicured because Tessa had hers done just like that all the time at Sally's Salon just down the block. "Nina! Stop taunting the client this instant or I swear, when we get back to the inn, I'm going to make you eat that bottle of sunscreen whole."

Nina flicked her fingers at a clump of Marty's burnt hair. "I'm not taunting her, blondie. I'm forcing her to face the reality of what just happened. You know, so we don't have to do the denial thing until we're fucking blue in the face?"

Mick's head shot up. "The client?"

Wanda patted his arm as though she were soothing a child. "You'll see what she means in a minute. Nina, wrap this up—*now*, Miss Nurturer."

Nina flipped Wanda the bird before returning her focus to a wobbly Tessa. "Where were we?"

Tessa tilted her chin upward, smearing more soot over her cheek when she used her forearm to push the burnt strands of hair from her face. "We were playing the blame game. Mick in the antiques store with a blowtorch being the obvious suspect," she offered in a reference to the game Clue. A game they'd played a lot of as kids at her parents' cabin.

Nina gave her head a brisk shake and cracked her knuckles. "Right. That's good. Okay, so what did the bad giant do with the blowtorch?"

Tessa's lower lip trembled. Obviously, she was battling with more disbelief. However, she caught herself and reared her shoulders back, putting on her tough-guy front. "*He* . . ." She paused, taking a deep breath that shuddered. "*He* set my store on fire. Like he was some sort of human Bic."

Mick winced. Yeah. *He* had. Strangest thing, too.

"And *how* did he do that, Tessa Preston?" Nina prompted, and if Mick was hearing her tone right, she did it with devilish glee.

Tessa was back to wavering, her eyes flitting from corner to corner of the store to avoid Nina's. She frowned, opened her mouth to speak, then snapped it shut again. Evidently she still hadn't passed disbelief. Instead, she jammed her hands on her hips and picked up the death glare where she'd left off.

Wanda tapped Nina on the shoulder. "I think we're addressing the wrong person here, Nina. Tessa's store can be cleaned up. Insurance claims filed, et cetera. She's but a by-product of this mess and only distantly involved other than the clear fact that she has a relationship with the big guy. The one with the real problem here is Mr. Malone. It would seem that he's the one most in need of our services."

Nina gave a sharp nod. "I don't like it, but you're right." She slapped Mick on his bare back, with a whole lot more force than he was comfortable admitting to. She was a girl, for Christ's sake . . . "So, big guy. How did *you* set your lady friend's store on fire?"

Mick shoved his hands in the pockets of his semi-charred jeans. They'd caught fire when he'd . . . well, just when. "Do you really need to hear me say it? Like, out loud?" Because all that "girly crap" he was supposed to keep on the inside just might find itself on the outside.

Marty shot him a sympathetic look and fluffed her crunchy hair. "Unfortunately, you need to hear it more than we do, Mick. Acceptance and all that therapeutic jazz."

Nina winked an almond-shaped eye. "So, dude. Who set the nice lady's store on fire?"

He scuffed his feet, feeling like he was in the principal's office with all these female eyes on him waiting in expectation. And he'd been to the principal's office more than once in his youth. "I did." *You, you, you, Mick Malone. Yes,* you *are essentially an arsonist.* Wouldn't that be the shit with the guys at the station? A fireman who'd set his best friend's sister's store on fire by . . . Shit. Shit. Shit.

Nina's smile was pleased. Grimly so. "Riiiight. And how'd you do that, Gigantor?"

Oh. He had an answer for that—or maybe it was more like a question. "I feel like you're supposed to tell me."

Nina nudged his foot with hers. "Answer the question so we can get on with this shit already. You know, the acceptance-thing bit."

He cocked his head to the right, opened his mouth to provide the much-anticipated answer, then closed it again, finding that he, too, couldn't quite articulate the events of the last ten minutes or so.

Eyes, four pairs to be precise, bored into his. There was even some impatient toe tapping.

Women and their need for unnecessary verbal ownership. "I don't know exactly *how* I did it." And technically, he didn't. In fact, what he'd done was nuttier than squirrel shit. To define it would mean going one step too far over the line of blithering idiot.

"I'll tell you how you did it, Mick," Tessa enunciated each word, her eyes finally beginning to settle into that familiar narrowing. The one that meant his ass chewing was about to begin. "You opened your big mouth again, which is no surprise, and stuck your nose in where it didn't belong. Again, no surprise—only this time when you flapped your gums with all your lame, overprotective bullshit, it set my entire store on fire. That's how you did it, Mick."

Nina and Marty looked at each other, mystification all over their faces—which, if they were who they said they were, didn't leave Mick with a reassured feeling.

Clearly, something had occurred here. Whether it had paranormal properties and he needed crisis management was yet to be decided, but it would certainly help if the crisis counselors in question didn't have such a fish-out-of-water look.

Yeah. That would help.

"Hold up, girlie." Nina eyeballed Tessa like she was on trial for murder. "I came in just as the flames erupted, but the way it looked from where I was standing, those flames came from his hands. He didn't do this with his fingertips? You know, like shooting fireballs from 'em?"

"Uh, no," Mick interjected. "That was just my fingertips on fire; I had to put my pants out with something." He held his hands up for inspection. Though not seriously burned, they were still a little pink.

Huh.

Tessa let out an exasperated sigh, the rise and fall of her chest making Mick instantly look away. Something he did often in honor of his best friend's memory. "No! How ridiculous. Who can shoot fireballs from their fingertips? That's insane."

Nina twisted her lips in a mocking smile. "I so dig that word. Oh, and I totally dig *ludicrous*, *ridiculous*, *preposterous*, *nuts*, *crazy*, and *certifiable*. Love 'em, like all big hearts and flowers-ish."

Wanda put her hand over Nina's mouth in a move so quick it was almost blurry. "Is it any more insane than Mick shooting fire from his *mouth*, Tessa?" Wanda admonished. "I, unlike our reluctant antiquer Nina, was the first in the door. The walnut jewelry box in the front window caught my eye. Of course, now that lovely piece is just a tragedy, but I saw what happened, and so did you, Mick." Her voice softened, as did her expression when she let go of the cagey Nina and set her aside as though she were lighter than a feather.

Yeah. Okay. He'd seen it, too. More to the point, he'd felt it erupt from his throat like boiling lava. Why wasn't that freaking out anyone but him and Tessa? For the first time, his shock was replaced with suspicion for these women who had all the answers. "You have a point."

"And seeing as the circus isn't in town, I imagine fire-breathing isn't what you do for a living, right, Mick?" Wanda asked, her voice soft and cajoling.

His spine went rigid under the women's scrutiny. "Um, right. Not a fire-breather. I put them out. I don't start them."

Wanda nodded, the soft wisps allowed free in her loosely pulled back hair frizzy from the effects of the explosion. "Exactly. So I bet you're wondering how you did what you did, right?"

Nina scratched her head. "Hang a sec. What did he fucking do, Wanda? I had him pegged as a demon. I was at the ready with Darnell and Casey on the voice-activated-dial gig, but now I don't know. So if he isn't a demon, then what the hell is he?" Nina asked.

"A demon?" Tessa croaked weakly, worry now creating lines on her forehead.

Mick's head began to spin.

Marty tugged on Nina's long hair, her lips forming a thin line. "Can it, mouth. Didn't we tell you the best way to keep a client calm is to always appear in control? You know, like you actually know what you're doing, Elvira?"

Wanda stepped in front of the other two women, blocking them from his sight while her eyes compelled Mick's to focus on her. "First, before we get into explanations, let me give you our credentials as paranormal crisis counselors."

"You have a degree in that?"

Wanda popped her lips at him. "Life is our degree, Mr. Malone. Now, we're going to share something with you that will no doubt leave you in more shock than you're already in. However, in order to prove we can provide services, it's a necessity. And as Nina said, I imagine you'll be able to handle it better being the big hunk of man you are. Women are far more emotional. Not to say that's a bad thing, but it can hinder the process when you're handing out tissues and dabbing tear-swollen eyes."

"The process . . ." he mumbled. Jesus Christ.

"Indeed." She nodded her affirmation, tugging at her gloves. "The process. I'd tell you to sit, but it seems we're fresh out of furniture for the moment. So how about you just steady yourself? You're a rather brawny man. It's all in the balance and placement of your feet."

"Maybe Tessa and I should go grab some dinner?" Marty asked, putting a hand on Tessa's arm, her expression one of visible concern, putting Mick at ease for a moment.

Until he remembered *the process*.

"Oh, the hell," Tessa responded. "I appreciate your concern, but I'm pretty tough, and I want to know what happened here, too, and what it has to do with demons. I don't know what a paranormal crisis is, or what you mean by *process*, but I'm dying to find out. I have to put *something* on those insurance claim forms." She gave Mick a pointed look.

Mick clenched his jaw. "I said I was sorry."

"Sorry doesn't bring back my Louis XVI chevet, now, does it?" she scoffed at him, thumping his shoulder with her hand.

"Are you sure, Tessa? What you'll see can be very disturbing . . ." Wanda warned, shrugging out of her singed shawl. What was so disturbing she had to partially undress for it? Mick wondered.

Tessa nodded her head, her resolve evident to Mick. He knew that look, too. It was the one that said, if you and my brother can plunge into the lake on a swing rope from twenty feet above, I can, too. Except, she'd broken her leg. "I'm sure. I can take whatever this is."

Nina shot Tessa a skeptical raise of her eyebrow. "That's what all the girlies say." Cracking her knuckles, she didn't wait for Tessa to respond. Instead, she glanced at her two friends. "Let's get it on." And then she laughed.

Which left Mick a little uneasy.

Well, a lot uneasy.

CHAPTER 2

Mick reached for the edge of a torched wing back chair, gripping it so he wouldn't topple over. He was, under normal circumstances, pretty solid. Nina hadn't nicknamed him Gigantor without reason. But what he'd just seen had left him weak and so close to mewling like a newborn kitten that he had to hang on to something to prevent his knees from buckling.

And the story that went with all that fur and power lifting? It was just this side of unreal. There were teeth accidentally lodged in another person's flesh, and poodles, and making potties, and dental hygienists, and blood drinking, and life-threatening illnesses, and levitation, and veterinarians who were cougars, and genies, and even an accountant who'd drunk a baby-making formula by accident and turned into a werewolf. All *accidental* incidences as relayed by Wanda. Wanda the halfsie. Half werewolf, half vampire.

It was a cornucopia of crazy.

Mick pressed the heel of his hand to his eyes and rubbed hard, forcing himself to say something—*do* something. He pointed at Nina, sucking in a deep breath. "You just . . ."

"Picked up a fucking car."

"With . . ." he faltered.

"One hand. Yeah. Nifty, right?" She repositioned a passed-out-from-fright Tessa on her shoulder like she was a blanket and not a one-hundred-and-forty-pound woman.

"And you have fa . . ." he grunted.

"Fangs," Nina provided with a saucy wink, stretching her free arm over her head and rolling her shoulders.

Had he really seen this woman's teeth jut from her mouth like she was an extra in that movie *Twilight*? *Yes, Mick. Oh, yeah.*

"And you! Jesus Christ, *you* . . ." Mick's gaze swung to Marty when his words continued to fail him.

"Shifted." Marty brushed at her boots to remove the stray bits of werewolf hair lingering on the suede, then broke out her compact to check her makeup and gasped at the sight of her burned hair.

"You looked like . . ." No. He couldn't say it. Would. Not.

"A dog." Marty let out a small, bored sigh. "I get that a lot."

Mick shook his head as if the motion would clear the visual that remained in his mind's eye. He looked to the most reasonable of the bunch. Halfsie Wanda. "What . . . ?"

"Just happened?" Wanda filled in.

"Yes." It was all he was capable of.

"We proved to you the paranormal exists. I told you our stories and how we ended up like this, and I have to say, this streamlining Nina suggested really is the best way to introduce a client to our world. No fuss, very little muss. So again, I'm a were-vamp, Nina's a full vampire, Marty's a werewolf, and my absentee sister is a demon. We were all turned by accident—well, of course with the exception of me. That was on purpose and never to be spoken of outside this circle. We've dealt with many paranormal incidents since ours, which is why we formed OOPS. So, in closing, you, sir, are as yet unidentified, but definitely paranormal from the looks of this place."

Nina tugged on a still-unconscious Tessa's hair with a gentle yank for someone so ready to rumble. "Hey, sissy pants—wake up."

Well, if nothing else, when Tessa did rejoin them, Mick had bragging rights on the last man standing during a paranormal event. With a roll of his head on his neck, he carefully pieced his words together.

He would take this like a man, and he'd gather the kind of information a man would hunt down and gather. Yes, he would. "So what does this mean for me? I'm not any one of those things you showed me—how does that make me paranormal?"

"You don't think breathing fucking fire means you're still human, do you, dude? You. Breathed. Fire. From your piehole, pal. Don't start with the delusional shit now, okay? I wanna toboggan down that big-ass hill, and if you're going to do the denial thing, these two saps are gonna wanna hang around and make your boo-boos all better. But me? I'm just not up to it today, buddy. I'm not up to it any day."

Wanda snapped her fingers in Nina's face. "Hush." She turned to Mick and said, "Obviously, this was the first time this has happened to you. So can you tell us what you did just before you blew Tessa's store to smithereens?"

"I came to the store to check on her like I always do." He kept his words purposely evasive. Not just because it was none of their business what his reasons were for coming to Tessa's store, but because he didn't exactly want to share the childish nature of his arguments with her. The neener, neener quality to them, as dubbed by Tessa, didn't exactly scream *mature*.

Wanda flapped one of her gloves at him and then rolled her eyes not just at Mick as one of the fingers of the glove broke free and fell to the soiled floor. "Oh, don't be cryptic, silly-billy, or I'll have Nina root around in your mind. You don't want that, do you? It's so invasive. Now, just tell us all of it. Even the smallest detail can factor into this mess you're in."

His skeptical eyes met Wanda's. "May I offer a misgiving first?"

"Fucking naturally. Anything to hold this shit up," Nina moaned. "I thought you were a bigger man than that, Mick. My bad."

"Shhh, Nina," Marty chided, giving up on restoring her makeup to shoot Nina a look of disgust. "He has every right to be suspicious, and ask questions. Or do we have to remind you of your turning, whiner?"

That's right. He had every right to ask questions. This way there'd be no buyer's remorse if he bought their desire to help him. "How do I know you ladies are on the up-and-up? Doesn't it seem a little suspicious that you three just happened to show up when this went down?"

"You don't," Wanda replied succinctly. "All you have is our word and the fact that we've helped several people in predicaments much like yours. Add in what we just showed you, and I'd think you'd at least consider our help. We clearly know a thing or two about the supernatural. So take it or leave it. We can remove ourselves at any time." She crossed her arms over her chest in a clear go-on-and-see-what-happens-if-we-leave-the-playground-and-take-our-toys-too stance.

The idea of them leaving did nothing to ease Mick's fears, either. What a double-edged sword they were wielding.

But what choice did he have? They definitely hadn't been lying about that process thing. He clenched his fists. Fine. "Like I said, I came to check on Tessa. We had an argument . . ." Like one of their biggest ever. Lots of yelling and name-calling. Only this one had had an edge to it he couldn't put his finger on.

"And what did you argue about?" Marty asked from behind him, poking her head around his back.

He bristled, then forced a calm response. "Why does that matter?"

Nina paced like some caged animal, Tessa still limp over her shoulder. "Dude, cough it up or I'll beat your ass with your lady friend as my stick, okay? And hurry it up. The night ain't gettin' any younger, and I wanna toboggan."

Mick didn't doubt Nina's words. He was used to intimidating people with his size—though typically it wasn't on purpose—but this slender, easily-riled-to-the-point-of-violence woman gave him pause.

Fine again. Maybe there was something in the details. "I got word from the guys at work that she's seeing a total jackass. I, being the good best friend I was and continue to be to her dearly departed brother, came over to warn her to watch out. She, being the confrontational, difficult, infuriating woman she is, threw something at me. Much screaming ensued."

Marty tugged at his shirt. "And then?"

"And then I had a headache—which is par for the course with Tessa. So I asked her for some aspirin. Only she never has the kind in the bottle—she's all about that hokey, organic crap when an Excedrin Migraine would do just as well."

Nina nodded her head, her eyes sharp and watchful.

Mick ignored her in favor of finishing his tale "Anyway, Tessa, and not without more yelling about what a pain in the ass I am, sent me to the back to the bathroom, where she said she had some packets of this powdered crap that would fix my fat head right up. I was desperate enough to take whatever she had, because Tessa could give even Mother Teresa a headache, if she were still alive."

"So you took something," Marty drawled as though she suddenly understood.

He nodded while trying to stay on track and go over every detail. For his own sake as well as the women's. "I grabbed the packet, washed it down with some froufrou designer blueberry acai juice she has in the fridge back there. Yeah, it was a little rough going down, and it got a little stuck in my teeth, something I can't say I remember happening the last time she gave me a powdered aspirin, but I was on a mission. So I come back up front to finish giving her hell. We go another round about the douche bag she's dating—she makes me even angrier because like I said, I'm just looking out for her. I open my mouth to yell some more, and this"—he spread his hands wide—"is the result. There was projectile fire flying out of my mouth like the kind of vomit ten drunks spew. The entire place went up in flames in seconds, but most of it burned out just as quickly. Then there was screaming and the sprinklers went off, and, well, you three were here. You know the rest."

"I'd bet Marty's ovaries whatever he shoved down his gullet was what did it," Nina guessed.

"What did it look like, Mick? Taste like?" Marty asked, her blue eyes shiny in the mask of black soot covering her cheeks and forehead.

He shrugged his shoulders. "It tasted awful and it looked just like the powdered aspirin she always gives me. But it was a little chunkier this time."

Tessa's head popped up suddenly as she hung from Nina's shoulder, her smooth hair stuck to the side of her mouth. She spat it away and raised those accusatory eyes at him again. "Which packet did you take, Mick?"

Mick took the two short steps toward Nina and looked Tessa in the eye, suspicious. "I took the one you told me to take, Tessa. The one by the fake flowers in the vase in the bathroom."

She struggled her way out of Nina's grasp, sliding down the vampire's body and landing on the floor with soft knees that wobbled.

Wanda came to her rescue, putting a hand at her elbow, but Tessa moved out of her grasp and stuck a finger in Mick's chest. "That's not the one I told you to take, you imbecile! I said the one on the stand by the *shower*! Oh, sweet baby Jesus. That was a client's! A client who paid me well over ten grand to locate it and have it shipped here from India. It's some rare spice he's been looking for for twenty years, Mick! Do you have any idea how long that took me to find?"

Mick planted his hands on his hips, his lips forming a thin

line. "Like I was supposed to know that? Why the hell would you leave something so rare like that lying around anyway?"

Tessa's eyes glittered at him. "Ohhh! I was in a rush, Mick. I had customers in the store when I got back from the post office. If you'd listen to me just once instead of blowing in here like you have some right to tell me who I can and can't date when I'm thirty-five years old, you would have heard me!"

"Hey!" Nina shouted into the room with a wince. "Both of you—corners, now. Shut the hell up. It hurts my ears when you screech like that."

"You mean your sensitive *vampire* ears, Nina?" Tessa challenged, her cheeks puffing outward.

Nina was in front of her in the blink of an eye. The. Blink. Of. An. Eye, he marveled. "Yeah, that's what I mean, loudmouth. You got the gnads to say otherwise?"

Tessa went a little pale under all the soot, leaning her upper body backward. "Sorry. Tense moment. A lot of money on the line. My apologies."

Nina gave her a sly smile and jammed her hands in the front pockets of her hoodie. "Okay, so, it doesn't take Angela Lansbury to figure this out. It had to be whateverthehell you accidentally took, Gigantor."

Tessa shook her head, her eyes wide once again. "But it was just a spice. How could a spice from India make him breathe fire? I mean, he incinerated my entire store with a spice? That's crazy."

"Lady, you don't know crazy. I bet a day or two ago, you would have called what we showed you tonight crazy. Now? Maybe not so much, huh? So can the talk about the crazy and save your 'oh-em-gee' for later when I'm tobogganing by moonlight and you're all alone freaking out while you replay the horror of Marty's shift in your mind. Right now, let's figure this shit out. Something I know Marty and Wanda are gonna make me do whether I like it or not while they swing the BFF bat in my face."

Wanda's nod was brisk and no-nonsense. "Nina's right. We're here to help however we can. I've tweeted some of our sources because, to be quite honest with you, I don't know of any fire-breathing paranormals. But we're a tight community and someone's always willing to lend a hand." She held up her iPhone to show she was on it.

Mick turned to Wanda, who'd begun scrolling through her messages on her phone. "I appreciate the help, and if you find anything, I'll give you my cell number or catch up with you at the inn, but for now, it looks like it's over. There's nothing to suggest it isn't. Maybe whatever it was that I took only had temporary side effects." *Yeah, you keep telling yourself that spewing fire is temporary, Mick.*

Forgetting his paranormal counselors for the moment, he turned to Tessa and shot her a genuine look of apology. "Okay, yes. I set the store on fire, and I'll probably end up apologizing for it for the rest of my life. I'll have the guys at the station come over and help clean up. Promise."

Tessa made a face at him and scoffed. "And what will you tell your Neanderthal firemen friends, Mick? How are we going to explain this? I can't believe that no one has shown up already. The glow from that blowout had to be visible from at least a mile away. Maybe it's not such a bad thing I'm tucked so deep into the village now, huh, Mick? Remember when I opened the shop and all those criminals you were sure were going to rob me blind right here in Valley View, Vermont, population four hundred twenty-five, were just waiting to use their deception on an innocent, unsuspecting woman?"

Yeah, yeah, yeah. He'd worried. But she was young and pretty, and they had a lot of tourists when the foliage changed. City tourists who thought a pretty woman was prey—Tessa, in particular. "Look, we'll just make something up. We'll figure it out. I'll take care of it all. For right now, everything's calm and my flaming vomit seems to have passed. Oh, and as far as I'm concerned, this is all your fault. Who leaves a packet of"—he swiped his fingers in the air to make quotation marks—"ten grand worth of spices in the bathroom, cupcake?"

"My fault? *Mine?*" Tessa squawked. "You have some nerve, Mick." She stopped short in front of him, and the confrontational glow in her eyes was suddenly doused, replaced by concern.

She reached upward, trailing a finger over his cheek. "You have blood on you," she said softly, her hazel eyes skating over his face. "Must've been all that flying glass from the shipment of mirrors I got in. C'mere." She swiped at his cheek with her thumb, nurturing and gentle.

Leaning into him, she stood on her toes and whispered like she was sharing a secret. The way she had when they were kids and he still didn't realize she was an icky girl. "Wow, what a day, huh?"

And so it went. Tessa could never resist baiting him, but she also couldn't stand to see him hurt. That meant his reaming was on hold for now. Mick swatted at her fingertips, soft and soothing against his skin. It was easier to go balls to the wall with Tessa than to give in to the fire she created in his gut. One he'd never give in to.

"Yeah, wow, and I'm fine. Stop hovering, and let's call it a night." He tacked on a smile to ease the abrasiveness of his words.

Wanda put a hand on his arm. "Maybe you should wait, Mick. I have a bad feeling, and truthfully, it's rather naïve to believe this is entirely over. No one launches fire from their mouth if something fishy isn't going on. Stick around for just a couple of more minutes while I read through these tweets. Just so we can see what we can see."

"Oh. Fuck," Nina said from behind him.

A chill ran along his spine. He was afraid to ask. But ask he did. "What?"

"Goddamn it. I want to go tobogganing. I sure as hell don't want to stick around for this shit," Nina groused with a stomp of her feet.

What shit?

She tapped him on the shoulder, forcing him to turn around. "Well, I guess we're gonna see what we can see whether we want to see it or not."

He cocked his head, his eyes catching Tessa's. Eyes that were filled with that special kind of horror reserved just for today. *"What?"*

Nina reached up and over his shoulder to flick her fingers at something, something that when flicked, sent the oddest vibration from the tips of his toes to the top of his head. "So, dude. How do ya feel about wings? On a big guy like you, you'd figure they wouldn't be so flattering, but I gotta say, you wear 'em well. Nice span."

"Ohhh," Marty cooed, clapping her hands together in delight. "What a lovely color."

His eyes searched each woman's. "Are you going to tell me that if I look in a mirror, I'll see wings on my back? *Wings?*"

"Yeah. Just like the kind on those feminine protection commercials, only not," Nina said on a cackle.

Before he had the chance to respond to this next batch of weirdness, Wanda began hopping around from one foot to the other, holding up her iPhone. "I know what you are!" she sang. "You, Mick Malone, are a dragon!"

Rawr.

CHAPTER 3

"Wings."

Nina helped Tessa out of her car, which she'd driven because Tessa couldn't stop shaking, and onto the sidewalk facing her tiny stone cottage without saying a word.

Tessa looked up at this beautifully pale woman who'd lifted a car with one hand and said again, as though Nina hadn't heard her, "Wings. Mick has wings."

Nina took her by the hand as one would a child and pulled her toward her mint green door. "Bet he can fly, which I'll give you, is crazy cool."

Tessa stopped dead in her tracks. *Fly?*

Nina clamped a hand under her chin and forced Tessa to look at her. "You're not ready for that, are you? Apologies. It's just like I said back at your bonfire—er, I mean store. I hate this part of the whole deal. It's a lot of whining and crying and sometimes thinking you can change shit you just can't. Marty and Wanda call me a bitch because of how impatient I get, but I prefer realist—because I know the GD score."

Tessa stared up at Nina and shivered. "I would *never* call you a bitch." Not ever. This woman would probably eat her face off.

"That's because you're afraid of me right now."

No point in lying. In fact, she'd read somewhere that if you gave your alleged captor personal information, relayed your particulars to them, it sometimes made you less a victim in their eyes—it humanized you somehow.

So if admitting she was petrified of this woman who really was a vampire would keep Nina from stealing her soul, Tessa had no shame. "I am. I'm terrified."

Nina cackled as though that brought her great satisfaction. "Then we're off to a healthy start. As long as you stay terrified, we're golden. Now gimme your key so we can get you inside and you can take a shower. You look like a weenie roast gone sideways."

Tessa gripped Nina's hand, clinging to it. A stranger's hand. Someone she didn't know, let alone trust, but she couldn't let go. "Why are you being so nice?"

"Didn't you just call me a bitch?"

Her eyes went wide in fear. "Oh, no. I said I'd never call you a bitch because I'm terrified you'll eat my face off."

Nina patted her icy hand. "Nah. Faces are overrated. But I would chew your arm off. Clean off."

"I'll make a mental note. But can you do me a favor?"

"Depends on the favor."

"If I ever incite you enough to want to chew my arm off, can you at least give me a warning sign? Because that would just be awful if you blindsided me. I can be pretty irritating. Just ask Mick."

"Yeah, so he says. You two fight like that all the time?"

All the time. It was her defense mechanism to keep herself from begging him to see her as anything other than his dead best friend's little sister. "It goes back a ways. We grew up together."

"It's goddamn annoying."

"I'm sorry. It's just what we do. It's how we communicate."

"Maybe you should learn sign language? You know, out of respect for the people around you who have sensitive ears?"

Her shoulders sagged. "He burned my store down."

"He did. He's the shittiest shithead-shit ever. But you two have much bigger problems than your store right now."

Horror filled her once more. "He has wings . . ." Mick had wings. He could breathe fire, and he had wings. Wings—beautiful, mythical, shiny, scaly wings. Just like in a storybook.

"That was some shit, I tell you. I've seen a lot, but can't say I've ever seen wings on a dude like that. My kid, Charlie, would love him. She's a big unicorn/Pegasus fan."

Tessa gasped in more horror, then slapped a hand over her mouth to muffle it. When she recovered, she asked, "You have children?"

"Just one. Why does that surprise you, Chicken Little?"

Because you're a beast? Because you swear like a drunken sailor? Because? Tessa hid her shock fast. "No. It doesn't surprise me. I'm sorry. I just thought that vampires—"

"Couldn't have kids. Right. They can't. She was a gift from a friend."

Tessa yanked her hand away from Nina's grip, a cold chill

washing over her. "Like a sacrifice gift? A kidnapped gift?" she squeaked.

"No, moron. I have a genie friend. She gave her to me."

A genie friend gave Nina a child? That's what all good genie friends did. "Is this legal in the vampire world? Because I don't think it's legal here in the mortal world."

Nina popped her lips, pushing the fabric of her hoodie away from her face. "It is now."

This was like a train wreck she couldn't look away from—couldn't stop herself from probing—gawking. "How?"

"Do you really want to get into how I managed to have a kid now? Or do you wanna figure out why your man's got wings?" She began to push her way past Tessa, but Tessa put a firm hand on Nina's arm to prevent her from going any farther.

"You can't come into my house." No. No. No. No vampires allowed.

Nina frowned. One of those frowns that said the vampire was displeased—heartily. "Say again?"

"Can I be honest with you?"

"Are you gonna do it confessional-style where you cry and carry on while you spew your guts?"

"I hope not. I know you don't favor sensitivity."

Nina motioned for her to continue.

"I'm afraid of you. Straight up. Yes, I've watched more than my fair share of vampire movies and television series. They don't always portray your, um, kind as accommodating. In fact, you guys are really aggressive, bordering on vicious. You suck souls out of people. You drink their blood. Try and look at this from my perspective. You know, your prey? What if you're trying to get me inside just so you can eat my soul—or drain me dry? This could all be a ploy."

Nina threw her head back and laughed, the cackle echoing against the backdrop of the snow-covered trees, startling Tessa. "I don't want your fucking soul, and I already fed for the day."

"Phew. I feel so much better. Wait. Fed?"

Nina's eyes gleamed, amusement in them. "Yeah. Drank the blood of a mortal. Had my yum-yums—whatever."

Tessa froze, her feet wanting to run but incapable of movement. "That's exactly why you can't come in."

Nina let her chin drop to her chest before she lifted her eyes and captured Tessa's gaze. "First, I don't drink blood from people. It's synthetic. Second, don't you think if I wanted to drink from you I could just do it right here—outside in the mountains of snow?"

"Maybe you like the game. A cat-and-mouse fetish?"

"Give me your fucking key, Tessa. Give it to me now. You're pissing me off, and you won't like when you piss me off." She held out her hand, waiting.

"I have to stand by my earlier reasoning and say no. No inside vampires allowed."

Bad, bad move, she thought just two seconds later when Nina picked her up, flung her over her slender shoulder, and gripped the doorknob. With a hard yank, she twisted the metal before bracing her unoccupied shoulder against the wood door and jamming into it, jolting both of them into Tessa's small entryway.

Nina unceremoniously dropped her on her puffy couch and scuffed her hands together. "Take note. Vampire on the inside." Then she grinned.

God, she was so beautiful. How could someone so beautiful be such a beast? Tessa's teeth chattered so hard she thought her jaw might break. "That didn't make me any less afraid of you. You broke my door. It was an antique."

Nina flopped down in the lounger just opposite the couch and nodded, pulling her phone from her hoodie's pocket and scrolling the screen with a lean finger. "Like I said, we're off to a healthy start. Go take a shower while we wait for your boyfriend and the rest of my nutjob friends to get here."

"I'm not leaving you alone—out here—while I'm in there." She pointed to the bathroom just behind the couch.

"Are you afraid I'll steal your silver? Maybe some of your old musty crap?"

"No. I'm afraid you'll eat my dog."

Nina's entire expression changed. She went from dour to light and smiley in mere seconds. "You have a dog? Dude—where?"

"He's probably in my bedroom, asleep. He's deaf. Wait! Please don't eat my dog. Please. Joe-Joe's the only man in my life who doesn't make me miserable."

Nina didn't bother to listen to her; she was up and out of her seat in one of those fast-forward movements Tessa still had trouble processing. She stalked her way to Tessa's bedroom and sat down on the bed, her hand reaching cautiously for Joe-Joe, letting him sniff it.

As Tessa rose from the couch, scrambling to get to her bedroom to save Joe-Joe's soul, Nina was already resting her cheek on Joe-Joe's head and stroking the white and black fur of his hindquarters.

"Pit bull?" she asked, scratching behind Joe-Joe's ears to the tune of his delighted moans.

"Ye . . ." She cleared her throat. "Yes. A rescue. He was a fight dog."

Now Nina's face was back to frowny and angry. "Assholes. If you wanna see me chew somebody's arm off, they oughta let me at one of those pricks." She waved a dismissive hand at Tessa. "Now go take a shower and let me and Joe-Joe get to know each other. Promise I won't eat him—or his soul." She chuckled to herself before returning to Joe-Joe, giving him belly rubs.

Voices coming from her living room made both Tessa and Nina turn their heads. "Gang's here. Time to start figuring this out." Giving Joe-Joe one last pat on the head, Nina cooed, "Come on, buddy. Let's go see how they managed to fit fireman Mick's wings into Marty's ugly, pretentious SUV."

To Tessa's surprise, normally shy and sometimes nervous Joe-Joe jumped off the bed and followed Nina out like the good cult member he was, never even acknowledging that Tessa was in the room with him.

Nina must have some sort of glamour magic or something. That was what they called it on TV, right? Vampires had the ability to play with your mind—put you under a spell? That had to be it. Joe-Joe took a long time to warm to strangers, and he never warmed like this.

Staying far behind Nina, Tessa watched Mick, now wingless, enter her cottage, his face still covered in sweat-smeared soot, with Marty and Wanda right behind him.

"Your wings are gone," Tessa mumbled.

"Yeah. Strangest thing," he said. "They just went away." He moved closer to her and smiled. "So all better, right?"

"Wrong," Marty chirped. "Our experience tells us that this isn't over. You don't just sprout wings and breathe fire and it all goes away. This isn't like a twenty-four-hour flu, Mick. This is a problem."

"A problem we need to get right on," Wanda said. "We need to know who bought that spice from you, Tessa. You did say they paid ten grand for it, right? That's a lot of money for a rare spice. So why don't you go grab a shower, because you're going to make an utter mess of such lovely furniture, and then look through your records. We need a name—a contact—something."

Mick grabbed Tessa by the arm and led her to her kitchen. A kitchen she loved to spend hours in since she'd restored it. It was shiny and clean, and had an old farmhouse appeal she'd managed to add modern touches to. "I know you were worried about the store, and what the guys back at the firehouse would say, but Marty says Nina has it all handled."

"Handled? Have you seen how she handles things? She can lift a car with one hand, Mick!"

He waved his big hands at her. "Yeah. She said she'll mess with their minds and plant an idea in there about how the fire started, so they won't dig too deep. I'll make sure she puts the right suggestion in their heads so this won't spin too far out of control. She said she'd deal with the insurance carrier, too."

Tessa's mouth fell open. "Do you hear yourself, Mick? She'll mess with their minds?"

His eyebrow rose. "Did you see what I saw? Do you disbelieve she's capable of it?"

Fair. Joe-Joe was proof. "Okay. You have a point. Maybe she can bend minds. But do we want her to bend the minds of the guys at the station?"

"Do you want to explain how I incinerated your store by breathing fire?"

She gave a resigned sigh. "So what now? How do we get rid of them?"

He frowned. She knew that frown. It was the one that said she was spouting crazy. "We don't. We need their help, T."

"But your wings are gone, Mick. It's over."

"Did you hear what that woman Marty said? She said it's *not* over."

"Okay, maybe it isn't. But what do we know about these people that would make us believe them? Maybe they're from the government. So say maybe you really did take something that gave you wings—"

"*Dragon* wings. I think I'm really a dragon."

Tessa slapped a hand to her thigh in disbelief. "Right, Puff. And maybe they've been watching us because I had the packet of pricey spices, and they know what the so-called spices are capable of. Maybe they've been watching me this whole time, hoping the guy who ordered them would show up and they could catch him in the act of taking the alleged spices from me."

He rolled his eyes at her in that very irritating way he had—just like when they were kids and he thought she was stupid. "Right, *Paranormal Activity*. Maybe they have been watching you all this time. Maybe they're on some covert mission, and we never noticed them in a town of only just over four hundred people," he said sarcastically.

"Maybe they're part of some special group of people—like Agents of S.H.I.E.L.D., or an X-Files kind of thing. Maybe, now that you have what they came for, they're going to want it back!" she hissed.

Nina poked her head over Tessa's shoulder. "Scully here—we're not fucking government or FBI or CIA or paranormal investigators. We're people who were once weak humans like you who had something crazy-ass happen to us. Now we try to help people who have the same problem we do. That's it."

Marty rushed over to intervene, placing a hand on Nina's back and grabbing her hoodie. "Stop getting pushy, Mistress of the Dark. They're speculating, hashing it out. They should. We did, didn't we?"

Nina pulled away, swatting at Marty. "I'm just trying to save them some time. Save us some time. I want to go tobogganing. Not play with dragons and their girlfriends."

Tessa narrowed her eyes. "I'm not his girlfriend."

Mick bristled, too. "What she said."

"Nina, go play with Joe-Joe." Marty pointed to the living room, where Joe-Joe sat at Wanda's feet while she cooed and stroked him. "Tessa, we need the name of that client *now.* Maybe he's someone the people in our world know, and if they do, they can offer us insight. If you don't want to freshen up, then make yourself useful so we can figure this out. If you don't want to be a part of this, give us the client's name, we'll take Mick back to his place, and you can process this alone."

In other words, shut up, Tessa. You're thwarting progress here. Besides, what choice did they have? These women appeared to at least understand the elements of an event this scary. Who else could they trust for now? "I'm sorry."

Marty's pretty face softened immediately. "Don't be, honey. It's natural to try and rationalize, but our experience is the faster we figure this out, the faster we can get Mick acclimated to his new life. And if he's not your boyfriend, then you really don't have much of a stake in this. So it's essentially not your problem."

"She likes him—it is so her problem," Nina called from the living room where Joe-Joe now sat on her lap as though he'd always known her.

Tessa stiffened. How could she possibly know that? Had she been fishing around in Tessa's head? "He's my brother's best friend," she offered lamely. "We've known each other all our lives. Of course I want to help him."

Marty's smile was as warm and as pretty as she was. "Then the client's information?"

That was a problem. A huge problem. "Burned to a crisp."

"Don't you keep backup of some kind, T?" Mick prodded, condemnation sprinkling his tone.

She squirmed, plucking at her burnt sweater. Of course she did. Just not today. "I didn't have time to put it in the computer before the store caught on fire. It just came in this afternoon."

There was a collective resigned sigh from all parts of the house.

Marty tried again. "Can you remember anything about him, Tessa? His initials, when he made the inquiry, where you got the stuff in India? If it was even a man?"

She took a deep breath, pressing her thumbs to her temples.

"It's been a pretty busy time at the shop, lots of orders and . . . and stuff." She couldn't think straight. Couldn't get past vampires and werewolves and genies that gave you babies.

She didn't know all her clients' names by heart—especially the ones who were one-time customers. She got orders from all over the world—shipped merchandise as far as China.

Forget that. *Think, Tessa. Think hard.*

Mick clamped a hand over her shoulder and squeezed—a familiar gesture she hated and lived for all at the same time. "Listen, go clean up, okay? Take a shower. Maybe it'll jar something. I'll dig around for some food. Think about it while I do that, all right? Don't stress."

She looked up at him—the man she'd loved all her life without him ever having a single clue—and nodded. "Okay."

He gave her shoulder a final squeeze as she pushed past him and went to her bedroom, closing the door behind her and locking it.

She sat on the edge of her bed, listening to the women and Mick talk, and found the pounding in her head was much louder when she was closed off from everyone's chatter.

That's when it happened.

An odd tingle in her feet that swept up along her body, reaching the top of her head only to swoop back down to her toes again. Pinpricks stabbed at her skin, and a strange crunching noise resounded in her ears.

The back of her sweater exploded outward with such force, it dropped her to the bed like someone had placed a hand on her back and pushed her.

But she popped right back up due to the bulk of something

heavy pressing into her spine, contorting it until her heart raced and she felt faint—dizzy.

A loud whirring noise thumped in her ears, a flapping, like the unfurling of a boat's sail.

And then whatever force was with her in the room propelled her from the bed, shooting her forward so hard that if she hadn't held her hands up, she would've cracked her head against the far wall. She fell to the floor in a heap, unable to move from the heaviness weighing down her spine.

Nina began pounding on the door and yelling—the ruckus foggy and distant. "Tessa! What the fuck is going on in there? Open the fucking door!"

Now Mick was banging, too. She heard his worry, the tension in his voice, but she couldn't get up off the floor. "T? Tessa, open the door!"

"Move!" she heard Nina yell before the entire doorframe crumbled in bits of splintered wood and chunks of broken wood.

Two vampire-mutilated doors down, she mused before trying once more to get to her feet.

Mick's face was the first thing she saw. Handsome, big, beautiful Mick. Would there ever be a time she didn't love him? Would she ever find someone who filled the void in her like Mick did? Who made her toes curl like he did?

He looked stunned.

In fact, they all did. Marty, Nina, and Wanda all had astonished looks on their faces.

And what the hell was keeping her from standing up?

She gave it her all, rocking forward only to fall back.

Fall back on something.

Something bulky.

At first there was silence as four faces with eyes like saucers stared at her.

Nina was the first to speak. She looked at Mick and slapped him on the back. “Aw, look, Fireman Mick, you’re not so alone after all, huh?”

CHAPTER 4

She couldn't breathe. She couldn't move.

She had wings.

Big, big wings.

Enormous flappy things that wouldn't allow her to stand upright for the weight of them.

Marty hunched down beside her and ran a finger over the edge of them, making Tessa scrunch her eyes shut as an odd sensation coursed through her veins. "They're beautiful—gossamer. I know this is going to sound vapid and utterly shallow, but the green veins running through them, the touch of gold and purple here and there suit your coloring, Tessa. Lovely."

Nina tugged on Marty's long, carefully highlighted blond hair. "Vain and shallow in the lead."

Marty made a face. "I'm just trying to make her feel better, big mouth."

Nina gave Marty a shove with the flat of her hand. "She can't even stand up with them, Marty. Who gives a shit if they're in her color wheel, moron?"

Mick knelt down beside Tessa and peered into her eyes—eyes she was sure were glazed over. "Did you have a headache, too?"

No. No headache. Just a weird pounding in her head. How had this happened? "No! I never even touched the stuff. I put the packet in the bathroom at the store. By the shower, just like I told you I did. I never saw it again after that."

Mick shook his head, the lines in his forehead creasing. "I don't get it."

She grabbed his arm and held on tight—because he felt real. "When do these . . . when do they go away?"

Mick winced. "Mine went away shortly after Nina left to bring you home."

"They just disappear? Just like that?"

He looked away, past her shoulder. He was struggling to speak in the same way he'd done when he'd had to tell her Noah was killed. That meant something bad happened to make his wings go away.

She twisted his arm. "What is it? Just say it, Mick!"

"It hurts a little when they go away."

"Explain *hurts*."

"Worse than a cut, but probably not as bad as an appendectomy without anesthesia."

Tessa blanched. But if Mick could do it, so could she. Hadn't that been her childhood mantra? All her life, she was always trying to keep up with Mick and Noah. "Okay. Help me up."

With two hands, he pulled her upright, steadying her when

she began to wobble to and fro like a drunk. She clung to Mick's forearms to keep from pitching forward. "They're so heavy." And enormous. She saw the span of them from the corner of her eye, filling up her bedroom. They were greater than the width of her annihilated bedroom door.

Mick edged around her, passing her to Nina, who gripped her forearms. "I'm going to try something so we can get you through the door," he said.

"Chainsaw?" she suggested.

Mick didn't answer. Instead, she felt his hand, but not on her limbs—on her new appendages. He used gentle fingers, running them over the edges of membrane.

Oh.

Oh. My.

Hot tingles coursed through parts of her that should not be tingling. A slow simmer began in her belly, molten like lava, stirring, churning as Mick fingered her wings.

Tessa fought a gasp that came out as a sputter. "Ssstop," she whisper-yelled, horrified once more.

Mick snatched his hands away. "Did I hurt you?"

No. On the contrary. Just that feathery-wisp of a touch had caressed her forbidden parts. As though Mick were touching all the places on her body meant to bring pleasure—the parts of her she'd had dreams about him touching since she was a teenager.

When Mick tried to touch her again, she shivered. "Stop!" she yelped, ignoring his question about whether he'd hurt her. "Let Nina do it—or Marty, you big oaf. You're about as subtle as a bull in a china shop!" He had to stop touching her now or she'd pass out or confess something she'd rather die than confess. Yelling was what they did. Baiting him was what she did. Calling him names, making fun of his size. It was how she'd survived all these years he'd ignored her. It was her wall.

"Here," Wanda said, crawling along the floor, over Tessa's feet, and behind Mick. "Let me help." She placed her hands on the wings, and waited. "Are you okay, Tessa? Am I hurting you?"

Taking a deep breath, Tessa nodded. Wanda's hands were like a cooling balm, soothing the raw nerves now connected to her back. She swallowed hard. "Better. Thank you, Wanda."

Mick grunted, ducking out and down to the floor, where Tessa watched his large body deftly navigate back out into the living room.

Wanda somehow managed to coax the wings to fold inward, like stuffing a poufy wedding dress back into its original box. She held them together while Nina guided Tessa back out into the living room.

The large mirror on the wall beside her front door beckoned her, calling her to look—to see the proof that this was real. Her eyes fixed on her reflection. She blinked.

She had wings.

What was next, a forked tongue and a deal with DreamWorks?

Mick came to stand behind her, holding his hands up so as not to touch. His face was a mixture of awe and wonder. "Holy shit."

"I don't understand. How did this happen to me, too?"

He shook his dark head, his longish hair falling around his face. "I don't know, Tessa. I still can't wrap my head around how it happened to me." Reaching around the front of her, he grabbed her hand and squeezed it.

It was rare moments like this, like after her brother's funeral, when Mick was at his strongest—when he wasn't teasing her or browbeating her with his imaginary job as her keeper—that she knew he only wanted what was best for her. That he was only doing what Noah had asked him to do. Watch over her. Protect her.

She squeezed his hand back, letting it go so she wouldn't linger. "So, we're in this together. Let's figure it out, because we can't wander around town with wings. I think people might point and stare."

He chuckled. "I think that's fair. You can't even stand up without help. We'd better figure this out soon before you fall on your ugly mug."

Everything was back to normal. She took another deep breath and fought to parse the transaction with the client she'd found the spice for. He'd been so nice. Very pleasant, had an accent. In fact, he was very British.

"British! The client I ordered the spice for was British."

Wanda nodded, an encouraging smile on her face. "Oh, that's good, Tessa! How did he pay you? Maybe we can track him through his bank account?"

Tessa frowned. No. She'd thought it odd at the time, but it was ten thousand dollars she really needed to stay afloat. "He sent cash. Via a courier."

Mick looked over her head and into her eyes still reflected in the mirror. "And you didn't question that, T? A cash deal? What if he was a drug dealer? Or laundering money?"

No, she hadn't questioned it. Money was tight. She had enough trouble keeping the store up and running in the slow months that the offer of ten thousand dollars for some research and her time was too tempting to second-guess. But she couldn't tell Mick the store was floundering.

He'd never shut up about it. He'd give her the "See?" speech. The one that went, "Should have stayed in college, Tessa. Your love of all things old and smelly isn't going to earn you a living. A degree will. I told you it was a stupid idea to take all that insurance money Noah left and invest it in a store."

"It never occurred to me that drugs had anything to do with it. I do large cash purchases for clients all the time."

Mick's lips thinned into a flat line. "For furniture. Not spices, Tessa. And you wonder why I'm always checking up on you? Jesus."

Nina poked him in the back. "Hey, big brother. Lay off, huh? She's got wings. Stop being an asshole know-it-all and focus on the point."

Tessa stuck her tongue out at Mick.

Marty came around and blocked her view of her reflection. "What was this spice supposed to be for anyway, Tessa? Who cooks anything with an ingredient that's worth ten thousand dollars?"

She shook her head, frustrated with not only her stupidity but her inability to remember much more than the promise of a ten-thousand-dollar finder's fee. "I don't know. I didn't ask him if he was going to cook with it. I'd never even heard of it before. I asked around in an antiques forum online. A guy messaged me and said he could hook me up—and he did. I sent the dealer a good-faith deposit, and the spice showed up today."

"That's good!" Marty coaxed, massaging Tessa's hands. "So who was the guy you messaged with online? Didn't you have to send him the deposit via a bank account?"

Tessa shook her head. "No. He disappeared after he gave me the name of the dealer he thought might have the spice. Never saw him online again. Come to think of it, I don't recall seeing him before that day, either. I'm familiar with most dealers and their user IDs. But he's unimportant. The person I obtained the spice from is important. I mean, who has something that turns you into a dragon just lying around?" What had she done? Had she been some kind of mule, transporting an illegal substance?

Was there even a law that prevented you from carrying dragon powder?

Her stomach turned. "But here's the real question. Why does someone want a spice, or whatever that powdery stuff was, that will turn people into dragons? It's insane."

Mick flipped through his phone. "I think it's safe to say this wasn't a spice, Tessa. What was it called?"

"I can't remember. It was some crazy bunch of letters I couldn't pronounce, but all that information burned in the fire with my laptop." She sounded more stupid by the second.

"Perfect," he muttered with the thick sarcasm he knew tripped her trigger.

"You know what, Mick? It doesn't help with you hounding me. All of my paperwork was back at the store. The store you burned down with your big mouth because you can't keep your grubby paws off what doesn't belong to you!"

Mick's eyes narrowed. "The store I burned down because you had some kind of crazy drug with no name, from some unknown person, a person who wants a pet dragon. Is it me, or does the buck begin with you, princess?"

Her anger spiked, racing along her spine, making her head

throb harder. She made a move to approach him and throw a finger in his face when she stumbled, wobbling from the heavy weight of her wings.

Her wings.

Wanda ran to her rescue, tilting her back up and smiling at her. "I know this is hard for you, honey. I understand you're confused and exhausted by the day's events. All of the yelling"—she gave Mick the eye—"is unnecessary. So if all parties with fingers to point don't stop pointing, someone's going to lose their pointer."

Tessa stuck her tongue out at Mick once more, just like they were kids again.

Wanda clucked her tongue. "Not helping, Tessa."

She let her gaze fall to the floor, contrite. "Sorry."

"Okay, so as it stands now, we need to find the name of the dealer who cashed your check—or you need to go to the bank and find out the name of his bank. Do you have those records? Can't you check online?"

They lived in Podunk Vermont with one bank to the town's name. And they certainly didn't have online banking. "His information was at the store, too. I know I entered his name into my computer as a potential dealer who handles rare inquiries. But we'll have to go to the bank to find out where the check was cashed because I won't have anything other than his phone number. And I can't go looking like this."

They all fell quiet again until her phone jingled from her jacket pocket, breaking the palpable silence.

"Better get that," Mick cooed. "It might be a text from your boyfriend."

It wasn't her boyfriend. She'd dumped him and just let Mick

think he was still her boyfriend, and she'd let him think that with smug satisfaction. Tessa struggled to move, but Nina grabbed the phone from Tessa's jacket and handed it to Wanda.

Tessa took it, scrolling through her text messages. Her eyes widened. The last text was from someone she didn't recognize. "I'd like to drop by tonight and pick up the spice you ordered for me. Please text me at your convenience."

She held up the phone, showing Wanda the text. "It's him! He wants to pick up the spice tonight."

Mick was already grabbing what was left of his charred coat. "Text him back and ask him when."

Nina put her hand on Mick's chest. "Hold up, fireman. You don't know if this dude's some kinda kook. You're not going alone. We'll go with."

Mick scanned her length with his skeptical eyes. "What if he's violent?"

Nina cracked her knuckles and grinned. "Then it'll be good times."

Mick blustered, always the knight in shining armor. "I can't allow a bunch of women to meet up with some strange man who could be dangerous. Not gonna happen."

Nina rose on tiptoe and stuck her finger under Mick's nose. "Did you really just say that to me, King Kong? To us?"

Realization crossed his face and he backed away. "Sorry. I keep forgetting."

Nina yanked the phone from Tessa's hand and texted back to the unknown number.

Tessa couldn't get a handle on Nina. If the vampire wasn't going to suck her soul from her very body, what purpose did it serve for her to be so helpful? What was she getting out of this? "Why are you helping us?"

Nina made a face. "Because those two make me."

Marty grinned and tweaked Nina's cheek. "That's not true and you know it. You love this as much as we do. You just express your love with filthy words and threats. To know Nina is to eventually love the devil's twin."

The camaraderie of these women, the way they'd taken charge of some complete strangers' situation like they were longtime friends, floored her.

Nina held up the phone, her expression stoic and above all, calm. "We're good to go for eight o'clock."

TESSA drew a ragged breath, sweat pouring down her face in rivulets of salty water.

Holy hell.

Mick rocked her, tucking her close against the sooty smell of his burned shirt. "You okay?"

If they could always just be like this, she'd be forever okay. But she couldn't—because he'd never go for it. She was Noah's little sister. End of story. Tessa lingered in Mick's embrace for only a moment before pushing away from him and nodding. "Definitely not as bad as an appendectomy without anesthesia. No big deal."

He chuckled, cupping her jaw and wiping her forehead with the cool cloth Wanda handed him. "It's a little rough."

Stretching her arms, she was happy to be erect again without help from their new cohorts. Her wings had decided to disappear without warning, and quite violently. But if Mick could take the pain of it, so could she. "Do you think it'll always be like this? Hurt like that?"

Mick's angular face went dark. "Jesus, I hope not."

"Nina said there's no changing it. We'll always be like this."

"You know, I was thinking about that. Technically, we're only half dragon. We have wings. But did you see when Marty did that thing . . . the . . ."

Tessa nodded, swallowing a hard gulp. "The shift. That's what she called it."

"Right. Shift. She was *all* werewolf. She didn't have a single human property left to her. Why didn't we change fully? You know, like the pictures of dragons we grew up with?"

"Good point." She paused as another horrifying thought crossed her mind. "Wait. You don't think we're going to turn into full-on dragons, do you? Like roaring, scaly, live-in-a-cave, fire-breathing dragons?"

Mick held up his hands. "I'm just gonna be honest here when I tell you, I have no idea what happens from here. But if they can be werewolves and vampires, I don't see a limit on this paranormal thing."

Nina had said acceptance was the hardest part. No truer words. "Okay. So let's go meet this guy who ordered the spice."

"No. You stay here and rest, T. I've got it."

"Um, no. I'm just as much in this as you are. I'm going, too."

Mick sighed, his wide chest inflating and deflating with that hiss of air that said he was becoming aggravated with her. "You just had a traumatic experience. Stay here. Rest. Shower."

"No more traumatic than you. I'm going. You have no say in

the matter." She grabbed her spare coat and threw it on, taking a hat and a pair of gloves from her countertop.

"I really don't think it's a good idea, Tessa."

"I know. You don't think anything I do is a good idea, Mick. But you know what? Tough shit. I'm going."

Nina snorted a laugh. "Leave her alone, fireman. She's got us. We'll protect her. Now let's go. Marty's got the car warmed up."

Tessa's stomach lurched again. Some of it was due to the wrenching pain she'd experienced when her wings decided they were done for the day.

It was god-awful—a searing stab of agony, a crunch of bones and flesh. But upon examination afterward, it was like nothing had ever been flapping around on her back.

But most of her fear came from the thought of finding out who this man was. Who would know about something as obscure as a powdery substance that produced dragons? Surely he knew what it did. He'd paid ten grand for it.

But why? To what end?

As they all piled into Marty's SUV, reeking of smoke and sweat, Tessa shivered violently. So violently, Marty slung an arm around her and tucked her close to her side, rubbing her arms.

While they drove through her small town, everything familiar and close to her heart passing by, Tessa knew deep in her gut—whatever they were about to find out would come to no good.

CHAPTER 5

Nina pulled up along the curb of Tessa's shell of a store, smoke still rising in small black puffs, a cavernous wasteland of piles of burned trash.

A tear slid from Tessa's eye. Three years. Three years she'd spent cultivating her love for, as Mick called it, all things old and musty. Three years of learning, and failing, and making contacts, and growing, and getting three steps ahead only to fall ten steps back.

Maybe Mick was right. Maybe this dream of hers had been stupid. Maybe she should have taken the money Noah left her and gone to college. She'd sure wasted a ton of time figuring out what she wanted to do with her life before he'd died.

And now it was all gone. The insurance would probably never cover the cost of some of her more prized antiques. So what would she do? Move on? Maybe even move away. There wasn't anything left for her here but Mick, and watching him from afar was like dying a little every day.

Maybe it really was time to try something else, somewhere else.

As long as it involved wings and fire-breathing, of course. She could join the circus. Be a sideshow. Do kids' parties, maybe.

Nina popped the driver's door open and looked back at them with a warning in her coal-black eyes. "You two stay here. Do not move a fucking muscle. If this guy is anything like us, you'll thank me."

She slid out of the car without another word, taking Marty and Wanda with her.

"God, they're badass, huh?" Mick commented, watching Nina skulk toward the side of the store while Wanda and Marty flanked the door and the other side.

"What's the catch?"

Mick looked at her, his brow furrowed. "What do you mean?"

She still felt uneasy about leaving all their eggs in this OOPS basket. "Do you think they want money?"

"Their website says they're nonprofit. I checked on my phone."

Tessa twisted around to look at him, still sore from her de-winging. "Then why are they being so nice? What's in it for them? There has to be a reason."

"I don't know."

"I'm telling you, I bet they work for the govern—"

A loud rumble, thunderous even, cut her off. A rumble and then a flash of lightning streaking across the sky. In the middle of winter in Vermont?

Tessa climbed over Mick to see where the noise had come from, pulling on the door handle just as she saw Nina fall forward, face-down, on the cement walkway leading to the door of the store.

Tessa pushed the door open and lunged from the car, tripping and almost falling on the uneven, snow-covered ground as she ran to Nina. In fact, as afraid as she was of Nina, she didn't even think twice about it.

She dropped to her knees, pushing the hair from the vampire's face. "Nina!" she yelped, giving her a hard shake. "Are you okay?" She grabbed her wrist and began feeling for a pulse. No pulse.

Nina groaned, rolling to her back. "Get off, dude. I don't have a pulse. Soul sucker, remember?"

Tessa's chest heaved, the exertion of simply running after her de-winging having sucked the energy right out of her. "What happened?"

"The fuck if I know," she growled, sitting up. "I was on my way in to see if anyone showed up, and the whole fucking world caved. What the fresh hell is going on?"

Mick went the other way, scooping up Wanda and Marty and helping them to their feet. The heel of Marty's boot had been blown clear off, but the women shrugged Mick off, rushing to Nina's side.

"What in all of heaven was that?" Wanda asked, her eyes sparkling under the moonlight.

Marty peered into the darkness of the store. "I don't know, but whatever it was, it's in there." She pointed at a dark lump Tessa couldn't distinguish from the pit of black at the opening of the store.

Nina was on her feet in seconds and flying toward the entry, her long hair streaming behind her in a ribbon of inky black. "Well, looky here, would ya!" she bellowed, dragging something up from the floor and dangling it.

Something that looked heavy—something bulky.

Mick shoved Tessa behind him as they all approached.

"Put me down, you animal!" a voice said. One that reminded Tessa of the voice of Pooh Bear from all those books she used to have on audio. Even in distress, it held childlike warmth to it, a sweetness she was sure would calm in times of trouble.

As they got closer, Tessa's eyes adjusted to the darkness. The shape was a man. Likely the one who'd texted her.

Nina let the man dangle from her fingertips as though he weighed nothing more than a pair of socks. She held him up to her face, assessing him before she asked, "Who the fuck are you, and why the fuck are you ruining my GD vacation?"

"Nina!" Marty screeched, coming to a halt at her friend's side. "Put him down—*now.*"

Nina didn't bother to sass Marty; instead, she dropped the man like he was a hot potato. He fell in another crumpled mess of limbs at her feet.

Wanda knelt down beside him, rolling him to his back. "Who are you, and what just happened?"

He groaned amidst the puddles of water and soot. "I'm here to meet a Miss Preston to pick up a package. What sort of shoddy customer service is this? Why would you treat me this way?"

Tessa stared down at him while Mick shone a flashlight over his face. He was, tops, maybe late forties, with a sweet, round face and gentle eyes. "You're the one who ordered the spice from

India?" She held out her hand to him, offering him help up, keeping in mind that he was a client.

He took it, pulling himself to his feet and brushing at his black coat, soggy from the debris. His blue eyes were watery in the glare of the flashlight. He had the sort of eyes that always looked as though he'd just rubbed the sleep from them. "I am."

Nina jammed her face in his, her confrontational manner in overdrive."So you got some 'splainin' to do."

The man leaned backward as if he found Nina's very existence abhorrent. His brow, shiny with perspiration, wrinkled. "Sorry?"

She poked a finger in his chest. "You damn well should be. Do you have any idea the bullshit you stirred up? You're fucking up a perfectly good vacation, weasel. So get on with the explanations."

He appeared to be aghast, his sweet, round face now scrunched in a bewildered tangle of confusion. "What did you call me?"

Nina nodded, affecting that menacing stance again. "Weasel. *Who* are you?"

The man puffed his cheeks out, his nose turning red, wincing as he looked up at Nina. "I'm Frank. Who . . ." His tone wobbled before he appeared to tap into some inner strength. "*Are you*?"

"Your worst fucking nightmare, Frank. So explain. Do it fast. Do it now. Or I'll chew off your short, little legs with my big, shiny teeth." In full threat mode, Nina flashed her fangs at him.

Frank trembled—visibly, his rounded shoulders quaking under his coat. "I don't know what you want me to explain. I'm here to pick up my order."

Nina bobbed her head and rolled her eyes. "Yeah, yeah. Nice play on innocent and light, buddy. Not fallin' for it. Now, this *spice.* What the fuck is it, and get on with it because I want to get the hell out of here."

Mick stepped in then, putting himself between Nina and Frank. "I'm Mick Malone. This is Tessa Preston. As you can see, we've had a bit of a mishap here at the store."

Frank took another step back, tripping on a torched ottoman before righting himself. "I see that."

Mick moved forward, but Mick often forgot how imposing his size could be. "So, this spice. What's it for?"

Frank inched backward again, his face now fearful and wary. "What business is it of yours? I paid good money to have it delivered here. That's really all you need to know. Now, where is the package? I'm rather in a rush."

Tessa tugged at Mick's arm, stepping around him, a the-customer-is-always-right smile on her face. "I need to know for my own personal records, Frank. That's all," Tessa reassured him, hoping to ease his obvious discomfort.

"So where is it?" Frank asked, shifting from foot to foot, his eyes scanning the landscape of the store. "I don't mean to rush you, but I really have to be going."

Tessa bit her lip. "There's been a bit of a problem."

"Yeah, there has." Nina inserted herself into the conversation again. "There's a big problem, Frank."

Frank's face took on a worried frown. "I don't understand. What kind of problem? You said the sca . . ." He cleared his throat, running his finger around the rim of the collar on his buttoned up jacket. "You said the spice was here."

Tessa bobbed her head, not even a little concerned with how crazy she must look to this man right now with her hair singed and her clothes covered in soot. “It was, but as Mick said, we had a bit of an accident.”

Frank tucked his chin to his chest, peering up at them with clear hesitance. “I’m hoping that accident didn’t involve my order.”

Nina slapped Frank on the back and grinned. “Guess what?”

He jolted forward, his meek eyes looking up at her. “I’m afraid to guess.”

“Try,” Nina goaded.

“It’s been ruined in the fire?”

Nina shook her head, the strings on her hoodie dancing under the flashlight. “Close, buddy. But not quite. Guess again.”

Frank gave his head a quick shake as though he were trying to clear it. “Please,” he fretted. “I don’t have time for guessing games.”

Nina rocked back on her heels. “Awww, c’mon. I miss my kid. She loves games. Humor me.”

Frank squared his shoulders, managing to straighten his spine. “You have children?”

Tessa winced, though, in all fairness, Nina was the least likely parent ever—even to a complete stranger.

Nina didn’t answer. Instead, she growled at him.

Frank began to posture, an odd sort of summoning of his will, mingling with a clear hesitant approach. “Miss, I don’t have time for foolishness. What happened to the spice?” he almost yelled, but instantly cowered when Nina gave him her death glare.

Tessa put her hands up, daring to step in front of Nina. She held her breath while she did it, but she did do it. If her soul was in jeopardy, so be it. They needed answers. Not gnawed-off limbs and mangled souls. “Um, Frank, here’s what happened—”

But Frank began to tremble—literally. His whole body began to shake violently, his arms and legs shuddering.

The sodden floor beneath them shook, too, trembling and quaking, kicking up spatters of water and sodden debris.

And then there was the wail—a screeching roar of sound—tearing through her eardrums, making everyone fall to their knees and clap their hands over their ears.

What the hell was going on? Fear rippled along her spine when Mick reached for her, grabbing her hand to yank her out of harm's way as the floor began to split before their very eyes.

And Frank. He *shimmered.*

Shimmered with tiny sparkles of light, making his body waver with color.

Then he began fading, coming into focus in vivid colors before the air felt like it was sucked out of the room. Chunks of the store's wreckage flew as though lifted by invisible hands, small cyclones of wet paper picked up speed, whirling through the space, and the roof began to collapse in hunks, raining down on them with hard pelts of roof tiles and soaked Sheetrock.

Tessa's eyes flew to Mick's before they both sprang into action, grabbing onto Nina, Marty, and Wanda and forcing them to run. "Get out!" she screamed above the unrelenting whir of the high-pitched buzz.

Mick pushed everyone ahead of him toward the store's entry, hustling them out just as the roof began to cave entirely.

As they reached the walkway, Tessa turned around to get a last glimpse of Frank, his image quivering in bright hues just as he screamed a name. A name that sent a chill down her spine "No,

Noah!" he croaked on a strangled cry before he disappeared entirely and the store collapsed in a thunderous moan.

Mick's eyes met hers in confusion before he looked back at the scene in the store. She rested her hands on her knees, panting for breath, drawing fresh air into her raw lungs, her mind reeling from Frank's words.

And Mick was there, kneeling next to her, running his hands over her back while everything around them exploded.

TESSA dried her hair, grateful for the fresh scent of shampoo after all that smoke. She'd stood a long time under the hard spray of her shower, absorbing the things she'd seen tonight. Processing what had happened to not just Mick but her, too.

The paranormal was real. She couldn't deny it. She wanted to climb into her bed, pull the covers over her head, and pretend this was all some nightmare, but she couldn't.

Nina was real. So real. She had fangs and drank blood, and she made Lestat look like a chump poser.

So she'd allowed herself a long, hot shower full of freak-outs and tears before she pulled herself up by her bootstraps and blew her nose.

Looking at her reflection in the mirror, she took deep breaths before tugging on a clean pair of sweats and a sweater.

If Mick could take this like a big boy, so could she.

Why does everything have to be a competition between you two, Tessa? She heard Noah's words, as loud and as clear as if he were right in the room with her.

Noah.

God, she missed him. She missed his insight, his laugh, his stupid, long-winded jokes with the pathetic, never-funny punch lines. For a long time, they'd only had each other after their parents died. They'd stayed as tight as two siblings could. She'd made sure of it.

Until he died of smoke inhalation, fighting a fire. She'd flopped around like a fish out of water for a long time after Noah's death, trying to figure out how she was going to face a future with just her in it. Her parents were both gone, a couple of years before Noah died, but his death had left her feeling like she was floating, without roots to tether her.

No purpose, no focus, no particular place to go. And alone. So alone. Until she'd found the store, and her onetime weekend antiquing hobby became her passion—a way to feel something other than empty inside.

That was all gone now. Burnt to the proverbial crisp.

And she had wings.

And you're skipping right over the part you spent the most time freaking out about, Tessa.

She nodded at her reflection as she ran a brush through her hair. She sure was. Because to ask herself what it meant, how, of all the names in the world, Frank had chosen her brother's, was to acknowledge that this was beyond real.

But why did Frank call out Noah's name?

There: addressed.

Oh, no, T. How did Frank know your brother's name? Why, of all the names in the universe, would he choose your brother's?

Another shiver ran up her spine, a dark, ominous shiver. Okay. Why did Frank scream Noah's name? There. Addressed some more.

She squirted some hand cream on her fingertips and began rubbing it on her chapped cheeks, noting that her eyes looked dull and her hair stringy.

But her reflection mocked her. *No, Tessa. You need to talk to Mick about it. He heard Frank yell it, too. Maybe it's a clue to what's going on.*

She couldn't talk to Mick about Noah. They always fought over what Noah would say or do in any given situation—even though he was no longer here to tell them what he'd do. They fought over who knew Noah better.

They fought.

Noah had become a sore spot between them. Instead of bringing them closer together, his memory came between them, and Tessa couldn't figure out why.

Mick wouldn't talk to her much after Noah died. They'd always argued when Noah was alive, but there'd been less of an edge to it then. It wasn't as go-for-the-throat as it was now. It had been far more playful back then. Fun, maybe even flirty on her part, when she really let herself go. But after Noah was gone, everything went sideways.

Mick had clammed up so tight, he almost hadn't spoken at all during that awful time.

He'd stood stoically beside her every step of the way, right until they'd lowered Noah's body into the ground. But if she even attempted to scratch the surface of his pain after the funeral, he battened down the hatches. And then, like a light switch, things had gone almost back to normal. Just like they used to be, but with a harder edge.

When Mick began digging at her, poking at her again, she'd welcomed it because she didn't know how to deal with the other Mick. The sad Mick. The deflated, sometimes broody Mick.

Mick had always been the less introspective of the two of them, or so she'd thought. Noah was the one who occasionally withdrew, brooding about one thing or another, but Mick had been the clown of the pair. That had died with Noah.

He did a good job of trying to cover it up, but there was always that niggle, something she couldn't quite put her finger on that was missing in action.

A knock on the bathroom door startled her. "Tessa?" Mick said. "You comin' out anytime soon? How long does it take for you to fix that mug?"

She smiled. Her mug. He teased her about it often, had as far back as she could remember. That was the old Mick—the one who rose up from the ashes of the remnants of the days when their families had picnicked together, shared holidays together, vacationed together.

She popped the door open, the steam escaping and shrouding Mick's face for a moment before it cleared, and he was looking at her with eyes full of concern. Eyes she'd fall so far into she'd drown in, if he'd let her. "What now? Are you reading minds? Scaling tall buildings in a single bound? Catching bullets with your teeth?"

He grinned, his perfect white teeth flashing. "Not yet, but the day is young. I just came to tell you there's pizza. Figured you had to be hungry."

"Pizza? Where did you get pizza at this time of night? Did Angelo open up the restaurant at this hour because Nina threatened to chew his tonsils out by way of throat?"

Mick grinned again, leaning his head against the doorframe. "No. But it's equally as fantastic."

"Did Angelo survive the blunt force trauma?" Worse, was his soul still intact?

Mick chuckled. She liked when he laughed; it always did something funny to her insides. "Angelo had nothing to do with it. She flew."

She flew. He said that as if it was natural, as though he'd said she'd jogged. *"What?"*

"Nina flew to New York and got some. It's pretty damned good. Come have some with us."

Her eyes widened. "You do realize you just said that like she did nothing more than throw a DiGiorno in the oven, don't you?"

Mick sobered, his eyes serious, his luscious lips flattening. "It's our reality now, Tessa. C'mon. Come eat. It's been a long day, and if those wings of yours come out again, you'll need your strength."

She pulled the door open all the way and followed his broad back out into the kitchen, where everyone had gathered at her breakfast bar with the shiny gray and black granite countertops.

They chatted as though the world hadn't just torn apart at the seams. As though no one had just sprouted wings, Frank hadn't disappeared into thin air, and Nina hadn't just flown to New York to get pizza.

They chatted like they were all old friends.

With a warm smile, Wanda held up a plate with a slice of

pizza covered in ham and pineapple. Tessa's favorite. "Mick told us what you liked best. Nina made sure she brought it back."

Nina sat on the plump sectional couch with Joe-Joe, stroking the dog's head while he looked at the vampire with utter adoration in his eyes. "Don't go thinkin' I did that out of the goodness of my undead heart or anything other than avoiding the potential bitch-fest Marty and Wanda would have if I didn't do their BFF bidding. I did it because they made me do it. I can't even eat fucking pizza."

Take that, you waste of skin and bones.

Tessa bit into the slice of pizza, realizing the moment it hit her taste buds just how hungry she was. "So I don't owe you a soul sucking? Because you really went way far out of your way to make sure I had ham and pineapple on my pizza. That says something. Like maybe someday, we can have a conversation that involves minimal snarling."

Nina held up her middle finger. "You're gonna owe me that snippy tongue of yours if you keep it up. Shut up and eat. You look like shit."

Tessa fought a giggle. She was probably delirious from the day's events, but there was something heartwarming about Nina telling her to shut up. "So, where do we stand now?"

Mick's eyes caught hers from across the room. "We don't know."

He was doing his best to avoid talking about what she knew they'd both heard just before Frank disappeared.

Marty smiled at her, patting her hand, looking refreshed after her shower at the inn. "How about you just eat right now—refuel, and we'll talk some more after?"

If Mick wasn't going to say it, she would. "Because we need to talk about Noah."

Mick visibly stiffened, his jaw clenching tighter as he chewed his slice of pizza.

Marty's brow furrowed. She tucked a strand of her vanilla-blond hair behind her ear, her ring flashing as it caught the beams of the recessed lighting. "Who's Noah?"

"My dead brother."

Mick clapped a hand on the granite counter, making her jump. "Jesus, Tessa! Do you have to say it like that?"

Tessa dropped her plate on the counter. "Say it like it's the truth? He's been gone for three years now. He's dead. That's just the reality. Quit acting like you didn't hear what I heard. So the question is, how did Frank know about him?"

Mick wiped his mouth with a napkin, crushing it up and lobbing it into the garbage can with an angry toss. "I know he's dead, T. I get it."

"So how does some random guy who can make himself disappear know about Noah?" She was pushing, because the only way to get a rise out of Mick was to push, and they needed to acknowledge what Frank said.

Wanda, also freshly showered and utterly gorgeous in crisp slacks and a black silk shirt, held up a hand. "Hold the phone, scaly ones—Frank knows your deceased brother?" She turned to Tessa, sympathy in her eyes when she grabbed her hand and squeezed it. "My condolences, of course."

Tessa rounded the counter, glaring at Mick before she answered. "I don't know. For all I know, Frank and Noah could be having beers at the afterlife bar and grill. All I know is, both

Mick and I heard him yell, 'No, Noah!' just before he disappeared. How does someone I've never met before, who has the ability to disappear into thin air, know my brother?"

"You don't know that he meant our Noah, Tessa," Mick scoffed.

Tessa rolled her eyes at him. "Right. So it was just a random choice out of all the names in the *Big Book of Baby Names* he could have chosen? You're delusional, Mick. This has some connection to Noah." The more she thought about it, the more she was convinced it was true.

Mick shook his head. "I can't sit here and listen to this."

"Then go home!" she retorted.

Nina popped up off the couch, strolling over to Mick and making the face that after less than twenty-four hours, Tessa knew meant shut up or prepare to die. "Hey, the both of you—quit this shit now or soul sucking is gonna be the least of your worries. Mick, I don't know what the fuck your shiz is about, but I sense avoidance. In fact, I could scoop it up and lick it off a spoon. Fuck that. Everything is subject to suspicion as of this second. So whatever your hang-up is with her brother, can it, and let's figure this out."

Mick fell silent, his brooding anger at being openly checked by Nina palpable.

Wanda took Tessa's hand and pulled her to one of the stools lining the breakfast bar. "Tell me about Noah, would you? I always wanted a brother. I have a terrific sister named Casey, but a brother would've been lovely."

Tessa's throat tightened. She'd opened the can of worms, but now that she'd spilled them all over the floor, her words wouldn't come.

"He died in a fire three years ago," Mick offered, his words tight like they always were, thick with something he just wouldn't or couldn't share with her.

Wanda smiled sympathetically while Marty leaned in, giving her a quick hug. "Oh, Tessa. I'm so sorry. How painful. Are your parents still with you?"

Tessa shook her head. Now she'd really done it. "No. Both of them are gone."

"And he was all you had left?" Nina asked, her voice oddly soothing and minus a snarl.

"Yes."

Nina was up and beside her in a second, giving her shoulder a squeeze Tessa didn't even cringe beneath. "Dude, I'm ever so fucking sorry."

Tessa shook her head to rid herself of the tears that so desperately wanted to fall from her eyes. "Frank said, 'No, Noah' just before he disappeared. I know Mick heard him, too. How, out of all the names in the world, could he have known Noah's name?"

"Good question," Wanda murmured. "Did any of you smell anything unusual about Frank? Obviously, he's not human. So what is he?"

Marty made a face. "I can't get the smell of smoke out of my nose. Now I wish I'd sniffed him closer."

Nina bumped Marty's shoulder. "Same here. I should have paid closer attention, but I couldn't stop thinking about how he sounded like the dude who does Winnie-the-Pooh's voice. Charlie loves Pooh Bear. We listen to the audiobooks all the time."

This vampire listened to Winnie-the-Pooh? What was next, long walks on the beach, cuddles on thc couch? "It's so odd you should say that. I thought the same thing about Frank's voice, Nina. So who, in your world, has the ability to disappear like that?" she asked.

Wanda shrugged like it was no big deal. "All sorts of people—in our world, anyway. Demons, genies. We need to get in touch with Casey and Darnell, maybe even Jeannie."

"Who're they?" Mick asked, suddenly not as sullen.

"Casey's my sister and Darnell is a friend. Both demons. Jeannie's, well, a genie."

Tessa gripped the edge of the countertop to anchor herself. They spoke of these paranormal entities so casually she had to remind herself she was still on planet Earth. "So what do we do after that? I mean, you say this dragon thing will probably never go away, right? How do we learn to control it? Live with it until we find out more about Frank? We can't go around setting things on fire."

Wanda began cleaning up the debris from the pizza. "Here's what I say. You look exhausted, Tessa. You've had a traumatic day, seen things you never even believed were real, got yourself some wings. You need rest. You'll probably need a lot of rest if your wings are going to sprout again—because that looks like it's going to take some getting used to. Now, I'm going to suggest we stay with you so we're close by if something comes up. Or if Frank comes back looking for his spice. I've already checked us out of your adorable inn here in town, so protesting is futile."

Mick moved forward, his dark hair gleaming under the recessed lights of her kitchen. "I can look out for her."

"The same way you looked out for my store?" She regretted the words the instant they came out. She was tired and cranky, and her bad mood was seeping from her brain via her mouth.

Marty popped her lips like Tessa's mother used to. "That's uncalled-for, and you know it. Stop being pissy and taking stabs at Mick for something that was an accident. A big, hunky man is offering to protect you. Where I come from, you don't let something like that go unnoticed. As to you, Mick." She turned to face him. "You're not equipped to deal with what we're equipped to deal with. Sure, you're the size of a semi, but we have the strength of an army. Between the three of us, we're like having five NFL teams and a bulldozer with a wide array of foul language. So we stay. Now, go do whatever it is you do when you're preparing for bed, and we'll stand watch tonight." She waved a hand at him and went to help Wanda clean up the rest of the kitchen.

Tessa eyed Mick. Wasn't it enough that she had to be in such close proximity to him because of their situation, but in the same house—overnight? She only had one bedroom. He couldn't sleep out in the living room if Nina and the other women were going to stand watch.

What if she had one of those dreams about him? The ones she'd been having since she was a young adult.

The ones where he threw her on her bed and made wild love to her the way she'd wanted him to for as far back as she could remember?

Without Noah's memory between them.

Just her and Mick.

CHAPTER 6

Tessa stared up at the ceiling, her back achy from her de-winging, her eyes grainy. The patterns made on the wall by the Malibu lights outside her window in her small garden usually soothed her, but tonight, she couldn't find peace.

Noah's face, handsome and strong, kept floating in and out of her mind's eye. She couldn't stop thinking about him, and she knew Mick was doing the same. She just didn't know how to broach the subject without him frying her house.

"You awake?" Mick called from the floor. She'd lobbed some pillows and an old sleeping bag at him before climbing into bed and shutting off the light.

"Yep."

"I can't sleep, either."

She pulled the comforter under her chin and tried to forget

what Mick looked like semi-naked in just some boxer briefs and flannel pajama bottoms. “It’s been a long day. I imagine our days aren’t going to get any shorter until we figure this out.”

“He did say Noah’s name. I heard him.”

“Yep. He did.” No more. It would only lead to an argument she wasn’t up to having.

“You’re angry?” His silky-deep voice rumbled around the room with the question.

“No.”

“Yes, you are. I can hear it in your voice.”

He didn’t mean she was angry about Frank. He meant she was angry because Noah was such a touchy subject. “I’m not angry anymore, Mick. I don’t know why you still are. Whenever we talk about Noah, you get your back up. So from now on, I’m choosing to remember him silently, because just the mention of his name sparks an argument I’m not willing to have with you anymore. Frank said his name. That makes no sense. I don’t even know how it relates to what’s happened to us, but my gut says it’s connected. If you don’t want to talk about it, even though it could be important, then don’t. But I’m going to—at least with those women.”

“I miss the shit out of him.”

That stung. Mick couldn’t claim all the rights to missing Noah, and he couldn’t behave like an ass because he did. “And I don’t? He was all I had left, Mick. You have your parents in Lauderdale and your sister in New York.”

“You have me.”

“On my back all the time. We have what I’m sure most psychologists would classify as a dysfunctional relationship. We're not healthy for each other."

Nothing. Only the sound of Mick's breathing. She imagined the rise and fall of his wide chest, stretched taut with olive-colored skin, rippled with muscle and just a sprinkle of hair between his pecs.

For a hundred years she'd wanted to lay her head on it, rest, inhale the unique scent of Mick.

But she wouldn't, because he didn't see her that way. It had begun with her silly childhood fantasies of chaste kisses and hand-holding, and had grown through the years into a full-on love affair in her mind. One she kept the deepest of secrets.

"I'm sorry you feel that way," he grumbled, his voice sexy and deep in the dark of her bedroom. She hadn't been in a bedroom with Mick since she was five and she'd snuck into Noah's room during a thunderstorm during one of their sleepovers.

She was raw tonight. Raw with the events of the day, raw with the surreal revelations she'd witnessed—just raw. "It's okay, Mick. Let's let it go for now. *Please.*"

Movement under the covers made her stiffen. Mick found her fingers and wound them around his. He squeezed before saying, "I just can't." His voice was tight, exactly like it had been the day he'd told her about Noah's death. Tight and thick, and holding back whatever it was that kept him from talking about his best friend.

A tear slipped from her eye and she fought a shudder of breath. Closing her eyes, she whispered, "I get it. But I can't anymore, either. Go to sleep, Mick. I'll see you in the morning."

Tessa let his hand go and rolled over, tucking the comforter under her chin, and stared out at the night sky until her eyes grew heavy and she finally succumbed to sleep.

"TESSA!" Winnie-the-Pooh hissed in her ear.

She batted at the voice with a weary hand. No-no wakey-wakey. She was having such a lovely dream about antiques shopping in Paris, and it didn't involve Mick naked at all. Not even Winnie-the-Pooh was going to disturb her serenity.

"Tessa! You must wake up!" Hands shook her shoulders. Soft, meaty hands.

Her eyes popped open, making her sit up and scoot backward on the bed as her heart raced. Frank.

Wait, Frank? In her bedroom?

"Frank?"

He pressed a chubby finger to his lips. "Shhh! You'll wake up the very large man sleeping on the floor."

Fear crawled along her spine. How had Frank gotten into her room? How had he gotten past the trio of beasts right outside her bedroom door? Tessa opened her mouth to speak, only to find there was more to this than just Frank in her room.

Frank was in her room, and Frank was floating.

A ghost? No. Ghosts existed, too? Oh, sweet baby J. No more paranormal surprises, please. "How . . ." She fought to keep her voice low. "*How* are you doing this?" She waved her hands around, her eyes widening when they passed right though his form.

His sweet face zoomed in, hovering right in front of hers. Hovering. Frank was *hovering*. Flying, lifting cars, fire-breathing.

She was this close to supernatural overload. "Never mind that," he said with urgency. "You have to listen before I disappear."

"Disappear?"

"Yes! I can't control my plane hopping. It's a defect. A pathetic defect that even in death, I can't seem to elude. So you must listen. Do you understand?"

Well, no. She didn't understand. Was plane hopping like train spotting? "Plane hopping?"

"None of that is relevant right now. You must listen to me, and listen well. I've done a horrible thing. So horrible, I can't even begin to describe the torture I'll endure because of it."

Her chest tightened. She would not pass out. *Do not pass out.* "What have you done?" Her voice quavered, making her angry at herself.

"You must get me more of the er . . . spice. I need it immediately or I can't tell you the pain we'll all suffer!"

His words startled her. She clung to the sheets and forced herself to ask, "We?" Was it going to be worse than sprouting wings? Because that had sucked big-time ass.

"Yes—we! How soon can you get more?"

"I don't know if I can get more, Frank," she whisper-yelled, afraid to tell him the spice hadn't burned in the store at all. "I have to relocate the dealer, and it took almost a month to get it here to begin with. What's so special about this spice that someone would torture you over it, Frank?"

His sweet face fell, his jowls quaking as he began to fade in and out the way he had back at the store. "Oh, nooo, no, no, no! That's not the answer I was hoping for. We're all doomed!" he cried dramatically.

"Frank!" she spewed his name in a harsh whisper. "What is this spice? What does it do? Why are we doomed if we don't find more? Do you have any idea what this spice has done to me . . ." She stopped short, gripping the sheets. She'd let him see her cards before she was ready. Crap.

His bushy eyebrows rose, his watery eyes glazed over. "What it's done to you? *You?* Oh, no," he groaned as though he were in pain. "It didn't burn with the store?"

She bit the inside of her cheek. "Well, the store did burn down because of it." Which was the total truth.

His face flickered in and out, becoming fuzzy, like an old movie on a television with rabbit ears. "What really happened to the spice? You must tell me now. *Now,*" he insisted.

She pointed to the floor where Mick lay, softly snoring. "The very large man took it by mistake," she said, wincing when she did.

"He ingested it?"

Tessa's gaze was sheepish. "If I say yes, then what happens?"

Frank clapped his hand to his heart, his fingers shooting straight through his ethereal form. "Things become bad. Very, very bad."

Tessa almost couldn't breathe now. "Why, Frank? Why do things become bad?"

"Because you've stolen something from someone who will *kill* you because of it."

Kill her? She went from afraid to very angry in two seconds flat. She wasn't no thief and she wasn't going to have Floaty Frank accuse her of such. "Excuse me? I didn't steal anything. It was an accident. Mick didn't do it on purpose. He took it because he thought it was aspirin. I didn't steal anything!"

"I can't tell you how much I regret hearing that, Tessa," he said, his voice becoming faraway.

Tessa scooted farther back and sat on her knees to face his shimmering form. "Don't you dare disappear on me, Frank! Who was this spice for, and why did they want to be a dragon?"

His watery blue eyes flew open. "A dragon? The large man is now a dragon?"

"Yes! And so am I! Now, who did you order that spice for, Frank?" she almost screamed before catching herself.

Frank waffled, his image beginning the fade in, fade out of earlier. "Oh, dear. Those spices were dragon scales! This is awful, Tessa! So dreadfully awful. Hell will rain down on you all for this!"

Dragon scales? She threw her finger up in the air, shaking it at him. "Frank, if you disappear, I'm going to hunt you down. Swear, I will! Why is it awful? It was a mistake, Frank. Nothing more. Now tell me who wants that spice, and how you know my brother's name!"

Frank began to drift away in plumes of colorful smoke. No, no, no! Her vestiges of fear turned to hot bolts of anger, shooting along her spine, spiking in her veins. "Frank! Don't you dare disappear on meeee!" she roared, so loud, so long, she almost passed out.

But passing out was the least of her worries.

She was more worried about the big hole in her far wall.

The big hole, now smoking and crackling, where her shoe closet used to be.

A charred shoe fell out and dropped to the floor.

No! Not the pink polka-dot ones. Damn. She'd just bought those shoes in anticipation of spring. They'd been such a deal, too, fun and flirty, and only $29.99.

Tessa gagged, spitting out the acrid taste on her tongue just before she tipped over from the weight of her wings and crashed to the floor, landing on top of Mick.

"TESSA! What the fuck is going on? Jesus Christ and a Wheat Thin, what's all the racket about?" Nina banged on the door.

Mick scooted out from under her, rubbing his eyes before he rose to crack the door.

Nina stuck her eyeball to the seam in the door, a shaft of light pushing its way into the room. "What the fuck, dude? If you two are in here consummating your unrequited bullshit and you can't keep it to a minimum, we're gonna have a goddamn problem. And why do I smell smoke?" She pushed the door open all the way, shoving her way inside.

Tessa lay facedown on the carpet, her wings flapping like the sail of a boat clapping in a breeze. She lifted her head, trying to push herself to her feet with no success.

"Oh, fuuuck," Nina said, planting her hands on her hips. She used one of her flannel footies to toe Tessa's shoulder. "You set your GD house on fire, Mothra."

Tessa coughed, a puff of smoke streaming from her mouth. "Can I get a hand here?"

Mick reached down to help but she swatted him away. "Not you!" She had to fight to keep from yelping so he wouldn't lay hands on her. Not after the last reaction she'd had. "One . . . one of the ladies, please." She couldn't bear it if he touched her wings.

Wanda poked her head in the door, her face covered in a green cream, her hair in rollers. "Nina, help me," she ordered, pushing Mick out the door.

Wanda slid her hands under Tessa's body while Nina got behind her and readied herself to catch her. As Tessa tried to help them lift her, her wings suddenly didn't feel like an extra appendage, but rather a part of her. Not as much a burden as an extension.

Once upright, and with Wanda holding her hands, she rolled her shoulders, sensing her wings rolling with them. This time, they didn't feel nearly as heavy.

Wanda looked her in the eye, her green face cream in chunks. "Why can't Mick touch your wings?"

God, these women were like mind readers. Wait. Nina was a mind reader. "I don't want to talk about it."

Nina cackled from behind. "I know! I know! Pick me, Miss Wanda," she singsonged.

"Nina," Wanda chastised, giving her friend a stern look, the goopy face cream wrinkling at the corners of her eyes. "Don't tease. It's ugly and mean."

Nina leaned around Tessa's right wing, pushing it out of the way to eyeball her. "It's 'cus it makes your lady parts tingly, right?"

"Nina! Hush, would you? Don't poke at her. It's cruel and rude to poke at the client."

Tessa lowered her eyes to the floor and grated a sigh. Why lie? It wasn't as if Nina couldn't probe her mind to find out if she really wanted to. God. The shame of all this. Her deepest secret lust revealed for all to see. "Yes."

Wanda's eyes went sympathetic and warm. She patted Tessa's

hand. "Aw, honey. I know this is uncomfortable for you, and Nina doesn't make it any easier, but it's a clue, and those are always good to have."

"To what?"

"In how to deal with these changes. Now we know Mick is off-limits to you when your wings are out to play. We'll remember that in the future."

How humiliating. "Why is this happening?" she asked, knowing it was pointless but asking anyway.

"I don't know, Tessa. I wish I had an answer. What made your wings come out anyhow? What made you breathe fire to begin with?"

Frank! How could she have forgotten about her encounter with Frank? "I was upset."

"About?"

"Frank," she said on a cough, clearing her throat.

"Frank?"

She nodded as Wanda steadied her. "Frank was here."

"And you didn't fucking call us? Dude, that's what we're here for!" Nina said.

"I didn't have time to call you. He just appeared out of nowhere again."

"Appeared?"

"Yes. Sort of hovering over my bed, all shimmery and fading in and out just like he did at the store."

Nina and Wanda gave each other that look that said they were communicating something they didn't want her to know before Wanda asked, "And what did Frank say?"

As she relayed to Wanda and Nina her conversation with

Frank, she refused to stop until she was done so as not to allow how insane all of it sounded to keep her from telling them everything.

"So you're sure he said Hell was going to rain down on all of us?" Wanda pressed, her eyes watching Tessa's.

"Yes. Those were his exact words. Every last one."

"Marty!" Nina bellowed. "Get Darnell on the fucking phone. We got Hell trouble."

More worry sprouted. She was almost afraid to ask, but she couldn't seem to remember. "Who's Darnell again?"

"A demon friend. A good demon friend. One we can trust," Wanda reassured her as though she'd just recommended her favorite investment banker. "No need to worry."

"You trust demons?" Tessa shook her head, her wings rocking with her. "Do you guys have a book with all this information in it? Because I feel like I didn't study for this test. How are demons trustworthy?" She'd been taught everything to the contrary. Demons were spawns of Satan who wormed into your soul and turned it black.

Which made sense if Nina knew this Darnell. But was Nina's soul black?

Or was that all just a front?

"I know it's a lot to get used to, Tessa. But all the things the two of you are witnessing are now second nature to us, and sometimes we forget this is a lot to soak up in a twenty-four-hour period. I realize it's rather like throwing you in the deep end of a pool, but sometimes, in cases like this where things begin to happen rather quickly, there just isn't a choice." Wise Wanda. So kind. So patient. Tessa didn't know how to feel about these women.

She gazed up at Wanda and gulped, clinging to her hands. "I

know you're only trying to help, but I'm really scared right now. I'm maybe even more afraid of the demon than I am of Nina." She didn't even have to look at Nina to know the vampire was rolling her eyes.

"Darnell's a pussycat. I promise, he's like a big teddy bear wrapped up in high-top sneakers and warm hugs." Wanda handed her over to Nina. "Hold on to her while I go find Marty and see what's up with Darnell."

Nina grabbed her hands from Wanda and walked Tessa backward until she was upright.

Tessa let her hands go slack, fighting not to pull away as her palms grew increasingly sweaty.

"Knock it off, chicken-shit. I'm not gonna hurt you."

Tessa was most afraid of Nina when she had to be alone with her. The others were less abrasive, less in your face. Just less everything. "Pinky swear?"

Nina rolled her eyes, her lips thinning. "I already changed out of my killing clothes for the night. You're safe."

Tessa took a deep breath, scanning Nina from head to toe. Maybe she could make friends with her. How many people could say they had a vampire for a friend? "I like your pajamas. It says something about a woman who's willing to wear Elmo flannels to bed."

"My fucking kid likes Elmo. I wear 'em for my kid because it makes her smile."

Her kid. Would she ever get used to the way Nina's child had come to be? Maybe if she tried to get to know her, personalize her, she wouldn't be so afraid of her. Still, her hands trembled when she asked, "How old is your baby?"

Nina's face went light again, her eyes shiny and happy. "In human years she's pushin' two."

Happy. Nina was happy. She liked happy Nina. "Human years?"

"Yeah. But in vampire years she's still crawling."

"Right. Because vampires age slowly."

"Yeah, but she's also half genie. So her dad and I keep wondering if that shit won't turn the vampire half of her on its ass."

"You have a husband?" Oh. Had that been surprise in her voice? Yikes. The angry look on Nina's face said yes. Tessa scrunched her eyes shut to prepare for the onslaught of bad language and threats.

"Yeah. I have a husband, or in vampire-ese, a soul mate."

She popped her eyes back open. "What's his name?"

"Vlad the Impaler."

Shut the front door. "No effin' way! Are you really married to Vlad the Impaler?"

"No, numbnuts. My husband's name is Greg."

"You act like I asked you an impossible question. How should I know if Vlad isn't still running around? After everything's that's happened today, anything is possible, right?"

"Yeah. Anything's possible. You talk a lot. You're almost as mouthy as Marty."

"Does that bother you? That I'm trying to get to know you?"

"I'm hopin' we don't have to stick around long enough to get to know each other."

Boo on the vampire. "Wow. That's sort of mean. You can never have too many friends, you know."

Nina's nostrils flared. "When you have Marty and Wanda for friends, you definitely can have too many friends. One more like 'em, and I'm liable to walk out into the sunlight tied up in garlic and shower with holy water."

"You don't really mean that, and I know you don't."

"How the fuck do you know what I mean?"

"Because I see the way you all work with one another. That doesn't happen if you're not friends. Good friends."

"Okay, so we're friends, yappy. So what?"

"And you're sure you don't want another one? Because I'm a super good friend."

"I'm all full up on super good friends."

"You really are mean, and I say that with tons of respect because my brain doesn't always get to my mouth to stop me from saying something I'm pretty sure will get me into trouble."

Nina bobbed her head. "I really am—mean, that is."

"Do you want to know anything about me?"

"I want to know what will shut you the fuck up before I have to go about finding out what shuts you the fuck up."

Why did she need this woman to like her? Why did she want to push her so far she might react and suck her soul right out of her? Because she wanted to know what made someone so unhindered by society's idea of appropriate behavior tick. "You would hurt me? I'm not sure I believe that."

Nina looked down at her, her eyes glittering. "Want me to show you?"

"No. No demonstration needed. I take that back. I believe."

Nina nodded, the dark curtain of her hair falling forward on her shoulders.

"You have amazing hair. It's so shiny. What kind of conditioner do you use?"

"The blood of yappy humans."

"I'm not a human anymore. I'm a dragon. Rawr." She giggled.

"Okay. The blood of yappy dragons." She flashed her teeth at Tessa and hissed. "Rawr."

Tessa was in the process of leaning back in fear when a new face appeared. Like, appeared.

Out of nowhere, right behind Nina.

Jesus.

"Nina, you beatin' down the new girl?" a warm, syrupy voice asked.

Nina's face lit up again, all wreathed in smiles and welcoming eyes. She was even more beautiful when she smiled. "Darnell, my man! Good to see ya, buddy!"

A large hand the size of a bear paw thumped Nina on the back. "You, too. How's my Charlie? Sho miss my snuggle bug."

"Missin' her Uncle Darnell. You know she loves you. She hasn't seen you in a month. Where ya been? You missed the last damn barbecue Marty had. Jesus, I could've used you for touch football. You know how pissy those ass-sniffin' werewolves get about a chick takin' 'em down."

Tessa was fascinated. Fascinated by the fact that demons and vampires and werewolves were friends. Fascinated by the idea they barbecued and played football. Fascinated that they chatted like old friends rather than sat around and plotted the end of the world.

"Dang, I'm sorry I missed that. I had some business to take care of is all. But you know I'm down with the next shindig. Wouldn't miss it.

"You must be Miss Tessa," he said on a grin, his wide smile full of white teeth.

"I am." She pulled a hand away from Nina's grasp to offer it to Darnell, who grabbed onto it and shook it. His touch brought with it a strange peace. As though when he was in the room, everything was going to be all right.

He rocked back on his heels, pushing his hands into his jeans pockets. "Pleasure, fo' sure. I hear you have some troubles, Miss Tessa. I'm gonna see if I can't help ya."

"I would really appreciate it. Because these"—she hitched her jaw at her wings—"are a lot."

"I like yer wings," he commented, chuckling. "They're right fine. Just right for a pretty lady like you."

Tessa's eyes captured his, warm and brown. "Thank you. So what do demons do? I mean, here on earth?"

"We stay outta trouble. I know all the stuff you been told about us, but some of us just got caught up in somethin' we can't get out of is all." He shrugged his shoulders and grinned again, boyish and sweet.

"Caught up in?"

Nina squeezed her hands, her eyebrows furrowing. "Jesus, you're like a dog with a bone, dude. Shut it with all the lame-ass questions, would you?"

"'S'all right, Nina. She's just curious." Darnell patted Tessa on the shoulder. "How 'bout we talk later? I'll tell ya everything I know 'bout Hell. For now, let's just focus on findin' out what's goin' on with this disappearing dude, okay?"

When he said it like that, Darnell made it sound like nothing wouldn't be okay while he was around. She nodded. "Okay. So, from the beginning?"

"Like all good stories start," Darnell coaxed, taking her hands from Nina to keep her from falling.

The moment he leaned in to steady her when she wobbled, Tessa relaxed, and relayed her story to Darnell.

When she said the name Frank, he held up a beefy hand. "Did you say Frank? Little round guy? Sounds like Winnie-the-Pooh?"

"Yes, that's exactly him. Do you know him? Is he a ghost?" If Frank was a ghost, he'd be like the lettuce in her paranormal sandwich.

Darnell's eyes flashed concern, but he hid it well. "He ain't no ghost."

Now she was worried again, despite Darnell's reassuring grip on her hands. "So what is he?"

"He's a minion for someone in Hell."

"And not the *Despicable Me* kind, right?"

"He's the kinda minion who's stuck. He doesn't really belong in Hell, but somehow he landed there. And I'm bettin' he wants out."

She'd lay bets the deeds were bad. "So give it to me straight, Darnell. I can take it."

"It means whoever he was getting those dragon scales for was probably somebody we don't want no part of, and whoever that somebody is, they're gonna be real angry when they find out he doesn't have what they asked him to get."

"But how does that affect Mick and me? Mick didn't take the dragon scales on purpose. Maybe we can just call this person up on the paranormal hotline and apologize?"

"Here's what I'm thinking, Miss Tessa. I'm thinkin' this guy Frank is stuck between our world and Hell. He wants outta Hell.

So he struck himself a deal with someone. Get the dragon scales, the demon he gives 'em to lets him out."

"Okay, so no problem. Frank doesn't have the dragon scales, right? So it's Frank's problem." Though she hated the idea someone would hurt Frank. He'd been the least scary of the bunch.

"Well, sho', Frank's gonna have some issues. But that's not the biggest problem. The biggest problem we have is, those dragon scales he got—they're rare. So rare they like hen's teeth."

Maybe it was lack of sleep, but she wasn't connecting the dots. "Still don't get it."

"This is what it means, Chatty Cathy," Nina cut in. "It means you and King Kong out there have all the dragon scales. You know, on you." She pointed to Tessa's wings. "That means someone's gonna come looking for you."

Her heart began to race, her palms going sweaty again, and that sick feeling in the pit of her stomach rolled like a tidal wave. "Someone bad?"

"Yeah. Someone bad. Someone really fucking bad," Nina responded with a tone suggesting she'd been to bad before, and it was really bad. "Someone who's gonna wanna skin you two alive."

CHAPTER 7

Mick sat with Wanda on the couch, Joe-Joe draped contentedly at her feet. They both stared at the fire he'd started in the fireplace, contemplating Darnell's words while Marty dozed on the love seat and Nina was in with Tessa.

Mick spoke first, though his words came out stiff. "Is what Darnell said true?"

Wanda sighed, tucking her legs beneath her. "Likely it is. Darnell's our hotline to Hell. If he says someone's going to want retribution for the missing dragon scales, he's probably right."

"He really lives in Hell?" Did he just ask that out loud?

Wanda shook her head with a smile. "No. He skirts Hell. Somehow he manages to fringe it. He's pretty good at it, too. But he has people there who keep him in the loop."

"So he's a good demon?"

"He's an amazing demon—one of the best pieces of our crazy,

patched-together paranormal family. I can't tell you how many situations he's gotten us out of."

"This goes against everything you hear growing up."

"Catholic?"

"Born and raised," Mick admitted, and struggling mightily with the idea that there were good demons. This wasn't a goddamn Disney movie.

"It's always hardest for those brought up in a strict religion to believe this life is anything other than black-and-white. But think of Darnell's situation like this: making the biggest misjudgment of character in your life, thinking you're doing it for the greater good, and then taking the hit for it so the people you love won't suffer."

"So he made a sacrifice? Like a deal with the devil?"

Her pretty eyes flickered by the firelight. "Sort of. He signed a contract with the devil for what he thought was a deal with a Major League baseball team. He ended up in the majors, all right. As a bat boy. Loopholes are huge with Satan. The gist of it is, Darnell was very poor. The deal he made was out of desperation and love. Not because he wanted something for himself, but because he wanted to help his financially struggling mother and sisters. Nowadays, he fringes Hell. Sort of lays low, gets lost in the fray and, in the interim, tries to help those who've been tricked like he was. It's rather like his perpetual penance, I think. He just keeps helping in any way he can."

"Damn," Mick breathed.

Wanda nodded, but her face was all business. "What we need to focus on right now is how we're going to keep our guard up until we can find out who wants your scales."

"They'd really skin us alive?" Jesus Christ. He had to find a way to protect Tessa. Not a goddamn chance in hell was he going to let anyone near her. Demon or not.

Wanda turned to face him, her usually calm face now fierce, her shoulders rigid. "We won't let that happen, Mick. We'll protect you, of that you can be sure."

"How did Tessa get involved in this? How did she become a dragon, too? I still can't figure it out."

"I don't know. I have no answers about that. To be honest, I don't have answers for a lot of the things that happen in our world. But I've got lots of feelers out to see what our people know about dragons."

"And how do we help Tessa? She can't go around falling all over the place every time her wings pop out. Aside from the fact that it hurts her when they sprout." He'd take that pain from her if he could. Take it and keep it.

"I don't know that, either. But we will. We haven't failed yet. I won't start now."

He admired Wanda's fierce determination. It had to come from a place of experience. "Can I ask you a question?"

Her face went light again. "Of course."

"The afterlife . . ." If the guys at the station could hear him, they'd call him a pussy. He'd call himself a pussy, too, except for the crazy shit he'd seen since yesterday.

"You want to know if it exists?"

"I don't know." He cleared his throat, righting himself on the couch. "Yes. Does it? Exist, I mean?"

"I don't know. I might never know because of what I am. But I hope so—because I couldn't bear the idea that after this, there's nothing. If that's the case, I'd venture to guess I don't mind living forever. But can I ask you a personal question now?"

"Sure."

"Does your question have to do with Tessa's brother, Noah, and what Frank said?"

Yeah. Yeah, it did. What scared the shit out of him was how Frank had known Noah's name. If there was a Heaven and Hell, no way a guy like Noah had landed down below. So what was the connection between them? If he just knew Noah was okay. That he forgave him for . . . "I guess it does."

"You were best friends all your lives, right?"

"We were. Since we were kids."

Wanda tucked a pillow to her stomach. "I can't imagine losing Marty or Nina. I'm sorry losing Noah still hurts you so much. I'm sorry it affects your relationship with Tessa."

"It doesn't—"

Wanda flapped a hand at Mick to hush him. "Of course it does. It's plain as the nose on your face you're in love with her, Mick. Though I'm far less crass than our Nina, I'm not one to tiptoe around. Whatever Noah's death has to do with this angst between you and Tessa, I'm still not sure I understand. I only know that it's driven a wedge between the two of you. You're holding something back, and in doing that, you're only hurting yourself. Think about that on this journey, would you?"

"I can't talk about it." God. He'd said that a million times since Noah had died. He wanted to talk about it. But every time he thought he might be able to, his words became thick and uncomfortable, stuck on his tongue like they were mixed with peanut butter. It was easier to fight with Tessa than confess to her how he really felt.

Tucking her chin under her hand, Wanda smiled at him, using her other hand to welcome Joe-Joe up onto the couch and into her lap. She stroked Joe-Joe's ears as she doled out advice. "Men say that a lot. 'I can't talk about it,'" she mocked, deepening her voice. "Then after they say that, they complain when they don't garner the reactions from us they want. You're all strange, strange creatures to expect us to guess at how you feel or why you're feeling it. But here's something to think about. You and Tessa are in this together. You're both in a helluva predicament. Working together is crucial. Learning about what happened to you both is even more crucial. Trust and communication are the two most important keys to making this work right now. I hope you'll think about that if Noah's death, and the aftermath of it, begin to get in the way."

Sage advice. Mick took a deep breath, reaching over to give Joe-Joe a scratch on the ear. "Why is she so uncomfortable with me touching her wings?"

Wanda shrugged, leaning her head back on the couch and closing her eyes with a smile. "Why don't you ask Tessa?"

Why didn't he?

And love. Was he that obvious? He thought their spats covered all of it up. Hid the way he felt. If he didn't keep arguing with her, he'd throw her down on any available surface and make the kind of love to her that fifteen years of pent-up longing could produce.

If fighting with her kept him from revealing his painful secret, he'd keep right on fighting with her.

Because her silence was what confessions from him would supply. She'd never speak to him again.

And he couldn't take her silence.

NINA rubbed Tessa's back with a soothing cream, massaging the muscles with the skill of a masseuse. Nina had helped her through the agonizing shift back to her normal state, rocking her, consoling her. Tessa never would've guessed she had it in her, but it led her to believe maybe she'd pegged the vampire all wrong.

"I set my house on fire." With her breath. *Dragon breath* had a whole new meaning now.

Nina wrapped her slender fingers around Tessa's wrist and twisted them in a gentle motion back and forth, working her way up her elbow and back down again. "You sure did."

"Everything's such a mess."

"A shitty one, for sure."

"My store is gone, too." So gone. It was all hitting her right now. Her store was toast. She had no way to make a living. Her brother was dead, and so were her parents. And she was a dragon. It was a good thing dragons lived in caves, because that's where she was going to end up at this rate. "I don't think this mess can be cleaned up."

"Messes can be cleaned up, kiddo. Even burnt-to-fuck stores. We'll help."

Tessa didn't speak. She didn't know how to respond to the kindness, especially after so much fear.

"But you hardly know me. Why would you help?"

"It's just what we do," she responded, her voice gravelly to Tessa's ear. Nina gave Tessa's back one last pat. "Better?"

"Thank you," she whispered into the pillow, fighting the sting of tears. There had to be a better way to de-wing, because the agony of that last bout felt like near-death.

Nina dropped to the edge of the bed, pushing Tessa's hair from her face. "It hurts. That sucks. I'm sorry."

She curled her fist under her chin. "Me, too. It should be way funner to be a dragon."

"At least you can still eat chicken wings."

"A sure sign I lucked out when it comes to gifts from the paranormal."

"Looks like."

"Do you miss eating?"

Nina stroked the top of Tessa's head just like her mother once did. "You bet your scaly ass I do. But I'd rather go through my eternal life like this than have missed out on my husband, my kid—my stupid-ass friends."

Tessa's laughter was weak, a frail wisp of sound. "Can I ask you something?"

"More questions? You're yappy." But her tone said it was all right.

"Will it always hurt like that?" Because she didn't know if she could survive that for the rest of her life.

Nina continued to stroke her hair, and just as Tessa's eyes began to close, she said, "I sure as fuck hope not, kiddo. But if it does, I'll stay with you until it passes."

"Will you really?" she whispered, her voice hitching, hating that she sounded so weak.

Nina grabbed her hand, tucking it to her chest. "Count on it. Go to sleep now. I'll stay with you."

Tessa let her eyes slide closed, clinging to Nina's hand like she was an undead lifeline in the choppy waters of the sea of life.

"HOW do you feel this morning?" Mick asked, leaning into her, smelling of fresh soap and spicy cologne. Whenever she saw him, her stomach always fluttered. His long legs, thick with muscle, encased in tight jeans, never failed to make her heart jump around in her chest.

But today, even the sight of Mick didn't perk her up. Everything felt all wrong. Like she was looking through a frosted window and could only make out hazy images.

"Hey," he prodded again, looking down at her with concern. "How do you feel?"

Not great. She definitely didn't feel great. Kind of warm, a little sensitive, like someone had steamrolled her body. Maybe a little lightheaded and dizzy and odd. Just odd. "Like I suddenly sprouted wings and someone ripped them off my back," she answered, sliding onto the breakfast bar stool and wrapping her grateful hand around the mug of coffee Marty supplied.

Marty laid her palms on Tessa's back and began making circles. "Aspirin? Maybe that'll help. Nina, check the bathroom for some aspirin, would you? Our girl's still achy."

Nina appeared out of nowhere, standing at the inside of Tessa's small pantry, her nose slathered in sunscreen. She crossed the room and chucked Tessa under the chin. "We sure it's the real stuff?" she teased, snickering as she made her way out of the kitchen.

"Funny. Very funny." She let her head rest in her hands, massaging her temples. God, she felt worse than she ever had with even her worst hangover.

Nina plopped two of the pills down in front of her, using the tips of her fingers to push them toward her. "Drink up, princess."

Tessa grabbed them and swallowed, washing them down with a hot splash of coffee. "So what's on tap for today? Are we going demon hunting? Vampire slaying? Full-moon frolicking?"

Marty chuckled, pinching her cheek before frowning and putting the back of her hand against Tessa's forehead. "You're staying here and resting, because you look absolutely green around the gills, and you're a little warm for my taste. Mick's going to the store with Nina to meet his friends from the firehouse so she can make sure her mojo stuck."

"Her mojo?"

"The one where she makes them scratch their heads at how they missed a fire like the one at your store. I hope her mindbend is in working order, because I imagine there'll be some mass work to be done with the people in town."

Nina snorted from the stove, where she was cooking something. "Don't you worry your pretty little airhead about that shit. I whammied your entire Podunk town last night. When they get up today, the fire will all be like a huge surprise."

Tessa looked to Mick, so strong and solid and obviously feeling much better than she did. "How are we going to explain it away?"

"I'll handle it, Tessa. Don't worry. But the girls are right. You do need to rest. You had a rough night last night."

She bristled. "No rougher than you."

Mick made a face, his strong jaw tightening, and grated out a sigh. "It's not a competition."

It was if you were always the little sister. But she was too tired, too achy to care today. "You're right. I just mean, you must be tired, too."

"I'm fine. I'm used to nights like this. Fireman, remember?"

Nina dropped a plate in front of Tessa with some fluffy eggs and buttered wheat toast. "Eat."

"You cook? Will your vampire wonders never cease?" She didn't feel like eating, but the dark mistress had cooked. Tessa had a feeling she'd better not screw up Nina's offering.

"Will your yappy mouth ever stay shut? I have a kid. She's half genie. She eats soft foods at this point in her life. Eat and shut up about it or I'll force-feed it to you."

Tessa smiled, despite her headache. "I'm not afraid of you today, by the way. Not after last night. Just in case you thought that was going to work on me. You know, your DEFCON fear factor."

"The day is young, Chatty McChatty. It could turn on a dime. So shut up and eat."

She tugged on the edge of Nina's hoodie. "How come you're awake? It's eight in the morning. Don't vampires sleep during the day?" Ever since Nina had reminded her vampires could burn to death under the sun, she had irrational fears about Nina turning to ashes.

"I've learned to build up a tolerance to vampire sleep. Good damn thing, too, with the kid and all. But come tonight, I'll be hanging upside down in your closet by my bat wings from fucking lack of sleep."

Mick's eyebrow rose. "Really?"

Nina rolled her eyes at him. "No, Gigantor. I was joking. I sleep in a bed just like you, dipshit."

Tessa glanced outside. The sun was bright, despite the cold weather. She was still figuring Nina out, but she didn't want to see her set on fire. "But won't you burn outside? From the sun?" That would be dreadful to find Nina a pile of ashes in the middle of a snowbank.

Nina shrugged into her jacket. "Nope. Built up a tolerance to that, too. That's why they call me badass."

But Tessa had found something in Nina. Something she'd been lacking for a long time now. Someone who made her feel safe. Comforted—even if it was done in the gruffest of manners. And she didn't want to lose that. "Promise you're telling me the truth?"

Nina's eyes raked over her face, searching. Tessa's head swarmed with an image of Nina for a moment, almost as if her brain had been nudged, and then it was gone as swiftly as it had come. "I promise I'm telling the truth, kiddo. I do it all the time. How else do you suppose I put up with these two?"

Where was this fear coming from? Why was she clinging to a woman she hardly knew?

"It's the fear of being abandoned," Nina provided.

Wanda was behind her in seconds. Her face had admonishment written all over it. "Nina! Shame on you. You know better than to read minds. Off-limits, vampire!"

Tessa pushed the chair back, wobbling when she rose. How invasive. How incredible. "You can read my mind, too?"

Nina held up a palm to Wanda. "Yeah. I only do it when I need to. So relax and listen to me. I make you feel safe. You haven't felt that way in a long time. Swear, I'm not going to fucking disappear on you like everyone else in your life. You're not alone. I'm coming back. Hear that?"

Crimson spots burned holes in Tessa's cheeks. Her worst fears voiced to a roomful of people she didn't even know and the man to whom she was always trying to prove how completely independent she was. But it was true. "I hear you."

Nina smiled. "Good. Now go fucking lie down because you look like shit. I'll see you in a little bit."

Wanda tucked her arm into Tessa's and pulled her toward the couch. "C'mon. Let's sit by the fire and rest. You look feverish, and that worries me."

Tessa let herself be led to the couch, taking one last peek at Nina as she and Mick headed out the door before allowing Wanda to tuck a blanket around her shoulders and settle her on the couch.

"YOUR woman's freaked out, dude. Fix that shit," Nina said on the ride to Tessa's store.

Mick gripped the steering wheel. "She's not my woman. She's my best friend's sister."

"And you feel responsible for her. That's a good front. Dude, she's lost a lot of shit in her life recently. Not just her family but now her store with all the old shit in it. Maybe a little love from you would ease some of her stress. Because she's clinging, and that's not healthy."

He glanced over at Nina. "She's not normally this way. Usually she's mouthy and determined to prove to me that she can handle everything on her own.

"Usually, she's not a dragon, dummy. Look, just go easy on

her. If she lobs you one, don't take the bait. I know it's your thing, but I don't like the feeling I get from her."

"You mean when you read her mind?"

Nina slapped her gloved hand on the passenger door. "Yeah. All right. When I read her fucking mind. There's a lot of shit going on in that nutty-ass head of hers, but she's scared. She feels alone. Like, really alone. The kind of alone that even upsets a tough old bitch like me. Where does she go if she has no job, dude? How will she take care of herself in this dive of a town? Who does she turn to if she can't pay her mortgage?"

"She can turn to me."

Nina shook her head as Mick pulled up to the store where many of his fellow firefighters had gathered. "She doesn't feel that way. She feels like you're holding something back, and she's GD right. You don't have to tell me what it is, because it ain't none of my business, but it's pretty important that you two trust each other, seeing as we can't find any of your kind anywhere. So get that shit together. The longer you two fight, the longer I have to reassure her. Not a fan of being somebody's Binky."

As he pulled to a full stop, Mick looked over at her. "I don't believe your tough-guy exterior. Not even for a minute. You're a good person. And while it's not like Tessa to be clingy, I hear what you're saying and I'll do my best to keep the fighting to a minimum, okay?"

"Good. Now let's go, Optimus Prime. Let me do the talking."

"But—"

Nina popped the door open. "But shit. Shut up so I can work my magic and Tessa can at least collect some of her insurance money. She's going to need it if she's still considering relocating."

Relocating? Wait. Tessa was thinking about leaving Vermont? He didn't have time to dwell on that as he dropped from the car and followed Nina to the circle some of the guys had made around the store's entry.

"Gentlemen," Nina said, sticking out her hand to the nearest fireman. "I'm Marty Flaherty, your guide to all things suggestive today. So who's up for having their brain matter tickled?"

Mick fought to keep from snickering when Nina introduced herself as Marty.

Deon Bateman shot Mick a look of confusion. "What?" he asked, the condensation forming a cloud coming out of his mouth.

Nina waved a finger under his nose. "You heard me. Don't play stupid, pal."

Deon nodded like a trained seal, pushing his hands into his down jacket. "Sorry, ma'am. I didn't mean to be stupid."

Billy Tobin clapped Mick on the back from behind, his thick fingers digging into Mick's shoulder. "You okay, buddy? How's Tessa? We couldn't believe it when we all heard. How the hell does something like this happen and we don't even wake up? It had to burn hot—just look at the place. It's a charred shell."

Nina whipped around, zeroing in on Billy. "Who're you?"

Billy glanced at her, his booted feet shuffling. "Billy Tobin. Why?"

"Listen up, Billy Tobin, that fire burned hot because fires are hot. You bunch of potential calendar boys came running right over the second the alarm bell rang and put it out, didn't you?"

Billy nodded his ginger head, his blue eyes glazed. "As soon as we heard the bell."

"Nobody was hurt, and we suspect it was an electrical fire,

which is what we're going to tell the nice man from the insurance company, right, boys?"

All of them, every last one of Mick's friends from the firehouse, nodded like puppets on strings. "Yes, ma'am" was muttered in one fashion or another from every set of lips.

Nina brushed her hands together. "Good. Now remember what I said. Auntie Q's burned down due to a clear case of faulty wiring. You got a call from nine-one-one, when someone anonymous called the fire in. You all answered the call and put it out like the good firemen you are. You're going to go back to your nice firehouse and write up that report. No one was injured. No further investigation needed. We clear?"

Ten or so sets of eyes, glazed and fixated on Nina, seemed to register her request. Then every man nodded his head in agreement.

"Good deal. Thanks, guys."

Everyone stirred then, feet shuffled on the frozen ground, words were murmured, and then all the guys were rushing at Mick, worry on their faces. "How's Tessa?" Deon asked.

Mick cleared his throat, marveling at more of the crazy. "She's pretty upset, which I'm sure you'd expect. She's taking the day to catch her breath."

Gil Ormon, firehouse lothario, a slick man who spray-tanned religiously once a week at Tan and Sand, leaned into him. "Who's the hot broad?"

"The one responsible for molding your pea brain like some goddamn piece of Play-Doh," Nina whispered from behind, her tone crisp and menacing. "So step off, Prince Charming. Because not even the loneliest day in the apocalypse would make me consider you."

Mick fought a bark of laughter when Gil instantly took a step back and changed his tune. "You got a handle on Tessa?"

Immediately, Mick's hackles were up. Tessa had turned Gil down on more than one occasion, but if what Nina said was true about her new vulnerability, he didn't want Gil and his dime-store charm wheedling his way into her life. "Tessa's at home dealing with the insurance and catching her breath. She's fine, just shook up."

"Mick! Mick!" a woman's voice yelled from across the road.

Damn. Sandy Giden. He'd forgotten all about her. He'd promised to help her with the school's fund-raiser for the fire-house last night.

Mick swung around, putting a smile on his face, only to see Sandy's look of horror. Her petite frame, wrapped in several layers of clothing, came to a complete stop. "Oh, poor Tessa!" she cried. "Is she okay? We all heard over at the bank, and I wanted to come and see if we could do something to help. You know the Ladies of the League are always willing to roll up our sleeves."

Mick dropped a hand to her shoulder. "Thanks, Sandy. I'll pass that on to Tessa."

"Was anyone hurt? I can't believe we didn't smell the smoke. I said to my Bernard just this morning, a fire like that surely would create enough smoke to wake up the people in the next town over."

Mick, at a loss for words, let Nina handle it.

"Mornin', Sandy. I'm Marty Flaherty. Nice to meet you."

Sandy peered at her suspiciously, tucking her chin into her hand-knitted scarf. "Nice to meet you. You new here?"

Nina slung an arm over Sandy's shoulder and began walking her away from the store, their feet crunching in the cold snow.

"Just a temporary visit. So let's talk about the fire last night . . ."

As the two wandered off, Mick let his mind revisit the idea that Tessa would leave Vermont.

She loved it here. She loved the snow and that she knew everyone's name. Why would she leave?

Because she doesn't know what to do with you, stupid-ass. Because you have to tell her. Because sometimes starting over is easier than hanging around.

His phone vibrated from inside his jacket pocket, pulling him away from his thoughts of Tessa. Mick scrolled through the texts, cupping the phone to shade the glare of the bright sun.

His eyes flew open at the text from Marty, his gut clenching.

Come home now! Tessa needs Nina. Don't ask questions. Get here fast.

Just as he was about to call out to Nina, she was scrolling on her phone, too.

When she looked up at him, he saw genuine concern on her face, and he knew, behind those big sunglasses, worry steeped her eyes.

She pointed to the truck.

So Mick ran.

Fast.

Because something was wrong with Tessa.

CHAPTER 8

Mick thrust open the door just as his wings drove their way out of his skin and settled on his back, slapping Nina in the face.

She ducked under them, making a dash for Marty, who was in the middle of the living room, pacing. “What the fuck, dude?”

Marty tucked her hair behind her ear. “We have a problem.”

“We’ve had one of those ever since we came to this damn town, Marty. What now?”

Mick heard the concern in Nina’s voice for Tessa, but rather than point it out to her, he decided to be grateful for it. Tessa had found comfort in Nina. Something he couldn’t seem to provide.

He fell back against the door, and with the tip of his right wing he knocked over a lamp Tessa had picked up at a garage sale, sending it skidding across the floor.

Wanda poked her head out of the bedroom, her face flushed

rather than that eerie pale. She took one look at Mick and sighed. "Marty! Wings at twelve o'clock! Nina, get your ass in here now!"

Mick began to move toward Tessa's bedroom, crashing his way through the entryway, taking coatracks and pictures from the wall with him, but Wanda shot up a hand. "No! You stay put. She needs a woman's touch right now."

"And *Nina's* that woman?" he asked, crossing his arms over his chest as Marty came up behind him and pushed his wings together like an accordion.

Nina glared at him. "Hey, fuckknuckle—vagina here. That makes me a woman, okay? Now go practice setting shit on fire or something. You know, so you don't burn down your ladylove's next place of business?"

"She's not my—"

Nina threw up a hand to quiet him. "I know. She's not your ladylove. Shut up and go find an airport hangar to rest those things in," she mocked before she disappeared inside the bedroom.

Mick tried to turn around, but found he couldn't quite maneuver in the small space. "Marty?"

"Mick?" she answered, muffled and strained, the scuffle of her heels resounding in his ears.

"What's going on with Tessa? Was Frank here again? Is she hurt?" He couldn't keep the panic from his voice. He wanted to be a real keep-it-close-to-your-chest man here, but it wasn't working out. Anything that had to do with Tessa sent him into irrational orbit.

"No Frank, and she isn't hurt," Marty grunted. "Now hold still, and stop moving around. These things are like trying to hold on to greased cats."

"Then why did she need Nina?"

"It's a female thing?"

"You don't sound convinced."

"I'm not sure what I am right now. How about we focus on making these go away?"

Right. His wings.

His wings.

Would he ever get used to that? What had made them pop out to begin with? "Do you think we're ever going to find anyone to teach us how to control this? Especially Tessa. You see how she suffers when she de-wings. How will she live like that?"

Marty sighed from behind him, scrunching his wings back together to keep from taking out poor Joe-Joe, who was sleeping on the sofa, blissfully unaware. "I don't know, Mick. I don't have any answers. Nothing. I'm just as in the dark as you. But why don't we see what brought it on? Let's explore where you were at when they popped out. What was going on inside your head?"

His chest tightened again and his fists clenched. "I was worried about Tessa."

Marty batted at his wings with light swats of her hand. Swats that sent pulsing vibrations throughout his body. "But you were angry when you spewed fire at the store."

He clenched his teeth. Seemed he was always worried about Tessa. "Yes."

"So maybe it has to do with a heightened emotional state? It makes sense, right? Anger, fear."

His wings shifted a bit, fluttering on his back, and he felt every fine bone in them as surely as he felt his feet or his legs—like an appendage or another limb. Rolling his shoulders, he heard Marty squeak.

She sputtered her next words. "Whoa, Nellie! Take it easy, huh? Anyway, you were worried about Tessa, and at the store you were angry with her. So focus on calming down and let's see where that gets us, okay?"

"Okay," he muttered, breathing deeply. As he inhaled then exhaled, his chest expanding and deflating, he began to relax and his wings began to fall to the floor like a parachute that had lost its wind.

"Oh!" Marty shouted. "That's it. Just relax and breathe, and if they're going to pain you like they did at the store, I'm here. I'll help."

"I'm here, too, man," Darnell said, appearing before him from out of nowhere in a mist of sparkling dust. His cheerful face gave Mick something to focus on as the demon assessed his wings. "Daggone, buddy. You got some spread there. Now look at ol' Darnell and breathe." Darnell put both his hands on Mick's shoulders and gazed directly into his eyes.

And it was like deflating a balloon this time. There was still the crack of bone, though less jarring, still the ever-present ache along his spine, dulled now, but it was working.

Darnell gave him an encouraging smile. "Good job, my friend. You doin' it."

But then Tessa screamed, setting off the rip of flesh as his wings reappeared, making Marty scream, too, as she was hurled back against the door.

What the hell was going on in there?

NINA, at the end of the bed, the burned-out closet as a backdrop, looked at Wanda over the top of Tessa's head. Wanda was sitting behind Tessa, holding her around her middle, which had grown to the size of a small beach ball.

And Tessa knew that look in the vampire's eyes. Something was wrong.

Duh, something's wrong, Tessa. Since you woke up this morning, your stomach inflated like some mutant hot air balloon. Definitely appears as though something's just a little off, don't you think? You look like you're having Rosemary's baby.

"What the hell is happening to me?" Tessa cried between grunts that came from deep within her throat. It had begun as a pain in her right side, which she'd attributed to gas. Eggs did that to her from time to time, and while Nina's eggs were yummo, they'd made her stomach feel heavy.

But by the time an hour had gone by, her stomach had grown before their very eyes, and she was screaming like a schoolgirl only half an hour later as one cramp after another assaulted her like knives in her gut.

This couldn't be what she thought it was. How? How was this possible?

"Wanda?" Nina yelled over Tessa's screams. "What now, paranormal crisis counselor?"

Nina didn't know what was happening? Not good.

If Nina didn't know what was happening, that was bad. Very bad. But it couldn't be what they were all thinking it was. What she knew they were thinking it was . . . How could it be?

Nina clamped her hands on Tessa's thighs and shouted, "Tessa, look at me! Look at me and focus. Stop screaming because you're killing my fekkin' ears, and focus. I don't know what the fuck is happening, but I'm here, okay? I'm here no matter what."

The shift in her stomach was excruciating, pulling her flesh so tight she thought she'd burst. Her eyes almost fell out of her head when she caught a glimpse of her belly, distorted and growing more enormous by the minute. Her belly rippled with life, rolling and twisting until the pain seared her from the inside out.

What. The. Hell?

Yet Tessa tried to focus on Nina while sweat poured from her forehead and her insides turned to gooey, molten lava.

Wanda rocked her, pressing her knuckles into Tessa's back to ease the pain there. "Breathe, Tessa. Just breathe. Let your body do what it will. Don't fight, honey."

"I don't understand," she said with clenched teeth. "How is this happening? Is this what I think it is? Because I call unfairrrr!" she yelped. "I haven't had sex in two years!"

Nina's face was grim, frightening Tessa, but when she looked up, the vampire's eyes were full of determination. "I don't know. Don't think about the how, for fuck's sake. Think about getting through this. Just keep looking at me, kiddo."

The urge to rise and squat came over her like lightning in a flash of crazy colors and desperate need. She pushed from Wanda's embrace, rocketing upward, shoving Nina out of the way in order to get into a position she instinctively knew would bring relief.

She dragged the blankets from the bed with her, letting the edges of them wrap around her hand, and then she began twisting them to form a circle.

"What the fuck are you doing, kiddo?" Nina's eyes were wide, her eyebrows arched in question.

A nest. She was making a nest. Where that answer had come

from was a mystery, but she knew it as surely as she knew something enormous was about to happen. "I'm making a nest!" she cried. "I don't know why. I just know I have to!"

Tessa didn't bother to question how she knew this. She didn't care. She only knew that whatever this was, it was going to rip her in half if she didn't get it out.

Squatting down over the blankets, she fought another scream—another terrified, earsplitting scream—while she gripped the edge of the bed and Nina braced her by holding her other hand.

Wanda pressed a cool cloth to her head, wiping away the sweat blurring her vision and whispering soothing words in her ear.

The urge to push became all she was, every fiber of her being, every beat of her heart.

So she pushed—pushed so hard she was sure her brain was going to pop out the top of her head.

With a roar she couldn't contain, Tessa bellowed a warrior cry, feeling something dislodge from her body, pull away. Something smooth and maybe round?

She couldn't tell, but she was grateful for Wanda's arms encircling her when she fell backward from the force of the object leaving her body.

Whatever it was fell to the floor with a thunk. Like a bowling ball dropping to the floor on a slick alley.

And then there was silence.

A deafening silence.

Nina spoke first, her gravelly voice barely a whisper. "Holy fuckers."

Wanda's chest pressed into Tessa's back when she inhaled a rasp of air after peering over Tessa's shoulder. "Oh, dear."

"What?" Tessa asked, weak and sore, her limbs feeling like butter.

"Well," Nina said, her voice once more rock-steady. "Tell me how you want this information delivered. Hot and fast, or slow and easy."

"Nina! Give poor Tessa a break. She's exhausted. Don't play games at a time like this."

Nina scoffed. "I just wanna know if she wants me to pussyfoot around or hit her hard."

Tessa took gulps of air before she said, "How would you like it, Nina?"

"Well, if it was me, I guess I'd just want to know. But this is you. And you're all fragile like an eggshell." She paused, cackling a laugh. "Hah! I crack myself up."

Tessa shook her head, struggling to sit up, but her stomach muscles felt like Jell-O. "I don't get the joke." Her frustration and exhaustion warred with each other until she decided whatever was going on down on the floor was something she needed to know about. "Just tell me. It's not like I can't take bad news. I mean, my store burned down, I set my closet on fire, met not one but two demons, and I have wings. What else is there? So just tell me what flew out of my body like a torpedo, taking most of my insides with it."

"Nina." Wanda used her behave-yourself tone. "Be gentle."

"Tsk-tsk, Wanda. Would I be rough with my new homeslice? Not in a muthafluffin' million. Okay, so listen up, kiddo, you're in for a shock. A big one. Gird your loins."

"I just did that, and they spewed all over my bedroom anyway. I have no gird or maybe even loins left."

Wanda propped her up so she had a clear view of Nina, who had something in her hands.

Something smooth, gold, and shiny flashed in the late-afternoon sun. Something approximately the size of an oversized Easter egg used for displays in store windows.

Nina held it up with a tentative smile. "Now, be strong, grasshopper. It's important you be strong."

Wanda whimpered from behind her, but she managed to fend off another gasp. She patted Tessa on the back. "Deep breaths, sweetie. Deep and long."

Oh, fuck breathing.

Who could breathe when they'd just laid a golden egg?

MICK looked at Tessa from across the kitchen counter and over the top of the incubator Nina had had her zombie, Carl, bring. "I . . ." He clamped his lips shut, shaking his dark head.

Tessa shook her head, too. "Me . . . neither . . ."

Carl stood at the edge of the counter, his lopsided grin embracing them with a warmth Tessa was at a loss for words to explain.

He was a zombie, Nina had said. A vegetarian zombie she'd rescued from a witch doctor. But he was a damn good babysitter. He watched her Charlie all the time. Because nothing said a mother's love like leaving your infant with a vegetarian zombie, right?

Sometimes, it was all Tessa could do not to run out of her tiny cottage, full of all these paranormal people, and scream at the top of her lungs.

Carl adjusted the heat lamp with stiff, clumsy hands, his crooked face strangely endearing. He thumped Mick on the back and smiled again before going off to join Joe-Joe on the couch, where her dog crawled into his lap and Carl happily watched the snow fall outside her picture window.

"So is everybody ready to talk now, or does the cat still have your tongues?" Marty asked, folding her hands in front of her, her shiny bracelets clacking together.

Tessa began, pointing her finger at the top of Carl's head. "Zombie . . ."

Nina's smile was wide and fond. "Yep. That's my Carl. He's a good guy. Gets loose sometimes, so you'll hear a lot of 'Where's Carl?' But he's the best babysitter ever when it comes to date night for Greg and me. That's why I brought him here. He'll look out for whatever the hell's gonna hatch like he's lookin' out for his own damn life."

"Egg . . ." Mick managed, his face pale, his eyes unfocused and glazed.

"Uh-huh," Wanda added with a grin. "You, Sir Scales-a-Lot, are a soon-to-be proud daddy. Yay, for impregnating a woman from one hundred paces. We shall call you and your little swimmies manly-man from this day forward."

Marty stifled a laugh, then straightened before forcing a serious expression. "So, let's talk about this. If this is in fact a baby dragon, wow, guys. Way to pollinate. Have you thought of a name?"

Tessa's mouth fell open again. Her jaw just wouldn't stay hinged. She gripped the edges of the counter. "I had an egg."

"You and *lover boy* had an egg. "

Tessa's eyes flew to Nina's face, humiliation dropping two red spots of fire on her cheeks. "You don't know it's Mick's. We don't know anything."

Nina planted her hands on her hips. "So, if it's not Gigantor's, whose is it? How many baby dragon daddies do you know?"

Mick ran his hand over his jaw, his eyes dark and stormy. "We don't even know if it's a baby, for Christ's sake."

"What the fuck else comes out of a chick's lady bits? I was in there. You didn't see what I saw. Fell outta her like a damn bowling ball. So for now, we have to assume it's a wee baby dragon—until it hatches, and we find out differently. Until then, it's fetus-dragon. I damn well hope it's a girl. Hollis and Charlie could use a playmate, right, blondie?" She nudged Marty and winked like this was some joke.

Marty nodded and grinned, her pink frosted lips tilting upward. "Wouldn't that be incredible? Once upon a time, in a land not so far away called Vermont, a werewolf, a vampini, and a dragon became BFFs. Oh, the fiery, winged, fanged, hairy playdates they had."

Nina high-fived Marty with a cackle. "So what were you two doing in there last night that made this? All that talk about how she wasn't your girlfriend, and now she turns up preggers. Explain that."

"I can't explain that!" Mick groused, stopping to take a deep breath. He was looking to keep his temper in check. Tessa knew that look. It was the one he used with her when she was doing something he disapproved of. "Tessa and I have never once . . . Well, you know. I can't explain this. I can't explain anything anymore. There are no explanations. All things explainable are totally unexplainable."

"It's true," Tessa finally piped in, pulling her sweater tighter around her. "We've never . . ." Nothing in this world made any sense anymore. She hadn't had sex in two solid years.

"Then this is the Immaculate Conception, Dragon Edition?" Nina queried, her eyebrow raised.

Wanda giggled before straightening and smoothing a hand over her hair to compose herself. "Okay, so we have what we suspect is a baby dragon, incubating—in an incubator like we used to do with baby chicks in Mrs. Margetti's science class in fifth grade . . ." She began to laugh again, and wrapping her hands around her midsection, she laughed until she wheezed and teardrops fell from one eye.

Finally, she bent at the waist and took in gulps of air before rising to look them squarely in the eye. "I'm sorry. So here's what we have. An egg. An egg we have no idea about. An egg that could contain a baby dragon. What do we do about it?"

The egg rolled then—or maybe the correct word was *stirred*, shifting ever so slightly under the incubator's lamp. But it was like a jolt to Tessa's system. She grabbed Mick's forearm. "Did you feel that?"

He made a face, his eyes narrowing. "Feel what?"

Tessa held up a finger to her lips and cocked her head. There it was again, an odd pulse when the egg rolled to the other side of the incubator. "That! Did you feel that?"

Mick's expression said she was out of her mind. "I didn't feel anything."

And then she heard something. A soft mewl—so faint, she wasn't sure she'd really heard it until it became louder. She was compelled to put her finger in the incubator, drawn by some instinctual force to run her digit over the egg's shiny gold surface.

The mewling became louder, rising and falling in a sound Tessa knew deep in her soul was the sound of contentment. Her heart raced, her belly fluttered, and her very core reacted as she stroked the egg, feeling the pulse of it beneath her fingertip.

From nowhere, a bolt of understanding hit her, an acute awareness, a sharply sweet pang of love so intense she almost fell over from the force of recognition. Tears streamed down her face, her hands trembling as she ran them over the egg.

Marty put her hands on Tessa's shoulders, her voice watery. "I understand. If I could only tell you how deeply I understand."

"I . . ." Tessa tried to speak, but her throat was so tight, so constricted with emotion, she couldn't even begin to express what was happening to her.

Nina gave her ponytail a tug, squeezing her shoulder. "It's indescribable. Don't try to describe it. Just feel it."

Wanda gathered Nina and Marty in for a hug, sheltering Tessa as they all looked down at the incubator.

Whatever had just happened, she couldn't define it. She only knew it went as deep as any emotion she'd ever felt. So deep it almost hurt.

This was her baby. Her child. How it had come to be, why it had come to be, ceased to matter. All that mattered was that inside this gleaming egg was her future. She felt it, breathed it, needed it more than she'd ever needed anything else.

She would protect it with everything she had in her.

Kill for it.

Die for it.

CHAPTER 9

"So, we have good news and maybe really good news, depending on how you look at this kind of shit. Which do you want first?" Nina asked, sitting down at the breakfast bar where Tessa sat, staring at her egg, still trying to grasp all of her thoughts. Trying to examine each of these new feelings swarming her from the inside out.

She peered up at Nina, seeing a whole different vampire. One who was smiling and a much lighter version of the vampire she'd met only twenty-four hours ago. "You like kids and animals, don't you?"

Nina reached in and tickled the egg, eliciting a soft sigh from it as it stirred. "Yep. It's adults I wish would all fuck off."

"I'm afraid to ask why."

"Don't be afraid. I'll tell you. Adults come with filters. They mostly never say what they really mean. They allude to it. They dance around it. They bullshit. Kids and animals have no agendas and no censor. I don't like to dance, and I fucking hate bullshit."

"Well, here's something completely unfiltered for you. I have a baby, er, egg . . . whatever. What do I do with a baby, Nina? How did I even get a baby? And even as I question that, I'd eat your face off before I'd let you hurt this baby. I might not win, I might not even make a dent in you, but I'd die trying. How do I explain that?"

Nina grinned, crossing her arms on the counter. "Oh, no doubt you'd die up against me. But you feel this way because all mothers feel that way, kiddo. It's instinct—raw, primal, chew-your-guts-up instinct."

"I've never even considered having children, and now, by some mysterious, magical event, I have a child, or what will be a child." That was a lie. She had considered it. She'd considered lots of little Micks and Tessas. She'd just given up hope that it would ever happen.

And with the way Mick was reacting to this, it was clear he'd never thought about it. He'd withdrawn to a corner of the kitchen, the way Mick always did when he needed time to process something, his hands jammed into the pockets of his low-slung jeans, his torn shirt falling forward on his shoulders from his wings' impromptu appearance.

But this time, while he wrapped his big head around the latest events, it hurt. This egg had to be his. There was no one else it could possibly belong to. If that was true, why wasn't he feeling the way she was? Why didn't he even crack a smile?

Maybe he didn't want to be a father—and that was just fine by her. She'd do it alone. But Mick would make the best father on the planet. All the kids in town adored him, and she knew he adored them back. He played Santa Claus for them every year at the firehouse dance.

Was it because they didn't know what was inside the egg? Was he worried that what might pop out was going to look like it came from a DreamWorks movie instead of a human baby?

The truth of it was, Tessa wanted him to feel the way she did. She wanted him to love this life forming inside an eggshell as much as she did. It hurt that he wasn't responding at all.

"So, that's what we have to talk about."

She looked up at Nina. "Huh?"

"The egg. We gotta talk about the egg."

Terror struck her heart, so hard, so fast, she trembled. "If you tell me something's wrong with my egg, er, baby . . . I'll die, Nina. Right here, right in front of you. Please tell me nothing's wrong. *Please.*" It was then she knew she'd beg, lie, steal, whatever it took to protect this amazing thing she'd created without even trying. With or without Mick, she was going to be a parent—to whatever. She didn't care if it wandered around on two legs, had a forked tongue, and said *rawr* instead of *mama*.

This egg was hers.

"There's nothing wrong, kiddo. But we got some word from some of our contacts about what to do next when you're a dragon with an egg."

"Did Puff the Magic Dragon call, and I missed it?" Tessa asked on a giggle, unable to hide her relief. "Sorry. How did you find out about what happens next?"

"Archibald. Wanda's manservant."

"Wanda has a manservant?"

"Yeah. A dude who was once a human, became a vampire because of a crazy circumstance, then turned back into a human because of another crazy circumstance. He'll be here in just a second."

A knock at the door sent all eyes to Wanda, who opened it and gave an elderly gentleman a hug. "Oh, Arch, thank you for coming on such short notice."

The older man was wrapped in a black wool coat and matching black galoshes, and as he looked at Wanda, his face wrinkled into a wide smile. "I daresay, Miss Wanda, you know that when you call with another paranormal adventure, I can't resist!"

"Arch!" Nina called out, waving him over to the incubator, where she and Tessa sat as Mick still hovered silently in a corner. She gave him a squeeze, taking his coat and draping it on the back of one of the chairs.

"Miss Nina! As always, a delight. So good to see you. Why haven't you been to visit with my Charlie? Surely she doesn't have enough stuffed unicorns from Grandpa Archibald?"

"One more stuffed unicorn and we're going to have to buy another castle, Arch. Promise to bring her around soon. For now, we have this," Nina said, pointing to the incubator.

Archibald clapped his hands together, his bright blue eyes crinkling at the corners. "What a wondrous world we live in, yes, Mistress Nina?"

"Damn straight, Arch. So this is Tessa, and her baby daddy, Mick, is the huge dude over there sulking in the corner."

Mick cleared his throat, coming out of the darkness and putting a hand out to Archibald. "Pleasure," he said.

Archibald took it, giving it a hearty shake. "Oh, congratulations, Sir Mick! I realize this was a surprise, but aren't all miracles full of surprises?" he said as Mick retreated back into the dark kitchen. He turned to Tessa, his smile so warm she wanted to wrap herself up in it. "And you must be Miss Tessa. The new mother. Pretty as a picture. Warmest of wishes to you—to you both."

Tessa wanted to bask in this moment—the one where this adorable man called her a new mother. She didn't care that this baby was unconventional or maybe even crazy. She was going to be a mother, and hearing the word brought a flood of love to her heart. "Thank you, Archibald. It's a pleasure to meet you."

Arch planted his hands on his hips, his suit, complete with silver ascot, gleaming under the lights of the kitchen. "Now, down to the business at hand. What must be done in order to ensure the health and well-being of the coming wee one."

Tessa nodded. She was all in. She didn't care if it meant she had to be skinned alive. She'd do it. "Whatever it takes."

Nina snickered, rocking back on her heels. "Yeah. About that."

Mick finally spoke up from his dark corner of the kitchen, coming out of the shadows to stare down at them. "What exactly will it take?"

Arch looked at Nina. She rolled her hand in a gesture that said the floor was his. "It is a delicate matter. May I speak openly?"

Wanda, who'd come to stand by Arch, winced.

Tessa's heart began that fearful thump again. "Please. Go right ahead."

"Sir Mick?"

Mick nodded his dark head, crossing his arms over his wide chest as though he were bracing for the worst. "Absolutely."

Arch bounced his head with a curt nod. "Now, I speak only from legend, as dragons are quite rare, even from my era."

"Your era?" Mick asked, his eyes unreadable.

Archibald's smile was devilish. "Yes, Mick. I was born several hundred years ago. Now, mind you, there were no dragons to speak of then. However, I'm well schooled in the mythology of dragons. Which is what brought me here today. Miss Nina asked that I come here to share with you both what comes next."

Tessa saw Mick's eyes cloud over, more paranormal overload, no doubt. She slid off the chair and grabbed his hand, squeezing it, drawing him closer to Archibald. "What comes next?" he asked gruffly, his eyes fixed on Archibald.

Archibald remained silent for a moment before he steepled his hands under his chin. "May I be direct with such a sensitive issue?"

Panic was beginning to seize Tessa. "Please."

"Fertilization."

Huh? Like hens? "Say again?"

Archibald cleared his throat. "You and Sir Mick must fertilize the egg."

Mick was quicker to react this time. He shot the question off at Archibald with rapid fire. "Meaning?"

"Meaning you gotta do the do, Gigantor. With your 'she's not my ladylove,' " Nina said, her eyes glittering with amusement.

Archibald stepped forward, placing a hand on Tessa's arm. "Let me explain. Within the egg is a child, simply waiting to hatch. In order for the child to incubate and come to term, you and Sir Mick must fertilize it by becoming intimate. Otherwise, the egg will die."

Oh boy.

"Hold the hell on," Mick shouted. "We have to have sex? Like me and her?" He pointed in Tessa's direction. "That's just damn crazy, and there's no way I'm doing it. You people are all nuts. Has anyone stopped to wonder how she got pregnant in the first place? How did I, when I never laid a single finger on her, impregnate her?"

Archibald shook his bald head. "I wish I had more of an explanation for you, sir. I can only tell you what I know. What I know is, Miss Tessa was neither a dragon nor pregnant before your accident. Correct?"

Mick's jaw went tight and hard. "Correct."

The manservant's shoulders squared, as though he were going into battle. "So then, sir, are we to believe Miss Tessa found another dragon to create this child with? Did she happen upon another man in the last twenty-four hours we're unaware of? Or are we to chalk it up to yet another mystery in the paranormal realm? Please, do tell me which you find most plausible. I shall wait."

Mick's lips tightened and a vein popped out in his forehead. "I don't have an explanation."

Archibald clapped his heels together. "Then, sir, you must accept mine. Please do so without the whine of a toddler. Now, if you'll excuse me," he said with prickly ice in his tone as he unplugged the incubator and whisked it off the counter, "I shall take the wee one elsewhere where he or she cannot hear the disparaging words of its father. Do keep in mind, Sir Mick, even in the womb . . . er, eggshell, a child can sense discontent, and I absolutely will not have this precious life marred by your incredible insensitivity. Carl! Come. We shall read baby dragon a story by the fire. What say you to *Goodnight Moon* this fine eve?" With that, Archibald turned on his heel and went to join Carl.

Nina popped her lips, looking up at Mick. "You've done it now, buddy. It ain't easy to piss off Arch, but when it comes to the kids, he's a ferocious mothereffer."

Mick exhaled hard, leaning his hands on the counter, letting his head fall forward. "This is crazy."

Tessa gulped. "So let me get this straight. We have to have sex in order to ensure the baby will live?"

"Yep," Nina said.

"Like I said," Mick mumbled. "Crazy."

Well, hold on a second. What was the craziest part of it all for Mick? Okay, she'd give him that the events leading up to this immaculate conception were definitely outrageous. She'd give him that this had been sprung on him from out of nowhere. She'd even give him that the idea they had to fertilize an egg together was right out of some kooky writer's imagination in some fantasy novel, but was it so crazy if it meant their child would live?

Call it hormones. Call it postpartum nutbaggery, but she lost it then. She was so angry that all Mick could think of was himself, her fury shot up her spine and right out of her mouth. "Archibald?" she yelled. "Cover the egg's, um, baby's ears because here comes some discontent!"

Then she rounded on Mick, standing on tiptoe, and waved a finger under his nose. "Here's what's crazy, Mick. It's crazy that you won't accept your part in this. If you didn't knock me up, then who did? You took the dragon scales. *You.* You infected me with whatever the hell you're infected with and now we have a baby. That's right, *a baby.* So here's a little something to chew on while you stew like a five-year-old who lost his fucking recess privileges—you didn't just give birth to something the size of a damn T. rex. I did. It wasn't you in there screaming like a damn teenager at a One Direction concert because you didn't know what the hell was happening to you. That was me. But it was you who started this, and it damn well will be you who finishes it, because the hell I'm going to let this child die because the idea of doing me doesn't suit your palate. So you'd better gear up for the fertilization of a lifetime, buddy, and you'd better do it fast. Not a chance in ten lifetimes am I going to let you screw with my kid's life!"

With that, she turned on her heel and made a break for the bathroom, popping the door open and fighting the urge to slam it shut so hard the house would rattle.

But of course, there was baby dragon's mental state and emotional well-being to think of, which prevented her from tearing the door from its hinges and lobbing it at Mick's big fat head.

"I'M sorry, Archibald. All of this . . ." All of this. What was all of this?

Archibald closed the book, adjusting his shoulder so Carl, who'd fallen asleep during *Goodnight Moon*, was more comfortable. He sniffed, tipping his nose upward. "I'm certain you are, sir."

Mick sighed. Jesus. He'd been an ass. A total ass. Not only with Arch, but with Tessa, too. But hell on fire, this was all a lot to take in. He was going to be a father, allegedly anyway, and he wanted to feel the things Tessa was clearly feeling—he just couldn't summon up much emotion over an overgrown egg.

Was that wrong? Probably. But in all fairness, this had been thrust upon him, too, and he hadn't given birth to it, either. He felt no attachment to it other than the fact that Tessa did, and he wanted her to be happy.

He shifted on the couch, facing Archibald. "No. I'm really sorry. I was rude to you, and that's not like me. Not like me at all. I'm overwhelmed. I'm worried. I'm . . ." Trying to keep my promise to Noah.

Oh, stop, Mick. It wasn't really a promise. It was a conversation you had where Noah expressed his displeasure.

Yeah. And then he died.

And now I have to sleep with his sister to fertilize her egg. I mean, our egg.

"Sir? May I be frank?"

"Absolutely."

Archibald set the book down and scooped up the incubator, placing his hands over the egg as though to cover its ears. "Clearly, you're distressed over this turn of unlikely events. Without a doubt, you have every right to question your circumstances—to question the outrageousness of this predicament. And make no mistake, I understand you don't feel the way Miss Tessa does about your coming child. In the instant she knew that what had come from her body was a child, she felt a mother's love. I saw it. Surely you did as well."

"I did." And he wanted to feel that kind of love, too. There'd been a million times he'd thought about him and Tessa in the long term. Wondered what it would be like to have her in his life as something more than an irritating replacement for her big brother.

When he'd let himself really dig deep into his fantasies about her, yeah, they'd included children. They'd also included making the children the old-fashioned way. She didn't even like him at this point, and somehow, they'd created a life.

"Then let me compare this to a surprise pregnancy, if you will. Unexpected, yes, but no less meaningful to the woman who carries the child. Now, let me take that a step further. As the woman carries the child, she becomes attached in a way you, as the cocreator, cannot. You may think you can, but you can never know what it's like to have a child grow inside of you."

"Are you sure?" Mick joked. "Because the rules don't seem to apply to the paranormal."

Archibald finally smiled. "The truth, certainly, sir. However, my point is this: Let this sit with you for a time. Adjust to the idea that you will, indeed, be a father. I know you've been blindsided, but hiding those feelings, making Tessa and this child feel supported, can only benefit the two of them. You mustn't let your feelings of hesitation seep into your interaction with them both—or you'll only create resentment. Resentment I suspect you do not wish from Miss Tessa."

"No. I don't want her or the . . ."

"*Baby,*" Archibald finished for him.

"Right, baby, to feel unwanted."

"Good, sir. Now, another thing we must address. Might I again be frank?"

"Please."

"You must fertilize this egg, and you must do it soon. It's my understanding that there are unresolved feelings between you and the fair Miss Tessa. Am I correct?"

He swallowed hard, fisting his hands together. "There are." So many unresolved feelings he'd lost count.

"But I'm not wrong when I suggest you're in love with her, am I?"

Shit. Shit. Shit. "No. No, you're not." For almost as long as he could remember. Since he'd come back from college and realized she wasn't twelve anymore. Then when he came back from living in New York to help his parents move and decided to stay here in Vermont.

And again a million times over the last ten years.

"Then I suggest this. I suggest whatever is between you, you hash out. I don't know what keeps you from making Miss Tessa yours, but for a man such as yourself, I expect it runs rather deep. However, all bets are now off, sir. There is a child to consider. A child Miss Tessa would certainly wrestle demons for—literally. Nothing will stop her from saving this child. Certainly not you."

This was tearing him up. Eating him from the inside out. "But I made a promise—"

"I care little for your past promises, sir," Archibald spat, cupping the egg. "I won't have you tell me this person you made the promise to would be so callous as to keep a child from its life. If that's the case, this person isn't worthy of your promises."

Mitch closed his eyes. "That's fair."

"Give me your hand, McAllister." Arch held out his wrinkled palm, waiting.

Mick hesitated for a moment, his head swirling with visions of Tessa and Noah, but he took a deep breath and placed his hand in Arch's in good faith.

The manservant scooped the golden egg up, placing it in Mick's palm, covering the top of the shell with his free hand. "Listen in the silence, Sir Mick. *Please.* Just listen."

Mick did as he was instructed, closing his eyes, breathing, thinking.

The egg stirred, made that sound all the girls had thought was so cute—one he couldn't hear over all their fussing.

Until now.

It was a coo. A sweet inhale of breath, a slurpy gurgle of contentment.

The egg grew warm, as if it was curling into his palm, as though it was snuggling into the shelter of his hand to ward off the cold night.

And it brought him to his knees, slashing at his heart, bringing the sting of tears to his eyes, leveling him so well, so instantly, he stopped breathing.

That was when he understood.

That was when he felt.

CHAPTER 10

Wanda rubbed Tessa's back while Marty and Nina scooped up the last bit of ashes from her decimated closet. Grateful for their help, she closed her eyes and took a deep breath.

"How do you feel, Tessa?"

She turned to Wanda, rolling her head on her neck to ease the tension. "Aside from the fact that the very idea of fertilization makes Mick want to jump off a tall building, and that I spit an egg that felt like it was the size of a bowling ball out of my body, I'm good. It's like nothing ever happened." It was the strangest thing. She felt just like the old Tessa again—pre-body split in two by baby-dragon.

"Bet dragons self-heal," Marty said.

Self-heal? She couldn't even touch that right now.

Wanda chuckled. "No one's jumping off a tall building. Mick doesn't feel that way, and I think somewhere deep down, you know it. But you use your quips as your defense mechanism as a just-in-case. It's a buffer for your real emotions. A protective shell."

"It's bullshit," Nina said as she held up one of Tessa's melted shoes, dropping it into a Hefty bag. "Remember what I told you about kids and adults? This—you and Gigantor—is exactly what I mean."

Marty blew her long blond hair from her face. "Did she give you the censor speech?"

Tessa laughed on a nod. "She did."

"I wish she wouldn't include me and Wanda in that speech. We're most certainly not afraid to tell her how we feel about her."

Nina flicked Marty's hair, fixing her eyes on Tessa. "All I'm sayin' is, whatever this stupid shit is between you two—fix it. Because if you let my baby dragon die, I gotta kick your ass. Then I'll suck your soul right the fuck out of you. Then I'll dip your delicate little fingers into my O neg and eat them. Maybe I might even hold the two of you down and make you do the wicky-wonk. I'd close my eyes, because the idea of the two of you slapping uglies almost breaks me, but the hell I'm gonna let your arguing hurt the kid. So figure it out."

Easier said than done. If she knew what they had to talk about, she might talk about it. But Mick had never budged. And now, out of all the crazy in crazy town, she had to have sex with him.

And have sex with him she would. It might not be the ravishing she'd fantasized about, but it would happen.

Tonight.

Tessa shivered. Clearly, it wasn't going to be the seduction of her dreams, with soft music and wine and a feast of cheese and crackers. Likely, it would be in her bedroom, smelling of smoke, on sheets wrinkled from a sleepless night, and maybe, if things got really hot, some Pandora on the laptop.

But let the seduction begin.

A sharp rap of knuckles at her door made her rise and pop it open to find Mick on the other side, his eyes softer than they'd been earlier, his gorgeous face lighter. "Can I come in?"

She just wasn't ready to let her resentment go—puppy-dog eyes or not. "To do what? Shit on something else?"

"Please?"

Wanda was up and off the bed in a shot. "Girls, let's give them some privacy."

Nina popped Mick on the shoulder on her way out. "Let the dragon baby fertilization begin."

Marty shoved Nina from behind. "Get out, mouth. Make them do the wicky-wonk?" she mocked. "What kind of crazy threat is that, Elvira? And don't you say a word. Move along. We need to Skype the kids."

Laughter followed the three women out of the bedroom as Nina protested and Wanda ordered Archibald to fire up her laptop.

Alone in the room with Mick, everything was too big, too much, too awkward.

"Wanna take a walk?"

"Off a cliff?"

"Work with me here, would you?"

"Where?"

"Down to the barn. You know, where you used to go play dolls all the time when you were little?"

The barn down by the creek. That big, red, musty place held so many great memories for her. She used to run behind Mick and Noah like some homeless puppy when they went to skip rocks at the creek. Where she'd followed them on her stupid pink bike, trying to keep up while they tried to ditch her.

The huge oak tree just outside the barn was where Mick had kissed Marianne Loomis for the first time while Tessa had watched from the loft full of hay. It was where she'd cried and cried because he wasn't kissing her.

It was where she'd wrapped herself in her mother's sweater and her father's gloves and sat on a bale of hay, sobbing, when she'd lost them.

Why would Mick want to go to the barn? "It's pretty cold," she hedged, looking down at her toes, covered in the gel socks Nina had found for her.

"But you love nights like this. When it's so cold your bones ache and the sky is so clear the stars look like they're winking. When we all complained about how damn cold it was, you always said the snow looked like frosting when it's like this, and who could complain about frosting? So, c'mon. Wear a warm jacket, put on some boots."

He remembered her saying that? "But the baby . . ."

"Archibald has it covered, and the girls are here. It'll be fine. Promise."

Her heart began to pound, and her throat got tight. But she relented. It was probably better to have mercy fertilization sex if they were at least nice to each other. "Okay. Let me change and I'll be right out."

Mick smiled—a smile she hadn't seen in a long time. "I'll wait out there." He strolled out of the bedroom, the width of his back filling the doorway.

As she shuffled out of her nightgown and threw on a pair of jeans and a heavy sweater, she tried to keep her fear to a minimum and remember this wasn't the love story she'd once hoped for. This was about saving their child. Nothing else, not their angry barbs, not their pokes or prods, mattered.

MICK grabbed Tessa's hand as they wended their way along the path from her house toward the deserted street. She loved it here. She loved the small-town feel, she loved that her nearest neighbor was almost a mile away.

She loved the split-rail fencing that lined the road, cordoning off old man Baker's farm. She loved the summertime, when his horses ran free and accepted carrots and sugar cubes from her. She loved the wildflowers in the field and the scent of sunshine.

As she and Mick crunched along in the snow, all of it felt new and strange now. She saw everything very differently since only this afternoon. She saw the danger that this deserted road she'd taken such pleasure in could present for a toddler on the loose. She saw the vast fields where a child could get lost in the tall grasses where the cows grazed. She saw it with the eyes of a soon-to-be-mother, critical and lavished with scrutiny at every detail.

"Penny for them?"

"I was just thinking about all the adjustments I'll have to make if . . . when . . ."

"The baby, right?" Mick said it as though he'd always been saying it.

To be fair, at least his tone wasn't dripping with scorn anymore. But she wasn't going to dance around about the issue. It was time to face this head-on. He would fertilize this egg with her if it was the last thing he did. "Yes."

"I'll help, Tessa."

She didn't say anything—she couldn't. Not right now. The future was so weirdly uncertain, all she wanted to do was focus on the task at hand.

Mick stopped at the end of the fencing, hopping over the top, lithe and strong. He held out his arms for her, picking her up and lifting her to the other side. Taking her hand again, he headed toward the barn, the moonlight shining on his dark hair and making it gleam.

A glow from the old barn's window stopped Tessa in her tracks. She looked down at the ground. Someone had dug a path to the barn, too. "Who?"

Mick smiled, his grin amused and oddly relaxed for someone who had a mercy fertilization on his plate. "Nina. She insisted."

"In the time it took me to get dressed?"

"Wanda and Marty helped," he admitted with a grin, his teeth flashing white against the black night.

"She's like the Flash. I don't know if I'll ever get used to her superspeed."

Mick chuckled. "You should have seen her today with the guys from the firehouse. It was like she was some crazy puppet master, yanking their strings. But you have to admit, it comes in handy," he said, pushing open the wide doors of the barn to let her see inside.

There were several lanterns scattered about, their wicks glowing with light, warm blankets spread out and pillows piled on a stack of hay bales, and even a kerosene heater. Wine and a platter of grapes and cheese sat on a makeshift table in the corner with one crooked, peeling chair.

Mick pulled her inside, bringing her to sit beside him on the blanket-covered hay. She folded her hands together, unsure what to say. She'd waited all her life for this very moment, and while what Nina had done to create a mood was lovely, it was uncomfortable and painful to think this was how it was all going to go down.

"Tessa?"

"Awkward, right? I know. You don't have to say anything else. But I'm here to tell you, I don't care how awkward it is. We're doing this, Malone. Besides, it can't be any worse than my first time with Denny Bradford."

Mick pulled off his gloves, dropping them on the dusty floor with a chuckle. "Denny was your first? I thought that jackhole Adam Monroe was."

She rolled her eyes at him, crossing her arms over her chest, feeling vulnerable. "Ugh. Adam Monroe? I'm surprised you think so little of me. He was disgusting."

Mick barked a laugh. "I thought everyone in your senior class was hot for him?"

"Everyone but me. And how do you know so much about my senior class—or who my first was?"

Mick shrugged, taking his jacket off. "You hear things. It's not like we live in the big city. Stuff gets around." He hopped off the bale of hay, his long legs taking strong strides to the far end of the barn where a small battery-operated CD player sat.

He clicked it on, the soft strains of Andy Williams singing "Moon River" drifting to her ears.

Mick had an enormous collection of CDs and records—he loved vinyl the best, and he loved Andy Williams because he said it always reminded him of visiting his Grandma Edith's house. Noah used to tease him about his fondness for the oldies, but there had been a time or two when she'd caught her brother humming a Mitch Miller tune.

As he walked toward her, Tessa's heart began to pound. This was not the way it was supposed to be was all she could think, despite how handsome he was in low-slung jeans and a thick knit sweater.

Mick held out a hand to her and hitched his jaw toward the barn's big floor. "Dance?"

"You hate to dance," she said with surprise, even as she slipped off the bale of hay and went to him willingly.

"Maybe not so much with you," he grumbled.

Walking into his embrace, Tessa closed her eyes, hoping her pulse would slow so it didn't pound as hard in her ears.

Mick had hugged her a thousand times over the years, and she'd often wondered what the shelter of his embrace would be like if she lingered, but she never had.

Turned out, his wide chest, the beat of his heart, his strong arms around her were just as heavenly as she'd imagined.

Mick let his head rest on top of hers, swaying to the music. "So, let's talk."

Tessa squeezed her eyes shut, her arms still uncomfortably at her sides. "We don't do that very well, Mick. Maybe it's better we just do this." *Get it out of the way so you can forget you had to do your best friend's sister like she was on par with having the plague.*

"How about we set our differences aside for now, okay? We have other things that need addressing."

She shuddered an uneven breath, tears stinging her eyes. "Okay."

He took her arms and wrapped them around his waist. "I'm sorry I was so harsh back at the house. I didn't understand what you were feeling about the egg. A lot of crazy things have happened, and just as I absorb one of them, something crazier happens."

"Try spitting a bowling ball out of you, and then we'll talk crazy. Until then, I have the market cornered."

"I didn't get it until Arch had me touch the egg." His voice hitched then, his thick words becoming husky. "I can't even begin to . . ."

Tessa nodded, her heart welling with love for an egg. An egg. "It's amazing, isn't it? I can't describe it, but I understood it in my very soul."

"I did, too."

She lifted her head, forcing herself to look into his eyes while she wrapped her arms around his lean waist a bit tighter. "Then you understand why we have to do this?"

His eyes, now darker, maybe even fiercer, captured hers. "I do. But I need you to know something, Tessa."

Here it came. This would mean nothing. It was for the sake of the baby. She tightened her fists to prepare for the hurt his words would evoke. "What do you need me to know?"

Mick cupped her jaw, his lean fingers caressing her skin, sending shivers along her arms, soothing her tension. "I need you to know that my reaction to this—what we have to do—wasn't out of disgust or anything even remotely like that."

Her words became like peanut butter, stuck on her tongue, almost choking her. "Then what was it?" she managed to sputter.

"This—what we're going to do—is something I've always wanted. I just didn't want it to be this way."

If words could take a person out, she'd be flat on the floor. Every nerve in her body responded, every bone in her body melted. Tessa couldn't believe what she was hearing. Maybe she wasn't even sure she was hearing right, but if she wasn't, she didn't want to.

Rather than speak, she stood on tiptoe, pushing her fingers through his hair until their lips almost touched. In this moment, she wanted to savor this brief second, remember what his lips felt like pressed to hers for the first time.

She wanted to reflect on every daydream she'd ever had about this very moment.

But Mick took control, pulling her close, capturing her lips with no hesitation, letting his tongue slide into her mouth until her sigh echoed in her ears. Her arms went around his neck, her body inched as close as it could get to his, her head swam with the delicious force of his mouth.

Mick tightened his embrace, his strong arms around her, his hands running along her spine as he and Tessa discovered each other, as their tongues dueled, as her body caught on fire.

"Won't this hurt you so soon after?" he asked, peeling away her jacket, his eyes heavy-lidded and dark.

"Marty said she suspects we self-heal like vampires and werewolves do. She said when she and Nina had their babies, they self-healed instantly. But I promise, it's like it never happened. I can't explain it, but I swear it's okay," she whispered back, her nipples tight with need, scraping against her soft sweater.

Mick groaned into her mouth when she lifted herself higher, hoping to get closer. "I never want to hurt you."

His vulnerability touched her, soothed the edges of her raw heart. Instinctively, she knew she had to take the lead or he'd treat her with kid gloves. Tearing her mouth from his, she pulled him by the hand toward the hay bales. Turning toward him, seeing him, his eyes dark with desire, the pulse in his jaw beating, made her heart speed back up.

Taking the bottom of her sweater, she lifted it up and over her head and dropped it to the floor. She'd never been shy when it came to being naked, and showing Mick that was somehow important to her. She wanted him to want her. She wanted him to want her the way she'd always wanted him.

His breathing hitched, became thick and raspy when she slid her panties and jeans over her hips and hopped up on the bales of hay, pointing to her boots. "Help?"

Mick's big hands, strong and sure, pulled at her boots, dropping them to the ground before gathering her up in his arms. Pressing her flesh to his fully clothed length was intoxicating, the scrape of skin against material, his hands roaming over her possessively, needy, made her feel wanton and wicked.

She wrapped her legs around his waist, whimpering when his lips raked over the sensitive flesh of her neck, clinging to him when he finally cupped her breast.

Colors flashed behind her eyelids, bright, brilliant colors of heat, exploding with her need, making her tighten her ankles around his waist, clench the thick strands of his hair in her hands.

Mick walked them to a larger hay bale and set her on it, then yanked his work boots off and dragged his sweater over his head.

She'd seen Mick semi-naked before. She'd seen his chest, bronzed from a summer spent baling hay, rippled with muscle, the sharp V at both of his hipbones, the light sprinkling of hair between his pecs.

It was when he went for his jeans that Tessa held her breath. She'd considered this particular part of his anatomy, but maybe her fantasy wasn't as fully fleshed out as the reality. Still, her mouth watered when he hooked his thumbs into the top of his boxer briefs and dragged them over his bulging thighs.

She loved his legs, so thick with muscle, flexing and tightening when he bent to remove his briefs.

Standing over her, Mick looked down at her, and Tessa's mouth went dry. Mick obviously wasn't ashamed of being naked, either. In fact, as he stood in front of her, the finest specimen of undressed man she'd ever seen, she understood why.

Everything about him was sculpted, defined, from his arms right down to his calves. His cock was erect, thick, smooth, hot to her touch when she reached for him.

Mick groaned as her hands went around his shaft, and he drove his fingers into her hair, pulling her closer to his abdomen.

Tessa let her cheek rest against his skin, let the heat of it warm her, spur her on as she explored him, ran her hands over his rigid abs, over his hard ass, kneading, touching.

Mick's hands went to her shoulders, pushing her backward until she lay before him. His eyes consumed her, scanned her length, burned her skin until he was lying beside her, pulling her to him so their flesh finally met.

It was like a jolt of fire skimming her veins, bringing her nerves to life. Mick's chest beat against hers, their breathing choppy. "I want you to remember this, Tessa. *I* want to remember it. Let's go slow."

Tears stung her eyes. This was nothing like she'd expected. There was nothing awkward or forced about this. It felt more right than anything she'd ever done before. "Slow," she agreed, her response husky as she cupped his jaw, letting her fingers spread out over his cheek.

Mick dragged her closer, skirting his hands over the undersides of her breasts, making her gasp when he tweaked a nipple.

Her leg automatically went around his hip when Mick slipped his hand between her thighs, sliding it into her wet flesh, fingering the tight bud of her clit. She drew him closer, keeping his lips pressed to hers, absorbing the decadence of his mouth finally on hers.

But Mick tore his mouth from hers, making her whimper for its return, and then he was sliding along her body, kissing his way across her shoulders and down along her collarbone until he was at her breast. When his mouth enveloped her nipple, Tessa gasped, arching against him, gripping his thick shoulders, digging her fingers into his flesh.

He nipped at the tight peaks, pulling, drawing them into his hot mouth, then rolling his tongue over them until she saw stars.

The moment she didn't think she could take any more was when Mick skimmed farther down her body, trailing hot kisses along her belly, until his head rested between her legs.

Hiking her thighs over his shoulders, Mick glanced upward at her, catching her watching him. "I've waited forever for this," he said, his voice hot and thick, before he lowered his dark head, spread her flesh, and swiped it with his tongue.

Tessa bucked upward against him, crying out at the contact, loving the slick slide of his tongue, needing it like she'd never needed anything before. Her hands went to the blanket beneath her, clenching it as Mick slid a slow finger inside her.

The feel of his mouth on her, the heat of his tongue made her cry out, writhe in achy desperation. He stroked her long and slow, tasting, swirling over her clit in delicious patterns while his finger drew in and out of her.

Her pulse roared in her ears, her veins hot with molten liquid when the rush of orgasm began to wind its way outward from the pit of her belly. Her toes curled, her breathing grew choppy, her fingers reached for Mick's hair.

Mick's head between her legs, his tongue at her core was all too much as a flood of raging tingles began to build until she was almost dizzy. As she found release, her legs went around his neck, her eyes rolled to the back of her head, her mouth opened in a silent scream of pure pleasure.

Her hips rocked upward, driving against the ecstasy of his tongue until she couldn't breathe anymore, until she was boneless and worn out.

Mick stroked her thighs, kissed them, whispered words she couldn't quite hear for the subsiding roar in her head. He slid upward, his skin against hers, his cock hot against her thigh.

She melted into him, draped her arms around his neck, clung to his body, ran her hands over his shoulders before his mouth found hers again.

His length was hard against her own frame, solid and tense. Tessa reached between them, grasping his cock, slipping her hand around it and pumping it, learning what made him groan into her mouth.

But Mick wrapped his fingers around her wrist to thwart her. "It's been a long time, Tessa. Go easy."

"Really?" Why had she asked that? It was none of her business how long it had been since Mick had made love. Whatever he'd done before tonight should be considered voided.

"Really," he murmured when she slowed her strokes, pulling her mouth from his and letting her lips follow a path along his rock-hard chest.

She sipped at his nipples, licking them, teasing until she fixated on his abs, running her tongue along each hard line, sliding downward until she was settled between his thighs.

Tessa snaked her tongue out, swiping the head of his cock, testing the waters, smiling when he tensed and grabbed a handful of her hair. She took him slowly into the recesses of her mouth, inch by inch, using her teeth to gently scrape his skin until she was at the base of his shaft.

Mick hissed, grinding against her before pushing her away and dragging her upward. "I can't," he said with clenched teeth, holding her close and burying his face in her neck.

Tessa clung to him for a moment, inhaling his scent, pressing her forehead to his before rolling him to his back and straddling him.

The view from where she sat was everything she'd ever imagined and more. Mick, his hair mussed, his eyes heavy, his cock strong and thick, his chest rising and falling rapidly. He was so beautiful to look at she had to fight back tears. She smoothed her palms over his bronzed skin, wisped her fingers over his nipples, soaking in every inch of him so she'd never forget this moment.

Placing his hands on her hips, Mick guided her to his shaft, letting her wrap her fingers around it and settle herself there. Their eyes met for a brief moment before Tessa lifted her hips and drove downward on him, relishing their unified gasps.

He stretched her, filling her up, making her heart crash hard against her ribs. She'd imagined this, wondered if making love with Mick was all just expectation, but she'd never thought it would exceed her dreams.

And she just wanted to luxuriate in the moment, savor the texture, the sounds, the smells of their lovemaking, but her need, this crazy desperate itch that needed scratching, wouldn't let her hold still.

Falling back on her palms, she placed them on Mick's thighs and let her spine arch her body forward. The stretch of her body opened her wider, letting her take in all of Mick's length, and when he drove upward, she was now the one hissing.

His thumb went to her clit, caressing it as she rolled her hips in time with his thrusts and moaned when heat assaulted her and her nipples beaded tight and hard.

Tessa's fingers dug into Mick's thighs, and she rode the white-hot wave he'd stirred in her, letting everything go but the sweet rise to release.

His hands went to her breasts, cupping them, rolling her nipples into stiff points, and then she was falling forward against the shelter of his chest, burying her face in his neck as he blended their bodies together.

She felt his orgasm as easily as she felt her own—the tension in his bulk, the flex of muscle, the tightening of his cock. Mick's hands went to her back, crushing her against him when he came, and the feel of his possessive embrace made her come, too.

It was brilliant in sound and clarity, so sharp it created a sweet pain that made Tessa's toes curl.

Mick tightened his embrace, keeping her near as their breathing slowed and their muscles relaxed.

Neither of them spoke, but she sensed that he knew they needed to. She needed to. She needed to understand his earlier words. She needed to know what he meant when he said he'd always wanted this, and why he hadn't said it sooner.

But for now, she just wanted to lie here with Mick, her head to his chest, listening to his heartbeat.

CHAPTER 11

“What do you think happens next?” Mick asked, pulling his jeans on while she admired his rapidly disappearing nakedness.

Tessa reached down for a boot, pulling it on. “You mean with the egg?”

“Did that do it, ya think?”

“I don’t know. Archibald didn’t say if we had to fertilize it more than once.” Did they? After tonight, she couldn’t imagine making love with anyone else ever—mercy fertilization or not.

Mick scooped her up until her feet were off the ground and they were eye to eye. “Would you mind if I said I wouldn’t mind if we did?”

She grinned. “What a load off. I was worried we were going to go right back to awkward.”

“Awkward sucks.”

“We do it so well.”

"Let's not do it anymore, okay?"

"Why did we do it in the first place, Mick?" Damn. She'd promised herself to just let it be, like he'd asked.

"We have to talk, Tessa. Really talk. But not right now. We have too much going on. And with the threat of this demon thing, we need to focus on eliminating that before we think about anything else."

She folded her hands together behind his neck. "Okay. But no more taking whatever you're grudging about out on me. It's part of the reason our arguments have gotten so ugly since Noah died."

Mick stiffened against her, but that wasn't going to fly with her anymore. Not after tonight. "Don't do it, Mick. Noah was my brother. He was your best friend for a million years. We should be able to talk about him. I should be able to talk about him without you shutting down. We both loved him. So sure, we can leave this for now, but once we figure this out—how to live with wings I can't even stand up with, how to keep from setting things on fire, how we're going to deal with a baby and what that baby is going to be—we talk."

"Sorry. Knee-jerk reaction. It's a deal." He planted a kiss on the corner of her mouth to seal it.

Tessa shivered suddenly and then there was warmth. So much warmth, her heart actually twisted inside her chest. It overwhelmed her, gripping her, stealing her breath until tears stung her eyes. And without question, she knew it had to do with the baby.

Mick cocked his head. "Did you feel that?"

She looked up at him in wonder. "You felt it, too?"

"I did."

"Sort of all-overwhelming and all-consuming warmth and . . . love." So much love, she had to gasp for breath.

Mick looked at her, his eyes full of the same wonder she was experiencing. "The baby? I don't know why, but that was my first thought. That it was the baby. Do you think that was whatever working its magic?"

She knew without a shadow of a doubt. "I don't know why, but yeah. I think we did it," she said on a happy grin.

Her phone buzzed in her jeans pocket, signaling a text, making Mick slip his hands inside her pocket and pull out her phone. His face grew grim as he read the text.

"We need to get back to the house. Darnell's there and he has some information."

Her chest instantly went tight and she gripped Mick's sweater. "I'm afraid."

"Me, too, but it'll be a cold day in Hell before I let anything happen to you or our egg."

Her heart fluttered. He'd said *our* egg. "So you've grown used to the idea that we'll have a child to raise?" Had she?

Mick's eyes were confused. "I think so. I'm still trying to figure out what's going to come out of the egg. I guess it'll be half human, half dragon like us, right? And here's something else to think about: We'd better be careful where we point our firebreathing. If that's what got you knocked up, we'll have more kids than we know what to do with, considering our lack of skill."

Tessa's head fell back when she laughed. "Do you really think that's what knocked me up? And as a PS, if it is, you'd better move to the next state—because wow, it was like giving birth to a Ford Fairlane."

Now Mick laughed, too, setting her back on the ground, but keeping her in his arms. "I'm sorry it hurt. I don't get how it happened, either. But I promise to watch where I spew my fireballs."

Tessa looked up at him, this man she'd loved since kindergarten, when he'd ambushed her Barbie with his stupid G.I. Joe tanker. "Can you even believe the conversations we have lately?" She leaned back in his embrace and made her best Nina face. "I'll suck your soul right out of your scrawny body, kiddo. So shut the fuck up."

Mick batted his eyelashes the way Marty did. "Oh, Mistress of the Dark, you hush or I'll were-out on you and eat your ugly black heart."

Tessa pulled her jacket over her head, imitating Nina's hoodie, and stomped around in a circle. "Yeah. He's my zombie. And he's a fucking vegetarian. You got some shit to say about it?"

Mick rolled his eyes just like Wanda. "Nina! Must you be so crass?" He put his hands on his hips just like Wanda. "Honestly, will you never learn?"

They both laughed until tears came to Tessa's eyes, before reaching for each other's hands as if they'd always done it, then turning off the lanterns and heading back to her cottage.

TESSA pulled her scarf off and braced herself when they entered the cottage, her eyes immediately straying to the incubator, where Archibald held vigil and Carl stroked the egg with a clumsy finger duct-taped into place. "What's wrong?" She rushed to Nina's side. If Nina was worried, Tessa knew it was for good reason.

Mick came up behind her, placing his hands on her shoulders, instantly warming her. "Nina?"

"They know about the egg."

Fear slithered up her spine. *"Who knows?"*

"Hell. All of it, actually," Wanda offered, her lips thinning.

Tessa reached for Mick's hand. "Wait. Hell-Hell? Like seven levels and Satan?"

"I think there's more than seven levels, and yeah, Hell-Hell," Nina replied.

Tessa's mouth went dry. "How do they know?"

Nina held up a slip of paper, shaking it in front of them before looking at Archibald. "Cover mini-dragon's ears. That fucking weasel Frank. Who the fuck else? He left us a note."

Tessa's fingers trembled when she took the lined paper from Nina—paper he'd gotten from her own kitchen, no less—and scanned it. Her stomach turned and her pulse throbbed in her ears. "If we don't give Frank the egg . . ." She couldn't finish. This couldn't be real.

Mick grabbed the note and read it in silence. "If we don't give Frank the egg, the world's going to end? Is this for real?"

Nina nodded, her eyes angry. "Maybe not the world, but it sure as shit will cause some damage. Darnell says it's true."

Tessa snatched the letter from Mick and ripped it up, throwing it into the fireplace, incinerating it as surely as she'd like to incinerate Frank. "Well, that's not going to happen. So Hell and everyone in it can go fuck themselves!"

Nina gripped her shoulder. "Look, Frank said you two have to meet him with the egg. I'll meet him, minus the egg, and kick his weenie ass from here to Mars. End of. No way that skanky mutha is gettin' hold of my baby dragon."

Wanda shook her head hard, her eyes flashing. "No, Nina. If we don't give him the egg, he'll report back to whoever's in charge of this disaster, and then we'll really be ruined. We need to contain this, localize the source."

Tessa had to sit, her legs were wobbling so hard. Carl made room for her on the couch, thumping her shoulder and handing her a blanket he tucked around her legs. "Why is the egg important to Hell?"

Marty perched on the arm of the couch, rolling her sleeves up with a sigh. "I don't think it's important to Hell. I think it's important to someone trapped in Hell. Darnell tells us brimstone and dragon scales mixed together can open the gates of Hell, unleashing whatever's trapped unwillingly inside."

Panic seized Tessa, and her fingers grew icy. "This is insane. I can't seem to say that word enough lately." She took a deep, ragged breath. "So what do we do? There's no way anyone's getting their hands on the egg." Wait. If all they needed was dragon scales, why not take hers? "Hold on. Why not just take mine? They can have my dragon scales, right? Isn't that the same thing?"

Nina's head swung back and forth. "Because you'll die, Tessa. They'll skin you alive. Not fucking gonna happen on my watch."

She didn't care. She realized she didn't care. Nothing was more important than keeping this egg safe. "I don't care! Take me to meet Frank. I'll do whatever he wants. It's simple."

"No!" Mick roared, scaring even Nina. He took a step back, running his hand through his hair before he said, "Mine. You take my scales. Take me to meet with Frank. I'll go willingly."

Wanda placed a hand on Mick's arm. "That won't work, Mick. The baby's scales are far more powerful, meaning yours become of no interest with that notion in the mix. They'll do whatever it takes to get the egg."

"Then I'll do whatever it takes to stop them," Mick spat.

"No. *We'll* help you do whatever it takes to stop them," Marty said with a fierce growl. "So let's give this some thought before we jump the gun. We need a plan. Nina, have you heard back from Jeannie? Because Wanda and I texted her with an idea."

Nina held up her phone with a grin. "She'll be here in three, two, one . . ."

A petite woman with blond hair and sapphire blue eyes appeared in a purple mist sprinkled with glitter, throwing herself at Nina and planting a kiss on her cheek. "MWA! I've missed your pretty face. How are you?"

Nina batted her away, but it was clear that she was very fond of this woman—whatever Nina's version of fond was. "Get off, genie. Jesus, with the hugging and shit." She set the small woman away from her as though she was moving a chair, and grinned. "How's your ass-sniffer?"

Jeannie rolled her eyes, dropping her arms to her sides, and grinned as she gave both Marty and Wanda hugs, too. "Will you and Sloan ever get over that game of touch football?"

"Only when he quits cheating because he can't take being beaten by a GD chick."

Jeannie giggled, light and tinkling, before she looked at Tessa and Mick. "And you both must be the proud parents! Congratulations all 'round! MWA told me all about you."

"MWA?" Tessa couldn't stop herself from asking.

In the midst of all this fear, Tessa couldn't help but laugh. There was something about this group as a whole, something about how they all worked together toward a common goal, even when they bickered, that made her warm inside. Her family had been just like that before death had taken them all away from her, leaving her here to fend for herself. She missed the kind of comfort that safety had once brought her.

Jeannie pinched Nina's lean cheek. "That's short for Meanest Woman Alive. That's what I call her. Do you deny she holds the world title?"

Tessa held up her hands. "No denial here. I'm just surprised she let you live after you gave her the crown."

Jeannie planted her hands on her slim hips. "Did she tell you she'd suck your soul out of your body if you gave her trouble?"

"I think I remember something to that effect."

Jeannie flapped a hand. "Don't let Miss Marshmallow kid you. Her center is soft and gooey. It's the hard chocolate shell you have to crack."

Nina rolled her eyes and flicked Jeannie's shoulder. "Listen, I Dream of, get to the business at hand. We have to meet this fuck-knuckle in an hour, and I wanna be ready."

Jeannie bent at the waist, running her hand over Carl's face. He used his stiff fingers to cup her hand to his cheek and grunted his pleasure. "How are you, Carl? I'm so happy to see you."

Carl nodded, his lopsided grin beaming. "Goo . . ."

"Look at you talking! All those speech lessons with Arch and Sloan are paying off. I'm so proud of you, Carl. And, Arch, when's the next paranormal potluck? I've been dying for your recipe for that crème brûlée." Her eyes twinkling, she gave his hand a squeeze.

Arch gripped it back, dropping a kiss on the back of it. "Oh, Miss Jeannie, it's ever so good to see you. Soon, we shall all gather—once this bother has passed. This much I promise—with Mick and Tessa and our newest addition."

Jeannie wisped a finger in the direction of the incubator. "So this is the little one? Ohhh, how perfect," she cooed, slipping her hand inside under the heat lamp to caress the golden egg. The egg responded by rolling inward ever so slightly, making Jeannie smile. "What a wonderful, fabulous, miraculous event," she whispered. "You're both so blessed."

Tessa sat still, marveling at the acceptance these people offered. Zombies and genies and halfsies and even baby dragons were all instantly welcomed. The world could learn a thing or two from this group. Their tolerance was so pure, so unhindered by any kind of bias, it left Tessa breathless.

Jeannie stood up and smiled at both Tessa and Mick. "So, I'm Jeannie Flaherty. Full-time djinn, evil overlord of a realm of out-of-control genies, and part-time caterer. I'm here to help in any way I can. I wish I could do more, but if I mess with the balance of good and evil, we might have more trouble than we bargained for. I want you both to know, if I could cast a spell and make this all go away, it'd be done."

Ah. This must be the woman who'd given Nina her baby. "So what are we going to do if we can't stop Frank?"

Jeannie's eyes sparkled. "We're going to trick them until we can find a way to nab the person who wants to open those gates to Hell. We're essentially buying time, but let's hope it's enough to identify the culprit and nip this in the bud—because trust me when I tell you, there are plenty of the damned who want out."

"I don't understand," Mick said. "I know I've said that a thousand times since this all began, but how can we keep that from happening?"

"If they want an egg, we're going to give them an egg," Jeannie said. "We want to keep them as far away from the two of you as we can until we can find a safe place for both of you and the baby until this is over."

"We're going to make an egg? How?" Mick asked, a frown forming.

Nina draped her arm around Jeannie's shoulders and grinned. "Watch and learn, Gigantor."

TESSA shivered in the cold night air, hunkering down against Mick. Nina hadn't liked it, but in order for the plan to work, Marty and Wanda insisted she let them go with her. Frank was more likely to fall for this if it was Nina who had the egg and she and Mick pretended they were trying to stop her from handing it over.

Nina glanced over at them, her eyes glittering in the dark shell of Tessa's store. "Okay, so you know the plan, right? I have the egg. I play like I'm giving it up because Frank will probably fall for the idea that I'm a totally evil bitch. You two rush in like you're gonna fight me for the egg. Put up a big fuss, call me crappy names yadda, yadda, yadda. I toss him the egg. We let him think he's won. The weasel takes the egg—we out. Clear? No questions, no bullshit. We need time to figure out who's fucking behind this. I need time to gear up for killin' the motherfucker who wants your kid—because I want it to damn well hurt. Do not vary from the script. Got that?"

Both Mick and Tessa nodded. "Got it, MWA. No heroic efforts. No questions. Nothing."

Mick held the egg Jeannie had created, a perfect replica of the real one.

And she'd done it with the snap of her fingers. It even moved like their egg, cooed like it, snuggled into your hand just the way theirs did.

Mick cradled it against his chest and wrapped it in one of Tessa's throws. It was almost comical to see, if this wasn't so dangerous. Tessa wasn't so much afraid of Frank anymore. She'd gotten past the idea that he was a minion from Hell. She was afraid this wouldn't work, or they'd be found out and Frank would catch them in this ridiculous lie they were about to turn into a stage show.

The crunch of feet on the packed snow had them all alert. Nina gave them the thumbs-up—which meant go time.

They'd practiced exactly how this was to go down.

Nina grabbed the egg from Mick, tucking it under her arm, strolling to the center of the store. "Get the fuck out here, Frank, and let's get this shit done before I get caught."

Wow. Nina was really good. Like give-Meryl-Streep-a-run-for-her-money good.

Tessa took a gulp of air and ran toward Nina, grabbing her arm in a clumsy effort to thwart her, repeating the words the vampire had coached her with. "Give me back my egg, Nina . . ." she said woodenly, sounding like she was a bad actor in one of the dinner theater shows the VFW Hall ladies put on every year.

Jesus. She'd roll her eyes if she didn't think they were being watched. That didn't sound like fear in her voice at all. It sounded like she'd read it off the back of a cereal box.

And then Tessa forgot what she was supposed to say. Panic-stricken, she looked to Mick in the shadows, her eyes wide.

He mouthed the words, *"Mick! Don't let her give them the egg!"*

Oh, right. Damn. How could she forget that? "Uh, Mick, don't let her give them the egg?"

Mick popped out of the shadows, squaring his shoulders and rolling his head from side to side to gear up for his part, like he'd suddenly turned into Christian Bale. "Nina! Give me our egg, you mean, evil vampire!" he over-enunciated, over-projected, over-everything-ed, almost making Tessa giggle.

"I see you brought the egg," Winnie-the-Pooh said, appearing from the black depths of the corner of the store, his face pained.

Mick and Tessa turned to face him. "You leave us alone, Frank!" Mick roared, again overly loud, overly dramatic.

Jesus. This was starting to sound like a fifth-grade play.

Frank's lower lip trembled, his round, sweet face scrunched into a wince, but he shook off his very apparent fear. "I can't do that. I'm sorry, very large man. I have to insist you give me the egg. Please, give me the egg." He held out his hand, a tremor visible.

Nina had prepped them for every possible scenario, including the possibility Frank might figure out this was a dupe. But Mick stuck to his lines. "No! No egg for you, Frank!"

Wait. Wasn't it, *You'll never get this egg, Frank?* Was he improvising? Damn it. Every time he did that when they'd practiced it messed up her rhythm.

Mick turned to Nina then, making his best angry face, pretend reaching for the egg. "Give me the egg!"

Tessa fought another roll of her eyes. He might as well have held his fist to the sky and muttered, "End scene."

Nina flipped Mick the bird, taking two steps back, her eyes hot, her fingers tightening on the egg. "Fuck you and your stupid egg. The hell I'm gonna let a bunch of demons get loose and take over the world because of one kid you didn't even know you were having. Giving the weasel the egg is for the greater good, dumb ass!"

God. Nina was really good at this.

Mick nudged Tessa, prompting her to recite her lines next. The idea was to coax Frank into a fight with them—so he'd be fooled into believing they weren't just going to hand over the egg, which went to their motivation, Marty said, or something like that.

Tessa made an angry face, too. Or she tried, focusing on what she'd looked like in Marty's compact mirror as she'd practiced her terrified/mad face. "No, no, Nina." She gave her head a vehement shake, advancing on the vampire. "Give me my egg. And you go away, Frank! Go away and tell your Hell people they can't have our egg."

"Hell people? Minions," Mick corrected under his breath. "They're *minions*."

Tessa rolled her eyes, trying to summon her inner badass. "Tell your minions they can't have my egg, Frank!"

Instead of inciting Frank with their struggle, he began to back away, terror in his eyes, almost as though he were being dragged. "Nina, give me the egg now!" he yelled, his watery voice echoing in the burned shell of the store. He wasn't advancing on them like he wanted to take the egg from them, though.

They hadn't planned for this scenario at all. So Tessa improvised, jumping in front of Nina and moving toward Frank, her feet crunching on the frozen debris of the floor. "I won't let Nina give you the egg, Frank!"

Something was very wrong. Tessa felt it—the vibe just before everything went to shit. She'd felt it just before Mick had blown her store apart, and she felt it right now.

"Please," Frank's hollow voice whispered, swishing around the room. "Please give me the egg!"

Okay, it was time to ramp this horrific performance up a notch. Turning and grabbing the egg from Nina, Tessa held it tight in one arm. "You'll never get this from me—not everrrr!"

That was when she realized her intuition deserved its due. Because everything did go to shit.

In wave upon wave of shit.

Black figures from the shadows of the store appeared, swirling around in a circle above their heads, climbing the burned-out walls, snarling, seething, picking up speed until the effect was a dizzying buzz of palpable anguish and despair.

The store grew hot, pulsing, the floor lifting up and slamming back down again, knocking both Mick and Tessa to the floor as she grabbed onto Mick's hand. And the roar of something ominous, something vibrating her very bones, began to howl.

A sudden and painful stab of helplessness, an ugly desolation gripped her, leaving her hands trembling and almost making her lose her grip on the egg. In an instant, as sweat poured down her face, Tessa lost all hope—all hope their baby would survive—all hope they'd ever live through this.

Why bother to try? Her fingers began to pull loose from Mick's. If she just let go . . .

Mick grabbed her by the waist, pulling her to him, rolling with the floor as it rose upward like a wave at the beach and shot them to the rafters. "Hold on to me!" he bellowed over the wall of heat flashing over their bodies like lava.

Tessa shook her head. She didn't want to hold on anymore. She was tired of holding on. Tired of trying to figure out why Mick was so angry with her. Tired of being alone. Just tired. She wanted to be wherever Noah and her parents were. The grip she had on Mick's hand began to slacken, the arid wind pulling her in the other direction.

"Tessa! Don't let go!"

She saw the strain in Mick's muscles. The force he was fighting with every ounce of strength he had.

And she didn't care. Nothing mattered but the end. She wanted this all to end.

"Tessa—hold the fuck on! Fight this!" Nina screamed in her ear, suddenly behind her—in the air right along with the oily black figures biting at her feet. "Don't let it win! Hang on to that baby, you hear me? *Fight! Hang the fuck on!*"

But why, she wanted to ask. To what end? She had nothing left now. Once these demons found out the egg was fake, they'd come find the real one, and it would be over anyway.

"Tessa!" Mick hollered, yanking her arm so hard he almost ripped it out of the socket. "Look at me, Tessa! You'd damned well better not let go! You're not alone! Stay with me, Tessa! Stay!" Sweat glistened on his forehead as the force of the wind whipped him around, but he clung to her hand like it was a raft in the swell of a storm.

Nina screeched, her anger so vicious it roared from her mouth. She rose up like some kind of villain in a Matrix movie and snatched one of the inky black figures from the air—plucked it up like she was picking daisies. "You motherfucker, I'll hunt your slimy asses down forever before I'll let you get your claws into this kid!"

But the demon roared back, his wide mouth opening, an endless pit of blackened despair, howling in Nina's face, sending her flying backward against the wall. She slammed so hard against it, Tessa feared she was unconscious.

But that couldn't be if she was already dead, could it? Nina dropped like a ton of bricks, crashing to the floor, scattering the demons who'd set their sights on Mick.

A rage so enormous, so frightening, rose up inside Tessa, screamed from the tips of her hurtling toes to the top of her head. Her hands were sweaty, her nails ripping from their beds as she clung to Mick and she fought to hold on to the egg.

The demons tore at Mick, twisting his body, shredding his clothes, sinking their ugly talons into the flesh of his back.

And she became more enraged.

A flash of Nina, broken and battered on the floor, was the last thing she remembered before she opened her mouth wide.

Fire flew from her mouth, tearing its way out of her lips, choking her, searing her gums. Nothing mattered but making these horrific things let go of Mick. So she twisted her head from side to side, spraying them like a fire hose, sending each of them hurtling, tumbling through the air, exploding into fiery pieces. Then her wings were there, knocking her like a ball from a cannon, shooting her forward, and sending her sailing straight for the far wall, dragging Mick with her.

Terror struck her in mere seconds. If she didn't stop the forward momentum, they'd crash into the wall with nothing but her hands to soften the impact. With everything she had in her, Tessa focused on her wings, forced herself to think of nothing but moving them, catching the hot air beneath them, visualizing the kaleidoscope of colors on the scaly surface.

Desperation began to take over just moments before they missed the wall and soared upward with an exhilarating sweep of wind from below. Tilting her body left and right, she was able to navigate the store, racing around the remaining demons, gripping Mick with one hand and the egg in the other.

If she could just get to the hole in the roof, maybe she could lead them out of the store? Out of the corner of her eye, she saw Nina move from below, and Tessa lost her focus completely, heading straight for the wide black maw of an incoming demon.

They crashed together, knocking the egg from her hands, sending it high up in the air where another demon caught it with his mouth.

A slow rumble of laughter, devious, maniacal, shot through the room just before the demon that had swallowed the egg disappeared and the inferno of air deflated as quickly as it had begun.

Tessa and Mick careened to the floor with whistling speed, crashing in a heap of limbs and groans.

She rolled to her side, her wings crumpling as she tried to

push herself from the floor to stand, gritting her teeth, determined to own these damn wings if it was the last thing she did.

Her toes just touched ground when she toppled forward onto Nina, covering them both in a heap of flapping wings and tangled limbs. She pressed her hands to Nina's face. "Nina! Are you okay? Nina!" Using two fingers, she pried the vampire's eyes open. "Speak to me, MWA. Please!"

"Get. The fuck. Off. Me. Mothra," she groaned, her eyes unfocused and glazed.

Joy flooded her entire body. She expressed it by kissing Nina's cheek, bracketing her face in her hands. "Oh, thank God, you're okay!" And then she remembered Mick, broken, his flesh torn.

Struggling to stand, she gave up and instead rolled to her side, squinting her eyes to locate Mick. He was to the far right of her, his big frame so still that more panic rose in her—a fear so great she almost couldn't move. But she would—if it killed her.

Using all of her strength, she pushed off the floor, rising to her haunches, clenching her jaw as her wings flopped to either side of her. Sweat fell from her face, the salty perspiration making her eyes sting. Bracing her hands on her knees, she pushed off, the force pulling her backward until she almost lost her footing.

Tessa stumbled backward, flapping her arms, tripping over the torn floor, and then it happened. Just like that, she and her will of iron managed to balance the heavy weight of the wings.

Taking slow steps, she picked her way across the floor to Mick, dropping to her knees, falling on the shredded wood. "Mick," she whispered, stroking his face, assessing the crimson slashes in his chest and arms. Placing her cheek to his chest, she rested there for a moment, clinging to his ragged jacket. "I'm sorry I tried to let go of you, Mick. I don't know why I did."

"Demons," Nina provided, squatting down beside her. "They prey on your worst fucking fears, dude. Then they magnify them. You have to fight that shit—if you crack, and they stick their wormy fingers inside that crack, they have a chance to break you wide open, and it's done."

She couldn't reflect on the despair she'd felt in those moments. They'd stripped her very soul.

Mick groaned, his slack face tightening into a wince of pain. The moment his eyes opened he said, "Tessa? Where is she?"

She put her hand on his chest and whispered, "Here. I'm here." Always.

Mick's beautiful eyes, scanned her face. "Your wings," he murmured. "You used them?"

She nodded her head, excitement and horror welling up inside her at the same time. "It was the most amazing thing ever, Mick. But forget me. Are you okay? You're all torn up. We need to get you back to the cottage and fix you up. Do you think you can walk?"

He sat up, wincing harder. "Jesus Christ, what happened?"

Nina clapped him on the back. "You shoulda seen our girl. She was like the GD Flying Nun, spewing all that fire and shit. Took out a bunch of 'em in one spray."

"The egg?" Mick asked, trying to rise to his feet.

"It's gone," a worried, watery voice said from beneath a pile of debris.

Everyone's head swung in the direction of the debris. Nina stomped over the piles of wood toward it. "If that's you, Frank,

I'm going to kill you. You know that, right? I'm going to chew your ass up and spew your guts all over this damn room."

"Please don't!" he said, his voice quivering with a whistling whimper. "I didn't have a choice. Please, please understand."

Nina pulled the planks of scorched wood away to find Frank huddled up in a ball of trench coat and galoshes. "Get up, Frank. Get up and behave like a man, you weasel. You were willing to sacrifice a kid to save your hide. That won't work for me—which means I gotta kill you."

Frank used his arm to cover his face, his voice riddled with terror. "No! No, that's not it at all. I'm begging you. Please listen to me. *Please*."

Tessa grabbed Nina's arm to stop her from plucking Frank from the ground. "Let's just hear what he has to say. Maybe he has some information we can use." She held out her hand to Frank, offering to help him up.

He grabbed it, his palm sweaty, his eyes wide with fright. "They wrote that note. I would never do something so awful."

"Who wrote the note, Frank?" Mick asked, jamming his face in Frank's round one, which was shrouded in panic.

"Her minions. They wrote it. They held me hostage. Put some sort of spell on me to keep me bound to them so I couldn't warn you. I swear," he sobbed. "I would never kidnap a child. Never."

"Who's *her*, Frank?" Mick asked, gritting his teeth.

Frank bit his lip, scratching his head. "I don't know. I only know it's a woman because someone said 'she' wrote the note. I'm just a minion, caught in the in-between. That's the honest truth. My supervisor promised me if I got the dragon scales, I'd be set free from whatever binds me to Hell. That's all. And now

I'm here, and I can't make my magic work. But I swear to you, I would never hurt a child!" His hysteria was clearly rising, and if Tessa had learned anything about fear, she'd learned it wasn't conducive to productivity.

Tessa put a hand on Frank's arm, patting it, going on a gut feeling. "Frank. Come back to the cottage with us and we'll talk this out, okay?"

He pulled away, his eyes wild now. "You'll kill me!"

God, it was so bizarre to hear Winnie-the-Pooh's voice speak of killing someone. "No, Frank. I won't let anyone hurt you. Promise. You're safe with me."

"Don't make promises you can't keep, Mothra. I'm going to kill this motherfucker. Kill him but good!" Nina yelled in Frank's face, her eyes glittering in the dark.

"No!" Tessa yelled. "Stop scaring him."

"Are you crazy?" both Mick and Nina yelled back in unison.

"No. I'm not crazy. We're bringing Frank back with us and he's going to tell us everything he knows. Don't fight me on this because my gut tells me Frank needs help as much as we do. Or are you forgetting Darnell and his Major League baseball career mishap?"

"Fine," Nina huffed, rolling her eyes. "But you bet your Christopher Robin ass, I'll squeeze the minion right the fuck out of you if you make one wrong move, Frank. Got it? One. Wrong. Move."

Frank shivered in response, cowering.

"Go!" Nina roared at him, poking him between his slumped shoulders and making a face at Tessa and Mick to express her obvious displeasure.

Tessa wrapped her arm around Mick, hearing his hiss of pain. “Can you manage?”

“You gonna carry me if I can’t, tiger?” he teased, looking over her shoulder. “Hey, your wings are gone. Did you feel it this time?”

Surprise! She reached around her waist to find nothing. “Holy cow—no! I guess I was too worried that Nina would kill Frank.”

“I don’t think bringing him back to the cottage is a good idea. You know that, right?”

“Noted. But I have a gut feeling. So trust me, okay?”

“Okay, but if Nina spews guts all over your cottage, you’ll have no one but yourself to blame.”

Tessa chuckled, helping him step over the threshold of the store and out into the night. “Fair enough.”

She prayed she was right, but something about Frank’s fear, something about the approach he’d used when he came into the store tonight, made her believe he was telling the truth.

And she was determined to find out what he knew.

CHAPTER 12

Darnell jumped off the couch the moment they all arrived back at the cottage. "You bettah get on up outta here, demon!" he yelled, moving toward Frank, who shrank behind Tessa and Mick.

Frank grabbed onto Tessa's sweater, talking into it. "Please, please don't let him hurt me!"

Tessa put her hands up to hold the demon at bay. "Darnell! It's okay. I brought him back here."

Both Marty and Wanda jumped up from the sofa and yelled, "Are you crazy?"

Archibald stuck his head out of her bedroom. "Hush, you heathens! The wee one rests . . ." He stopped short, his nostrils flaring, his eyes narrowing in suspicion. "Who is this?"

"This is Frank the minion, Arch. It's okay. Go back to the baby. I've got this." Tessa took Frank by the hand and pulled him over to the couch, setting him down beside Carl. "Don't move," she ordered.

Nina pulled off her hoodie, hanging it on the coatrack. "I told her she was fucking crazy. But why would she listen to me? Someone who has experience in the kind of crazy exactly like *Frank*!" she yelled, craning her neck over his shoulder to yell in his face.

Frank jumped, shaking the whole couch, the tremor of his fear so violent he vibrated from head to toe.

Tessa put her hand on Nina's arm. "Please don't scare him, Nina. Trust me."

Nina narrowed her eyes at Tessa. "Fine, but when this all goes to shit, it's on you, kiddo." She stomped off to flop down on the section of the couch farthest from Frank.

Tessa took a deep breath, rolling her shoulders and taking a seat next to the terrified minion. "Okay, so tell me how you ended up a demon."

"Minion," he corrected. "I'm a minion. I'm stuck between upstairs and Hell."

"Which is why you kept fading in and out in my bedroom and at the store?"

"Yes. I'm afraid I'm not a very good minion. I'm bumbly and awkward, and all I want to do is get out of there. It's so awful." He shook his head, tucking his chin to his rounded chest.

She decided a gentle tone was best. "How did you get there to begin with, Frank?"

Frank blew out a breath of air, his shoulders falling forward. "I wasn't a bad person here on earth. I lived a modest lifestyle. Quiet, simple. I loved to garden and read. I read to the children at my local library once a week, because I realized I sounded like

Winnie-the-Pooh, and the children loved it. Sometimes, as a hobby, I tinkered with ham radios—which is how I know a bit about antiques, and it's also what led me to your store, Tessa."

"We don't fucking want to know if you like fuzzy kittens and *The Bachelor*, Frank," Nina taunted from the opposite end of the couch. "We want to know why the fuck you were in Hell. Get to it—and hurry because I'm bored with your simple."

"I don't understand it very well. After I died, I woke up in a line. A line I think meant I was going uptown." He used a pudgy finger to indicate the ceiling.

Tessa had to fight off the idea this was all impossible, and forged ahead. "How did you die, Frank?"

"It's rather embarrassing."

Carl reached his stiff hand over to Frank and thumped him on the shoulder to indicate that it was okay to tell them. He gave Frank a lopsided grin, his sweet face light and encouraging.

"I'd still like to know," Tessa prodded.

"I was a gardener—roses were my specialty. They once called me the Rose Whisperer, able to take out aphids with just a glance." Frank let out a soft chuckle at the memory, but his laughter soon soured when he continued. "I worked for many elite families in and around the tristate area, but as I got older, the workload became cumbersome. So I hired some part-time help. His name was Skeeter. Nice enough fellow, passed the background check—something I always do when I hire an employee for the safety of not just myself, but my employers. Skeeter was a thief, and I led him right to the doors of some of my most valued clients."

"And this explains how you died, Frank? Get on with this shit before I beat you up," Nina crowed.

"Nina. Please?" Tessa begged as Frank cringed again. "Finish, Frank. Please. I'd like to hear."

"Skeeter, of course, knew all the schedules of my clients because I knew them. I had all the security codes to their mansions and such. One night, after work, he held me at gunpoint and made me open the home of one of my clients, who was away in Bali. All so he could steal a flat screen TV." Frank shook his head in sorrow. "Long story short, one of the statues he'd cased was very valuable, but it was high up in an arch above their entry doors. So Skeeter got a ladder and made me climb it to retrieve the sculpture. My hands became quite sweaty, but I remember thinking there was nowhere for me to go. I lost my grip and the last thing I remember is falling. I assume I hit my head on the marble floor below."

Tessa winced. If his story was true, Frank had suffered a misfortune similar to Darnell. "So, how did that land you in Hell?" Was the man upstairs really that unforgiving?

Frank's breath shuddered in and out. "I was waiting in the line just like everybody else, waiting to see what was up ahead in the white, puffy clouds, and someone knocked me out of line—cut right in front of me. Next thing I knew, I was falling again—forever it seemed. I ended up in a big heap at Hell's gates. I don't remember much after that. Next thing I know, I was in a room with a bunch of other people like me. People who were granted only limited power until they'd proven themselves, is what they told me. My supervisor, Gary, told me I wasn't a full-fledged demon. I was just a minion, and if I wanted to come back to earth, I had to perform tasks . . ."

"Like buy dragon scales?" Mick asked.

"Yes. I can't tell you how long it took for me to locate you and your store. The Internet in Hell is slow, slow, slow. But I promise you, I didn't know what they were for."

Tessa sighed. One step forward, twenty back. "And you don't know who wanted the dragon scales?"

"Oh, no. I don't ask questions. I just do as I'm told. They promised me that if I did this one last thing, I was free."

"Aw, now, you know that ain't true, Frank," Darnell said, waving his finger in the air. "They sellin' you a bill of goods, pal. Ain't nobody gonna let you outta Hell that easy. Likely, the best you could do is live here on this plane on the fringe like I do. Lyin' low so nobody finds me."

"Oh, dear," Frank whimpered, his watery eyes looking to Tessa.

"So all you know is they want my egg because a baby dragon's scales are powerful enough to unlock the gates of Hell. Is that right?"

Frank nodded. "Mixed with brimstone, they can create all sorts of havoc, as you saw back at your store."

"So why were you at the store tonight?" Nina asked, her face relaxing.

He shook his head, his eyes sad and miserable. "They made me go with them. I swear that's the truth. When I found out you'd laid an egg, and they wanted to take it, I refused to go. I told them to put me in the hole for good. But they knew the only way you'd show up was to use me as bait—because you'd want to know what I know about what's going on down there and they assumed you'd all think defeating me was easy because I'd shown you my weakness. So they forced me to go—to draw you all out. There's no getting away from their magic. You saw what they did."

Perfect. "Any ideas who might want the egg, Frank? I mean, if you were guessing?"

"I don't go past a certain point in Hell's corridors. We're not allowed. I don't know any of the people in charge. I only hear rumblings about them. But whoever wants the egg has been pretty tight-lipped. It has to be someone trapped in there—against their will. Someone who's played along long enough to get some rank, but can't leave because they can't be trusted."

"Okay," Tessa said with a nod. "Thank you for telling me."

Nina's mouth fell open. She clapped her hands on her thighs. "That's it? No torture? No mutilation? You're just going to say thank you very much, nice minion? What the fuck's wrong with you?"

Frank leaned into Tessa, his lower lip trembling. "I'm so afraid of her."

Tessa smiled. "Yeah. I know the feeling. Let her warm up a little before you judge, though. She's not so bad."

"So now what, Frank?" Mick asked. "What happens to you?"

"I don't know. I can't seem to access the portal to Hell like I could before. Believe me, I tried when those demons were chasing you around."

Darnell rose and came to hover over Frank, sniffing him. "He's still got minion on him. Maybe his powers are weak now? It ain't over for you, Frank. I can tell ya that much. They're gonna come lookin' for you 'cus you failed the task."

Tessa patted Frank's hand. "Then we'll keep him here with us."

"Are you out of your Mothra mind?"

Tessa made a face at Nina. "What, you can have a zombie, but I can't have a minion? Why do you get all the fun?"

"Carl's harmless, twit. He didn't try to steal an egg!"

Frank suddenly grew a spine when he yelled back, "But I didn't, either! I just came to pick up a package I ordered."

"Is that you gettin' in my face, Frank?" Nina asked, flashing her fangs and making Frank cringe into the couch. "I didn't think so, nimrod. You stay the fuck away from me, got that?"

Frank sucked in a gulp of air, his bravado gone. "I promise."

Wanda put herself between Frank and Nina. "Nina, cool off. We'll make sure Frank stays put."

"This is bullshit, Wanda, and you know it. And if you give me that crap about the client always being right, I'm going to pluck your arched eyebrows right off your face."

"You're emotionally invested now, and you're not seeing things clearly, Nina. You know I'm telling you the truth," Marty said.

"Oh, screw your mumbo-jumbo psychotherapy. This isn't just a client anymore, Marty. We've got a kid on our hands. The fuck I'm letting Satan himself take a kid. This jackhole was in the mix. As far as I'm concerned, he's under suspicion."

Tessa tugged on the edge of Nina's shirt. "Nina?"

She rolled her eyes. *"What?"*

"Please trust me." She knew Frank meant no harm. Knew it. She just had to convince Nina.

Nina looked down at her and chucked her under the chin. "Who trusts a chick with wings? I'm goin' in to hang out with mini-dragon. You dumb asses figure this one out without me." She stomped off to the bedroom, leaving the room calmer.

Mick squatted down in front of Frank, looking him in the eye, his jaw hard, his face stony. "One wrong move, and it won't just be Nina up your ass. I will kill you if you hurt Tessa or our egg."

Frank swallowed hard, his jowls bouncing. "I don't want to

hurt anyone. I really don't. I just want to go home," he said on a weak whisper.

"Mick, let him be. I know you're angry, and you think I'm crazy, but please, just let him be. If what he says is true, he ended up in Hell by mistake. I know we don't know for sure, but we have to give him the benefit of the doubt. Just like everyone gave Darnell the benefit of the doubt."

Mick's jaw tightened, but he stood up, giving her hand a squeeze, and left the living room.

"So, quarters are tight here, Frank, but I bet you need some sleep."

The minion hunkered down on the couch, shivering. "I don't think I'll ever sleep again. Not after tonight."

Her heart shifted in her chest for Frank. "I have a really great blanket I always use, and if I didn't set it on fire, you can borrow it. It'll help you sleep. But before you go, can I ask you a question?"

"Sure."

"Back at the store. The first night we met, do you remember calling out a name?"

"I was trying so hard to stay on this plane, it's fuzzy."

"You said 'Noah.' Why did you say that?"

"Oh, yes! I do remember that. He was in the store."

"Noah was in the store?" A little impossible, seeing as he was dead, but she didn't reveal that to Frank.

"He was. Right there in front of me. A tall man, with brown hair and a nice smile. He said his name was Noah. But everything went haywire then and when he tried to keep me from leaving by grabbing my arm, I yelled, 'No, Noah.' I didn't want to take him where I was going. I don't ever want to take anyone there."

Tessa couldn't speak, and she had to bite the inside of her lip to keep from crying or asking more questions. For now, she'd have to let it go in favor of giving Frank a break. She began to rise from the couch, achy and sore, but Frank grabbed her hand.

"That wasn't the real egg? You tricked them?"

She grinned. Still pleased they'd somehow managed to pull it off. "Yeah. We did."

He looked up at her then, his shy, watery blue eyes actually staring into hers without looking away or cringing. "I'm glad. I'm so, so glad."

Tessa smiled at him. "I'll go get that blanket, okay?"

"Thank you," he murmured, letting Carl show him the book Nina said the zombie never left home without.

She made her way toward her laundry room in the back of the house to grab the blanket, knowing she'd done the right thing by keeping Frank with them.

Not a doubt in her mind.

HE'D self-healed. Jesus Christ. As Mick pulled his torn shirt off, he glanced at his shoulders and chest in the mirror to be sure he wasn't seeing things. Those demons had latched onto him for all they were worth, tearing at his skin, leaving gaping wounds that burned like the damn devil.

And they were almost completely gone.

He leaned forward on the sink, bracing his palms on it and stretching his neck. This dragon business was damn hard work. Probably harder than being a fireman ever was.

Flashes of Tessa, naked and willing, seared his brain. Of all the things to come of this, making love with her was worth what they'd gone through so far.

But Frank and what he'd said that first night they'd met the minion worried the shit out of him. What if Noah was stuck like Frank? Because of some crazy mistake?

What if the condolences and sympathetic words people handed out when someone died weren't really true? What if there was no peace after all was said and done?

He gripped the sink. He couldn't accept that. Refused to accept that.

Noah had been a good human being. He'd committed more than one heroic act in the time they'd worked together. How could a guy like that end up in Hell?

And how could you break your promise to your friend?

He had to believe Noah wouldn't have objected to the reasoning behind breaking the promise—had to, or he wouldn't be able to look at himself in the mirror.

And the future, Mick? What about the future?

There was that. No way was he letting Tessa go now—even if it meant fighting his personal demons forever.

Because he was in love with her. He'd always been in love with Tessa, and now they were going to have a dragon together.

He was so lost in his thoughts, the knock on the bathroom door startled him.

"Mick? You okay in there? Do you need me to help you clean those wounds?" Tessa asked.

What he needed her to do was not be so damn tempting. Not in the middle of all this. He opened the door to find her pretty eyes inquisitive and worried. "You okay?"

Opening the door wider, he pointed to his chest without saying a word.

Tessa drew her fingertips over his skin, her mouth open in a now familiar expression of WTF. "It's just one freaky thing after another around here, huh? It's like it never happened."

"What exactly did happen? I don't remember much after I told you to hang on."

She let out a breath of air. "I had the worst yet most exhilarating five long, drawn-out minutes of my life is what happened. I got mad just like you did, and fire shot from my mouth and my wings popped out and there was flying and demons and all sorts of things I can't explain."

"You flew? That's amazing. So I guess that makes you the expert?"

"I don't know about expert. I do know we almost bought it crashing into a wall, but you can control it. You just have to focus. Maybe it was the adrenaline of the situation, but somehow I managed to pull it off."

Mick ran his finger down the slope of her cheek. "You're a bigger badass than I gave you credit for. Noah would be proud."

She blushed, smiling up at him. "Speaking of Noah, more freaky news. You ready to hear it, or do you want to keep our pact and not speak his name till this is done?"

She didn't look upset, so whatever she'd learned, it couldn't be what he feared most. "Go for it."

"Frank says there was a guy named Noah in the store that first night, and that's why he called out his name. He described him and everything. The description was a little vague, but it fits Noah. He said Noah was trying to tell him something—even grabbed him by the arm, but Frank shook him off because he was afraid he'd drag Noah back to Hell with him."

Mick's stomach tightened, so hard that he had to take a deep breath. What if Noah wanted to tell Frank to pass on a message to Tessa? What if that message was what they'd argued about the night he died? "Do you think Noah's hanging around? I mean, Jesus—it's possible, right?"

Tessa leaned against the doorframe, crossing her legs at the ankles. "I guess it is. But why is he hanging around? And how long has he been doing it?"

He put a hand at her waist, curving it around to her spine and pulling her close. "I don't know, but I hope he saw you with that schmuck whatshisname—"

"Matt," she offered teasingly.

"Yeah, him. I hope he saw you with him and was trying to tell you he's a total dick."

Tessa wound her arms around Mick's neck, wiggling closer to him. "I agree. He was a total dick. But I have to doubt Noah would have much to say about it. He was pretty good about staying out of my love life. Unlike you."

Mick hauled her upward, wrapping her legs around his waist, trailing kisses along her cheek and down to her earlobe. He bit the soft flesh with a gentle nip, making her shiver. "I was just trying to look out for you. Is that so wrong?" *I was also trying to keep you from having a life, knowing I couldn't have one with you.*

Guilt stabbed his gut.

"Was it because you liiiked me?" she whispered into his hair, arching against him when he slid his hands under her sweater and cupped her breasts. He loved her breasts; soft, perfect, her dusky nipples tight and sweet.

"Maybe. Some secrets are better left secrets," he taunted on a chuckle, moaning into her mouth when she captured his lips in a kiss.

"For the love of horndogs. Didn't you two have enough of this back at the barn?" Nina said from behind them.

Tessa slid down Mick's body, guilt all over her flushed face. She looked up at Nina. "Are you still mad at me for keeping Frank here?"

Nina made a face. "Carl likes him, so I guess he's okay. I'm not crazy about it, but if my zombie likes him, I'm down with it. Carl, believe it or not, is a pretty good judge of character."

"He said he saw Noah in the store that night," Tessa revealed. "Do you think that's true? Have any experience with ghosts?"

She twisted the ends of her ponytail, her usually antagonistic eyes softening when they fell on Tessa. "Nope. No ghosts yet, but if there's a Hell, why the fuck can't there be a Heaven, too?"

Tessa seemed satisfied with that answer. "Would you ask your paranormal friends? If Noah was trying to tell me something, I'd probably give my left arm to know what it was."

Mick's pulse sped up. He had to tell her before Noah did. No matter what the consequences. If they were going to do this, he wanted to do it right. If she was going to walk away because of what Noah said to him that night, then he'd have to learn to live with it. But he had to be the one to tell her.

Nina tugged a strand of Tessa's hair. "You bet, kiddo. Now the both of you move the fuck out of the way. I need a shower and some quiet from all the yappin'. If I don't get some vampire sleep tonight, you don't want to know the level of cranky I can produce."

Tessa put her arms around Nina and gave her a hard hug. "I like you, Nina Blackman-Statleon."

Nina's arms remained stiff at her sides, but her eyes twinkled when she caught Mick's gaze. "I don't like you—not even a little. And I damn well don't like hugging. Get off of me, Mothra, before I pluck those wings off your back and sauté 'em."

Tessa chuckled, clearly ignoring Nina. "Night, marshmallow." She grabbed Mick by the hand, and he gave Nina a smug smile before letting Tessa lead him off to the bedroom.

MICK slipped into bed beside Tessa, pulling the thick comforter someone had kindly washed the smoke from over them both. He reached around the incubator between them, entwining his fingers with hers.

So much peace came with just that simple gesture, Tessa sighed. For the moment, they were safe and the baby was, too. Somehow, everyone had managed to find a place to sleep out in the living room, sprawled on the couch or sharing air mattresses on the floor. Her small cottage, overrun with paranormal people, was quiet.

The snow outside her window fell in fat white flakes beneath a half-moon while stars twinkled in the crystal-clear sky.

"What do you think is going to come out of that egg when it hatches?"

"I don't know, Tessa. I don't care. It's ours. That's all that matters."

Tears stung the corners of her eyes. She didn't care, either. They'd figure it out—together. "What's going to happen when those demons find out the egg was a fake? Jeannie said the spell only lasts twenty-four hours." She was afraid. She was so afraid they wouldn't be able to protect the egg. Where could you hide when demons popped up out of nowhere? There was no hiding place.

Mick sat up, taking the incubator from the bed and setting it on the nightstand. He opened his arm to her, and she gladly snuggled into his embrace. "I imagine it'll be a lot like what happened today at the store. But you're gonna show me how to use those wings and we'll give them a run for their money. Nobody's getting that egg or you, Tessa. I swear it on my life."

She clenched her fist against his warm chest. "Don't say that. I don't want to be without you. *Ever*," she murmured. Not after this. Not after finding out Mick felt the same way about her that she did about him. She had so many questions—why he'd waited so long to tell her, for instance—but she knew it would only complicate things if she brought them up now.

Yet she knew they'd have to clear the air eventually.

Tightening his hold on her, he pressed a kiss to the top of her head. "Then we'll prepare."

Putting her palms flat on his chest, she raised herself up, an urgent need to be as close as humanly possible to Mick canceling out everything else. "Make love to me again. *Right now*," she ordered, pushing the covers back and throwing her leg over his torso.

She grabbed the edge of her nightgown, pulling it over her head and tossing it to the floor. Mick's shaft hardening beneath her ass was an instantaneous reaction that pleased her.

He grinned, almost relaxed, something she hadn't seen in a very long time. "While everyone sleeps just outside the door? You're saucy. I like it."

"We just have to be quiet. No screaming 'do me harder,'" she joked.

"But what about dragon junior?"

She giggled, stretching like a cat, letting her hard nipples caress his chest, more comfortable with Mick than she'd ever been with anyone. "The baby can't see anything yet. I have it on good authority."

"Arch?"

"He's like Ask Jeeves. He knows everything."

"We owe him big. If not for him, who would have known we had to do this in order to ensure the baby hatches?" Mick wiggled his raven eyebrows, grasping her arms and kneading them.

Tessa sat back, rolling her hips against his abdomen, relishing the hard outline of his cock straining against his underwear. "Out of the million and two ways we could have gotten together, leave it to us to turn into dragons and somehow conceive an egg."

Mick's eyes became serious. "Did I tell you before that you're beautiful? That you're everything I thought you'd be and more?" he asked, reaching up to tug her nipples to life.

She splayed her fingers over his chest, running her fingers through the sprinkling of dark hair between his pecs. "I don't remember."

Mick ran his hands over her naked flesh, caressing the indent where her waist met her hip. "Then let me tell you now. You're as perfect as I imagined," he said, husky, low, his words thick with desire.

Leaning forward, she licked at his lips—luscious, delicious, full lips. "Did you imagine me like I imagined you?" She needed to hear the words. She needed to know he'd wanted her as much as she'd wanted him for so long.

Slipping his fingers between her legs, he grazed her already wet flesh. "I imagined you over and over. It was always you, Tessa," he groaned against her mouth, licking at her lips.

Her heart clenched. So much wasted time. "Why didn't you ever tell me?" she asked, shoving his boxer briefs down over his legs, setting his hot shaft free. She settled it between her thighs, letting the head of his cock caress her clit. Soft heat began to simmer in her belly, her nipples tightening.

"I'm telling you now," he growled out the words, rolling her to her back, spreading her legs, and driving into her.

She planted her open mouth on his shoulder, fighting a scream of exhilaration as he filled her, stretched her wide. Her legs instantly went around his waist, taking all of him.

But Mick stilled for a moment, the tension in his body vibrating against hers. His fierce eyes stared down at her, glittering in the dark. "I need you to hear this, Tessa. It's always been you, and it always will be. Now say it," he demanded.

Tessa curled into him, wrapping her arms tight around his neck. "It's always been me."

Mick stared at her hard one last time before he drove upward inside her, hard, forceful, stealing the breath from her lungs. She clung to him, her eyes closing, her body responding to his muscled bulk above her, pressing into her, filling her up until she thought she'd scream from the pleasure.

As their bodies fused together, Mick's lips found hers, and he slipped his tongue into her mouth, thrusting into her until release seized her and she came in hot bursts of intense pleasure and a sharp pang of ever-growing love in her heart.

Mick stiffened against her, his lips falling away from her mouth, his hands slipping under her ass as he took one last thrust into her, whispering her name against her ear.

Burying her face in his neck, Tessa gulped for air, holding Mick, keeping this new bond they'd forged as close as possible.

She needed this to sustain her, to tide her over.

Because she'd had people taken away from her before.

Those demons were out of their minds if they thought she was giving this up without a fight.

CHAPTER 13

A beautiful platinum blond woman greeted Tessa from the living room couch when she padded out of her bedroom to muster up some coffee. The strange woman's smile was somehow comforting.

She'd slept better than she had since this had all begun. Being wrapped in Mick's arms was the healing balm she'd so longed for.

"Morning, Tessa!" Wanda said cheerfully, rising from the couch and rushing into the kitchen to hand her a plate of eggs and freshly made biscuits smothered in butter and marmalade. "This is Katie Wood. She's a veterinarian and a former client, now a good friend, and the closest thing we have to a doctor for baby dragon. We thought it'd be a good idea for her to take a peek at the egg. Just to be sure everything's all right."

Tessa rubbed the sleep from her eyes and smiled, silently trying to figure out what kind of paranormal Katie was as the veterinarian made her way across the floor toward her. She was beautiful in a fresh summery way, long limbs in jeans, a curtain of braided hair, and beautiful clear skin.

She reminded Tessa of sunshine and buttercups.

Katie grinned again, sticking out her hand. "Cat. Cougar to be precise," she offered, then threw a hand up to keep Tessa from apologizing. "Don't bother to apologize. It comes with being a part of the OOPS family."

Tessa took a cup of coffee from Marty with a grateful smile. "I'm still adjusting. Sorry if I was staring."

"No big deal," Katie said, pushing her long braid behind her shoulder. "So can I take a peek at the egg? I don't know that I'll be a great deal of help. I mostly specialize in dogs and cats, the occasional exotic, but nothing quite this exotic."

"I don't mind at all." She ran to the bedroom to get the incubator and realized that Mick wasn't in bed anymore. But the rumpled sheets brought a smile to her face. It was like they'd always been together. Like they'd always climbed into bed with each other every night. Like they'd always made such fiery love.

And she didn't want it to end.

Scooping up the warm box, she drew her hand over the egg. "Morning, sunshine," she whispered. The egg rolled into her palm, nestling against it just like it had the night before.

As she made her way to the kitchen, she heard Nina greeting Katie with warmth. Yet another friend these women had made along the way to forming their crisis hotline/support group, making Tessa wonder how many of these crises they'd handled.

Nina tugged on Katie's braid with a grin. "How's Shaw and those babies? Haven't seen them since last Christmas."

Katie's smile brightened. "Shaw's terrific. He's in school, studying to become a vet now. We finally decided the twins were old enough to go to day care. So he gave up being a stay-at-home dad to start school. And the twins—yikes. What a handful. They're into everything as always—shifting, shedding, eating way more protein than I can seem to keep in the fridge. But it's an amazing life," she said on a happy sigh.

"Teeny?" Nina asked with another one of those fond grins. "How's my favorite smart-ass?"

Katie lifted her shoulders. "Teeny's, well, still Teeny. My grandmother," Katie said on a laugh as an explanation to Tessa, settling into one of the breakfast bar chairs. "We're still hiding cigarettes from her, and she's still giving everyone in town hell."

Tessa set the incubator down in front of Katie, plugging it into the outlet.

Katie was silent for a moment, shaking her head, a tear slipping from her eye. "Honest, I don't know that I'm ever going to get used to the kind of miracles this life brings us. Who would have thought you could have a baby, Nina? And now this. It's amazing—I'm so awed."

Nina clapped Katie on the back. "It's good to see you. I'm out for a little bit, but don't leave without saying good-bye, huh? I don't see you enough."

Katie gave her a hug. "You bet."

And again, Tessa was flabbergasted by Nina—flabbergasted by the friends she'd collected along the way. Astounded by the strength of her loyalty.

Nina grabbed a coat and a scarf from the coatrack, now nearly so full with coats from so many different people you almost couldn't get out the door, and waved Carl to the door. "C'mon, Carl. You and me got a date with a toboggan, buddy."

"Wait! What if someone . . . you know, sees him?" Tessa asked, keeping her voice low so as not to insult Carl, but fearing for him just the same.

Nina popped the tip of Tessa's nose with a fingertip. "I'll make 'em forget. Now go listen to baby dragon's heartbeat."

Frank sat alone on the couch, his hands folded neatly in his lap, his watery eyes staring at the fire. Tessa put a hand on his shoulder. "Frank? Did you eat?"

Nina pulled Carl's stiff hands through the sleeves of the jacket. "Of course he ate. I made sure he did. C'mon, Frank. You're coming, too."

"Oh, no," he whispered with a hitch in his voice. "I'm fine here, thank you."

From behind the couch, Nina pulled a hat over the top of his head and patted it into place. It was pink and had earflaps, but it would do. "Nope. You're comin' with us, minion."

Frank shivered, looking up at Tessa, his eyes pleading. "I'm afraid of—of . . . *her*."

"It's okay, Frank. I promise you. I wouldn't let you go with her if I thought she was going to hurt you."

Nina wrapped a scarf around his neck, too. "Yeah, Frank. It's okay. Now get up. You're keepin' me from the fresh powder. You don't want to do that because I'm just startin' to adjust to the idea of you. Darnell says I should give you a break. I say he's a damn bleeding heart, but I respect his judgment."

"You promise you won't eat me?"

"Can a vampire eat a minion, Frank?"

"I don't know," he blustered.

"Then don't make me effin' find out."

Frank rose, but it was with stiff legs. He made his way around the couch and toward the door, his pink hat crooked, his purple and blue scarf trailing along his back.

As the door closed and Tessa returned to the women in the kitchen, she realized Nina was taking Frank at his word by including him in her outing with Carl. That maybe he really was like Darnell—caught up in a bad situation he couldn't get out from under.

Katie pulled a stethoscope from her jacket pocket and held it up. "May I listen?"

Tessa nodded, taking a sip from her coffee mug, watching intently as Katie warmed the stethoscope with her breath before placing it on the egg. Her face didn't register anything serious, allowing Tessa to breathe comfortably.

Katie shook her head; her face had more wonder written all over it. "The baby's heartbeat's strong, Tessa. Really strong. That's good."

Tessa inhaled, leaning into Marty when she wrapped an arm around her shoulder. "Thank goodness."

"So Wanda tells me you've been hearing cooing noises from within the egg?"

"Yes. We all heard it."

Katie tucked the stethoscope back into her pocket. "So call me crazy, but I have nothing to go on but gestation for, say, a chicken egg. Now, I know that's an odd comparison, but an egg's an egg. Usually, when you start to hear peeping from the egg, it's close to hatching. But Arch tells me in order for the egg to actually hatch, you have to fertilize it? A little backward, I suppose, to have movement and sound before fertilization, but it is a dragon, something we mostly know nothing about."

Her stomach fluttered. "So we're almost there?"

Katie nodded, her eyes warm. "Likely. And that's mostly all I can tell you. I don't know if I'm right or not, but it's probably best to start preparing for the baby's arrival."

Tessa finally asked the question she knew the other women were wondering. "What do you think will hatch from the egg? I mean, will it come out human like Mick and me, or will it be a baby dragon?"

Katie's lips curved into a smile. She reached over and patted Tessa's hand. "Well, we've all had human babies with paranormal abilities—because we were impregnated by full paranormals *after* we were turned and we're all half human. That goes for Marty, Nina, and me, too. So I'd say chances are, you'll have a baby that looks human who'll sprout wings and breathe fire eventually."

It didn't matter to her. Not really. She'd already decided that if the baby came out looking like Puff the Magic Dragon, she'd take it somewhere secluded and figure it out. She loved it just the same, but being able to raise this child amongst the rest of the world would be a relief. She'd do what everyone else in this group had done.

Blend.

And there was something else she was concerned with. "The egg, it's so small. I mean, relatively speaking. It doesn't look much bigger than those oversized eggs the stores use for decoration at Easter. How can that possibly produce a baby who's full-term?"

"That I can't answer. I've researched from here to kingdom come since Nina emailed me, and I can't find anything on dragons that doesn't have to do with supposition and folklore. Everything is very vague. But if the baby is of preemie size, I'll be here to help, okay? Nina will fly off to get me just like she did today, and we'll figure it out. Don't stress about anything right now. Everything outwardly looks good. I'd do an ultrasound, but because the baby is in an eggshell, I worry about exposure. So for now, we'll just have to be surprised."

Tessa stayed silent, overwhelmed. At least with a human pregnancy, you had nine months to prepare, read a book, take a class. But this . . . everything was happening so quickly.

"I can see something's troubling you, Tessa. Why don't you tell me about it?"

She looked into Katie's face, so kind, so open, and more tears formed at the corner of her eyes. "It's all happening so fast. I don't know anything about being a parent. Not a single thing. My mother . . ." She gulped the words back.

"Is gone, right?" Katie asked, rubbing her arm.

"Yes. I . . ."

Katie cocked her head, her eyes connecting with Tessa's. "We'll help you, Tessa. We're not your mother, and no one can replace her kind of wisdom. But I'm willing to fumble through it if Nina, Marty, and Wanda will help."

Wanda pulled Tessa into a hug, surrounding her with the

sweet scent of lavender. "Of course we'll help you. You're part of the crazy now. There's no running away from that, so don't even try," she teased. "We can be here in the blink of an eye if you need us. Right, Marty?"

"Like you could stop us from sticking our noses in baby dragon's life even if you wanted to? Don't be ridiculous. We're nosy, opinionated bitches. The lot of us, and all you have to do is send us a text. We'll be here faster than Nina can suck your soul right out from under you."

Tessa giggled, still overwhelmed by their generosity. Pulling out of Wanda's embrace, she said, "Thank you."

Marty pulled her in tight to her side, her perfume lingering in Tessa's nose, soft and pretty just like Marty. She reached for a tissue and handed it to Tessa. "So, seeing as baby dragon's in a rush to get here, you know what this means, don't you, girls?"

Tessa wiped her eyes. "What?"

"Online shopping!" Wanda said, flipping open her laptop with a grin.

Katie peered over Wanda's shoulder. "Oh, my God—did I tell you girls about the cutest outfits I found for Alistair and Daniel? They're my twins," she said over her shoulder to Tessa. "It's the most adorable online store ever."

Tessa's kitchen filled up with laughter, with women who supported one another—with perfume and hair spray and varying shades of the very definition of beautiful.

"Well, get over here," Wanda said to Tessa with a grin.

"Yeah. We can't shop without the new mom telling us what she likes," Marty added, waving her over.

As Tessa joined the cluster of women, she knew, no matter

what, she wanted them to somehow be involved in her future. Carl, Nina, Arch, all of them.

"A'IGHT now, Mick, it's time to get mad, brother!" Darnell shouted from the field behind Tessa's cottage. For the most part, it was deserted—a good place to test these wings of his.

He was damned well going to learn how to fly if it was the last thing he did. Whatever it was that set him and Tessa off and made their wings sprout needed to be under control.

He'd begun to find it by taking deep breaths when his wings had bloomed from his back yesterday, but settling down enough to get them to disappear wasn't the same as flying.

Darnell came running at him from across the field, a look of concern on his face. He stopped short in front of Mick. "No go, man?"

Mick scraped his hand over his head, tossing his hat on the ground. "Fuck!"

Darnell held up a big paw. "Don't get frustrated. Get downright pissed off. What makes Mick madder 'n a hornet?"

"I dunno."

Darnell flattened his palm against Mick's shoulder and shoved him hard, almost knocking him down. "Yeah, you do, brother. Whatever's goin' on between you and Miss Tessa makes you mad. What is it?"

He couldn't talk about it with someone he hardly knew. He clamped his lips shut.

Darnell spread his arms wide, backing away from Mick, and yelled, "What's keepin' yo' chicken ass from telling her what the what, dude? Is it because you're a big ol' pussy? Afraid to tell her how you feel? Why didn't you stand up like a man when she was datin' other guys? You too afraid of a little competition? What made you let her warm another brother's bed? She sho' is fine. Hmm-mm. Got that nice, tight—"

Mick lost it then, saw red, felt a rage so keen it knocked him to his knees. He opened his mouth, letting out a roar, and along with it came a stream of fire, burning the interior of his mouth.

His vision blurred as his wings tore from his back, flying open like one of those fans you got at the county fair. And then he was on his feet, running at Darnell, charging him, wanting him dead for even thinking those things about Tessa.

He didn't even feel his feet lift off the ground until he realized his target was beneath him and he was actually airborne.

Holy shit.

Focusing the way Tessa had explained the night before, he put all his attention on these new appendages on his back, arching his spine to make them move, catching the freezing air beneath them.

Mick almost forgot to look up, he was so intent on looking down, until he caught sight of Darnell waving his big hands in the air and yelling something he couldn't quite make out.

His head snapped up just in time to see the enormous bare oak tree headed straight for his face.

"Pull up!" Darnell screamed, running along the ground, his thick legs pumping, the thump of his sneakers a distant but clear thunk in the snow.

Pull up how? Instinct took over when he arched his neck upward, the sun glazing his eyes with its sharp glare as his wings took over and began to furiously flap.

And then he was truly flying, soaring over the landscape dotted with rooftops and smoke coming from chimneys, swooping, swerving, circling until he understood the mechanics of his new appendages.

Jesus Christ. He was flying.

By hell, he was flying.

Pressing his arms tight to his sides, he ignored the freezing temperatures, the way his perspiration iced on his forehead, and just let go, rolling with the wind, catching it, commanding it, surfing through puffy clouds, exhilarated. He found keeping his arms close to his sides streamlined him, gave him speed.

Maybe more speed than he could handle at this point, he noted as he realized he'd lost sight of Darnell, and if anyone caught him up in the air, just the sheer size of him would send people into a frenzy.

So he circled back, finally seeing the top of Tessa's cottage and the small figure of Darnell by the old woodshed.

And then he realized something else. How the hell did he land?

Slowly, carefully, something told him. Mick rolled his shoulders, visualizing his wings, making them slow their movement in his mind until he began to descend.

Unfortunately, he hadn't given himself enough lead time as he slowed, and he hit the ground hard, knocking Darnell over like a bowling pin and sending the stacks of wood flying.

The crash tangled up his wings, wrapping Darnell in the cocoon of their glossy web.

Darnell began to laugh, his belly rippling, the thick chains on his chest clashing together. "Aw, man, that was somethin' to see!"

Mick eyeballed him, still a little angry. "I should smother you with these damn things, Darnell."

Darnell punched him in the arm. “C’mon, now. I didn’t really mean any of it. Nina told me what to say to rile you up is all. I was doin’ it so we can fight the good fight to save yo’ baby, brother. Side by side.”

Mick chuckled, spitting splinters of wood from his mouth. “I’m sorry. I should’ve known.”

Darnell began to untangle himself, peeling a flap of Mick’s wing up so he could duck out from under it. “Still don’t mean you don’t gotta talk to her. ’Cus you do. I ain’t much for interferin’ with matters of the heart, but I do know women need all of you. Not just some parts.”

He liked Darnell. He liked him a lot. His advice was sound. “Do you have anyone special, Darnell?”

Darnell grinned. “Nope. I’m a free bird right now. Too busy worryin’ all the time about this bunch.”

“They’re good people.”

Darnell nodded. “You bet they are. They sacrifice a lot. Can’t say I knew many like ’em when I was alive, but I’m sho’ glad I found ’em when I got dead.” He offered his hand to Mick to help hoist him up.

Mick gladly took it. “You ever wish you could go back?”

Darnell shook his head. “Not so much anymore. Not since I found the girls, their husbands, and Arch and Carl, too. We’re like a family. Kinda jacked up. Kinda kooky, but ain’t nobody better ’n those three in there when you’re goin’ into battle.”

“So you’ve had to do this before?”

“Aw, yeah. It ain’t always pretty, what we’ve had to do, but won’t no one fight harder for you than my girls.”

"Why do you do this? Give so selflessly? Put yourself in such danger for complete strangers?"

"Why do you do it? A fireman ain't exactly a desk job. You gotta care about people to wanna rush into a burnin' building, don't ya?"

Mick looked down at the ground. "I guess you do, but it's not like I'm facing demons and evil vampires. It's a little different."

"It ain't so different, Mick. They do it for the same reason you do it. It's why I do it. They don't seem like much on the outside, with Nina always growlin', and the other two fashion queens would have you thinkin' they don't care about nothin' but shoes and purses. But they got hearts bigger 'n your whole daggone state. They know what it's like to be afraid of the unknown. They know what it's like to face this world with a monkey on your back. Bein' different and all. So they invite you in. I don't take that invitation lightly or for granted."

Darnell's words, his conviction, his genuine love for this group of people hit Mick square in the gut—explained why he trusted them and their instincts.

Not just because they'd been living this paranormal lifestyle longer than he had, but because they asked for nothing in return.

They moved into your life like they'd always been there. Cooked, cleaned, nursed your wounds, stuck around while demons tried to kill you, helped birth unknown entities, were willing to protect you from what you didn't understand, and offered you shelter from your fears.

And there was no price attached.

It wasn't often you met people like that.

Which made him determined to cherish their invasion of his life. To listen and learn from them.

"You ready to head back now, or you want another go?"

Mick slapped Darnell on his shoulder. "Nah. I'm pretty cold, and the sun's about to set. Let's go back and see if we can bribe Nina into making us some hot chocolate, then tease her because she can't drink it."

Darnell's laughter rang out across the wide-open field, rich and hearty. "I dig a dude who likes livin' on the edge."

As they made their way back to the cottage, Mick took in a deep breath of the cold air, smiling as the sun began to fade and enjoying the company of a demon named Darnell.

CHAPTER 14

"Tessa, honey. Wake up," someone called, running a gentle hand over her arm.

She didn't want to wake up from this state of contentment. After an amazing meal of pork tenderloin, scalloped potatoes, and tomato salad, all made by Darnell, they'd sat around her living room, laughing, playing Trivial Pursuit, and just enjoying one another's company.

As she'd watched Mick team up with Nina, as he'd laughed, really laughed, smiled, and joked with everyone, she'd decided that if it all ended tonight, it would be on one of the best notes she'd experienced in the years since she'd lost her parents and her brother. This was the happiest she'd been in a very long time.

Most of her nights were spent eating a bowl of oatmeal or canned soup, catching up on TV—alone. Almost all of her time was devoted to the store because there was nothing else outside the store but her cottage and Joe-Joe. She'd conned herself into believing it was enough—until tonight.

She'd forgotten how much she missed being a part of something. Being a part of a group of people who loved one another, who had weekly meals together, who played touch football, had family picnics, gathered because they wanted to.

She'd shut all that out because it was too painful to wish for what was, and now she recognized how lonely she'd been since Noah's death.

"Tessa, sugarsnap. Wake up," the soft voice, floaty and surreal, called again.

Her brain began to surface, fuzzy and muted. Her mother had called her sugarsnap right up until the day she'd died.

Tessa snuggled deeper into the comforter, automatically reaching for the warmth and security of Mick, sure she was dreaming.

"Tessa. You heard your mother. Wake up, buttercup."

Dad? Her eyes flew open, blurry from sleep. She rubbed at them, trying to focus.

And then she felt it, the sag in the bed, just like when she was ten and afraid of thunderstorms and her mother would come in to comfort her. Someone was rubbing her arm, soothing her.

"Tessaaaa," the voice sang out.

She was afraid to believe it was true—afraid to look at her arm. "Mom?" she croaked, swallowing hard, her mouth dry.

"It's me, honey. Look at me, sweetie."

Oh, God. Please don't let this be a dream. Please don't let this be something I hatched from my brain because I was missing my own family. Please let this be real. If she could be a dragon, why couldn't her parents be alive again?

"Tessa, honey. Look at me."

Tessa forced her gaze upward along her arm, seeing the familiar hands that had once soothed her pains, kissed her boo-boos. As her eyes traveled upward, her breath caught in her throat. "Mom? Oh, my God, *Mom?*"

Her mother's eyes met hers, soft, loving, kind, their deep brown still only lightly lined around the corners. "It's me, sweetie. How are you, Tessa? It's so good to see you." She brushed Tessa's hair from her face, making her reach up and capture her hand, cupping it to her cheek.

This couldn't be real—could it?

Why can't it, Tessa? Vampires and werewolves are real.

Her father stood behind her mother, his hand on her shoulder. "Hi, pussycat. How's my girl?"

"Dad?" Her throat started to close, choking with emotion. Her father, Jack, stood tall and lean, his face as handsome as the last time she'd seen him.

In fact, he looked exactly like he did the day he and her mother had left for what they'd called their newest adventure—camping. They'd bought a house on wheels and they were going to travel the country, they'd told her over one of the family meals she missed so much.

And she'd sent them off with hugs and kisses and promises to call at each stop. But they'd only called twice before a tractor-trailer T-boned them, effectively wiping out their cute mobile home and her parents' lives.

Tears slipped from her eyes. "Is it really you, Dad?"

He smiled wide, the distinct dimple in his chin widening. "Tell her it's really me, Genevieve," he teased his wife good-naturedly.

Her mother nodded, squeezing her arm again. "It's really us, sweetheart. We've come to see our grandbaby. We're so excited for you."

Tessa tried to sit up, but her mother placed a hand on her shoulder, soothing her back into the bed. "You're tired, honey. I can see it in your eyes. Rest. We'll help you with the baby."

"It's an egg," she murmured, unsure how to tell them the crazy things that had happened.

"We know, Tessa. We know all about it. We know about you and Mick and those women. We know it all. We're so happy you found Mick."

A small thread of panic began weaving fear in her. "How? How can you know?"

"Where we are, we can see everything," her father said, pointing upward.

Oh. Of course. That explained everything. If Darnell could pop in and out of Hell, her parents could certainly drop in from Heaven. Right? "Noah. Where's Noah? Are you all together?" She swallowed her sadness. "Up there, I mean?"

Her mother's smile lit up her eyes. "We are, honey. He couldn't come this trip, but he sent his love."

Tessa's fear was swept away by the complete joy she experienced seeing them, hearing that Noah was with them. But then suspicion reared its ugly head. "Why didn't you come sooner? If you were able to now, why didn't you come see me before this?" she asked, swiping at the tears falling from her eyes.

"It's not an easy trip, Tessa. It's not like we can just get in the car and drop by. We had to get special permission. But we told them seeing you now, when you need us the most to protect you, was very important," her mother reassured her, stroking her cheek.

Tessa closed her eyes for a moment, savoring her mother's touch. "I've missed you both so much. I'm afraid, Mom. I'm afraid of what's going to happen to the baby."

Her father ran his finger down the line of her nose, just like he'd always done. "That's why we're here, pussycat. To keep the baby safe."

Relief flooded her veins, warming her from the inside out. "You can do that?"

Her mother nodded, the moonlight from the window shining across her pale skin. "We can, honey. We will. Until this is over. I promise you. Now you rest, and your father and I will take care of everything else."

She'd trust her parents with her life; there was no doubt in her mind they'd take care of the baby. But how would Mick feel about it? "Wait. Let me ask Mick. He's part of this, too. I want him to be involved."

But both her mother and her father shook their heads. "No, sweetie. Don't wake him. Look how tired he is. Besides, it's us, sugarsnap. We loved Mick, and he loved us. He trusts us, just like we trust him with you."

She glanced over at Mick, the rise and fall of his chest steady and slow. It was true. He was exhausted from the events of the past three days. Would he really mind if her parents took the baby until this was over? If it meant the baby would be safe?

Knowing Mick the way she did, knowing now how he felt about the baby, she knew if there was a way to keep the baby from harm, he'd be on board.

"Where will you take it?"

She ran her fingers over Tessa's eyes, closing them, whispering, "Somewhere safe, honey. But we can't tell you. If you know, they might try to get the information from you. It's safer this way. You understand, don't you, Tessa?"

"But you'll come back as soon as this is over, right? Please say you'll come back. I miss you both so much," she murmured, her eyelids so heavy, her heart tight with longing.

"Of course we will, pussycat," her father rumbled, his voice muffled and distant. "We love, you, Tessa, and we love the baby. Sleep now. Rest up."

"I love you, too, Dad. Both of you," she managed to mutter before the warmth of her mother's hands and the soothing grumble of her father's voice took hold of her, easing her, calming her until she allowed herself to fall into the soft spot they provided.

The last thing she remembered was a long, relived sigh slipping from her lungs before she succumbed to the security of having her parents with her again.

"TESSA! Wake up!"

She frowned. Gone were the soft voices of her parents from last night. Gone was the secure warmth as Mick shook her with hard hands. She sat upright, forcing her eyes open. "What's wrong?"

His eyes were wild, still lined with sleep, his hair mussed, his face hard. "The egg's gone."

She smiled and stretched. "I know, but it's okay."

Mick gripped her shoulders and gave her a shake. "You know? What the hell are you talking about, T?"

She put a comforting hand on his arm, enjoying the feel of his biceps beneath her palm. "I said I know. Calm down, Mick. My parents took the egg. They're going to keep it safe until this is over."

"Your parents? Tessa, that's crazy. They're dead."

She cupped his face in her hands. "I know. But Nina's a vampire, and we're dragons. Why can't they be ghosts?" That's what they were, wasn't it? Of course it was. What other explanation was there?

Mick grabbed her wrists, his fingers wrapping around them. "Tessa, that's crazy."

"Oh, c'mon. Is it any crazier than me having an egg? Or you knocking me up without even looking at me?"

He shook his head, his lips going flat. "No, this is wrong. Why would your parents suddenly show up after all this time?"

She shrugged her shoulders, still comforted by their lingering presence. "Why would Noah be in my store? Maybe because they were looking out for me all this time. Isn't that what ghosts do?"

"Honey—something's wrong. I can feel it," he urged.

Why was he always stomping all over everything she did independently of him? Jesus. This was a lot like the time he'd browbeaten her with a million questions before she'd bought the store. Or taken her to task when she'd gone out all by herself and bought a brand-new car. "Why can't you just trust my choices, Mick? I'm not your little sister. I was Noah's!"

Mick's face got harder still, the tic in his jaw popping out. "Tessa, this isn't like that. I'm not trying to run your life. I'm looking out for the baby. *Our* baby."

She gave his chest a shove, sliding off the edge of the bed. "Is this how it's going to be, Mick? Are you going to question every little thing I do with the baby? Because you can forget it if you think I'm going to have you breathing down my neck every time I make a decision about the baby!"

Mick stomped after her as she reached for the dresser drawer. "This isn't like deciding whether the baby should be breast-fed or bottle-fed, Tessa. You just handed our baby over to someone!"

Whirling around, she tore her nightgown off and threw it on the floor, pulling a shirt over her head and throwing on some yoga pants. "Someone?" she yelled. "Someone? They're my parents, Mick!"

"Who are *dead*, Tessa!"

"Heyyy, what in the ever-lovin' fuck, people?" Nina bellowed when she crashed through the bedroom door, her Elmo pajamas rumpled. "What is wrong with you two? I thought we were past the hump and onto the humpty-hump. Why the fuck are you in here screaming at each other like you're cage fighting?"

"The baby's gone," Mick spat, shoving his legs through his jeans.

Instantly Nina froze, her eyes flying to the nightstand where the incubator had been. "Say again?"

Tessa rolled her eyes. "The baby's not gone. It's with my parents."

Nina's head cocked to the right, the curtain of her beautiful hair glimmering in the early-morning sunlight. "Kiddo, your parents are dead."

"I know, I know. Mick reminded me. Listen, they showed up here last night and told me they'd take care of the egg until this was over. The baby's safe."

Nina grabbed her by her shoulders, gripping them so tight it hurt. "Tessa, that can't be right."

If Nina said it wasn't right, that made it not right, right? Well, not this time. "Why can't it? If you can be a vampire and Carl can be a vegetarian zombie, why can't my parents be ghosts? And get off me, Nina. You're hurting me." She tried to push Nina away, but that only made the vampire grip her tighter.

"Listen to me, Tessa. Those weren't your goddamn parents. They were fakes. Remember what I told you about the demons and how they prey on your fears? How all you have to do is show them a crack in your emotions and they'll worm their way the fuck in? Do you remember me fucking telling you that?"

Her mouth fell open, words escaping her, but only for a moment. She did remember. She also knew her own parents.

"Do you?" she roared the question.

"Yes! But that's not how it was. They were exactly like my parents. They looked like them, talked like them. My mom even called me sugarsnap. Just like always."

Nina shook her head, her eyes hot with fury. "They were *not* your parents, Tessa. They were shapeshifting demons that can take on any form and personality trait. Darnell? Get your demon ass in here!"

Darnell stuck his head inside the door, sleep still in his eyes, his flannel pajamas askew. "Why you yellin'?"

Nina let Tessa go and grabbed a framed picture of her parents from her dresser. "Look at this picture, Darnell. This is Tessa's mother and father. Show her how you shapeshift."

Darnell's eyes searched Nina's, worry in them.

"Do it!" she screamed at him.

Darnell glanced at the picture, his eyes roving over it for a few seconds before he melted away and her mother appeared before her.

No.

Oh, God. No.

Her mother rolled her head on her neck and then she morphed into Tessa's father. Just like that.

Oh, my God. What had she done? Her hands began to shake, her stomach revolting, churning acid bile.

"Do you see, Tessa? Do you?" Nina roared, jolting her out of her misery. "You handed them the fucking egg like you were giving out Halloween candy! Fuck!" Nina gave her a shove, storming out of her bedroom.

Tessa looked at Darnell and Mick, helpless. "I didn't know. I swear, I didn't know," she sobbed.

Darnell reached for her first, enveloping her in a big hug. "If it's any consolation, they probably put a spell on you. Even if you did know they were fakes, you wouldn't have been able to move anyway, Miss Tessa. I'd say likely they came as your parents to keep you calm. So you wouldn't wake the rest o' us up. They tricked you."

She bit back another sob when Darnell handed her off to Mick, who drew her in tight to his chest, running his hands over her back. "It's okay, honey. You couldn't have known."

"Now don't y'all worry. I'm gonna go find out what we can do. I won't let nobody hurt the baby. Promise you that much," Darnell said before pushing his way out the door to join Nina.

She gripped Mick's chest. "I swear to you, Mick, they looked and sounded just like my parents. I didn't know. I never would have let them have the egg if I knew." Terror seeped into her bones.

"We'll figure it out. Now let's get dressed and see what Nina and everyone else has to say before we panic."

Oh, God. How were they going to get the egg from Hell?

Who wanted her egg?

She couldn't afford to break down now. She had to be strong so she could help. *Stay strong, Tessa. No matter what.*

She pushed her way out of Mick's arms and straightened, fighting back more tears. "We need to do something and we need to do it fast. Me falling apart isn't going to get the egg back. Katie said it was about to hatch. We have to get the baby back before that happens. I won't settle for anything else."

Mick smiled, though it was fraught with worry, and dropped a kiss on her lips. "Then let's go kick some of Hell's ass."

YET another stranger was in her living room when both she and Mick entered it. A petite woman with dark brown hair and big round eyes. She popped up off the couch, where everyone had gathered. "I'm Casey Gunnersson, Wanda's sister, and a demon by accident. I'm so sorry we're meeting like this." She held out her hand, taking Tessa's in hers and pulling her into a tight hug.

Casey pulled away, putting her hands on Tessa's cheeks. "I promise you, I'll use all my connections, power, whatever to get the baby back, okay?"

Tessa took a deep breath of air. "Okay. So what's the plan of attack?"

"I'm going in," Casey said, planting her hands on her hips. "Me and Darnell."

Mick's brows knitted together. "Didn't someone say the two of you live on the fringes of Hell? In order to keep from getting caught? Won't you be in danger?"

Darnell chuckled. "S'okay, Mick. I been in and outta Hell more times than I can count. Haven't caught me yet. I'll take on a minion's form—somethin', but never you fear. We'll find out who's doin' this and end it."

Mick ran his hands through his hair, worry etched on his face. "So you need to pinpoint the source of this? But who's to say more souls trapped in Hell won't try the same thing? If Tessa and the baby and I are the only dragons, won't someone always try to get the baby's scales? Won't the egg always be in danger?"

Tessa's stomach plummeted. How were they supposed to hide from demons that could shapeshift into your own parents? Would they always have to look over their shoulders?

Casey's eyes gleamed. "Not if I tell Satan what's going on. You don't really think he wants this soul released, do you? This person is in Hell on lockdown for a reason. None of which can be good. Clearly, whoever it is is hard to control."

"Satan?" Tessa asked woodenly. "You'll talk to the actual Satan?" This got wackier by the second. Who just walked into Hell and asked to see Satan like they were asking to see the doctor on call in the ER? Was it that easy?

Casey grinned. "Something like that. Mostly, I'll spread a rumor. Sort of like playing the telephone game. It'll get back to him because Hell is full of busybodies and ass-kissers, and when it does, when he finds out someone's trying to one-up him, that's when chaos will reign."

Tessa shook her head. She'd done this. She'd fix it. "I don't want anyone else hurt because of my mistake. Let me go. Shift me into something, Darnell. You can do everything else—why not turn me into a minion? I can do this."

Nina shook her head as she stroked Joe-Joe's muzzle. "Not gonna happen. First, Darnell can't turn you into anything. Second, you know jack shit about Hell, yo. You're a novice. Just because you used your wings once doesn't mean you're all of a sudden ready to take on a bunch of vicious motherfuckers like those demons."

"At least take me with you."

Frank spoke up then, lifting his eyes, not nearly as fearful as they had been just yesterday. "No, Tessa. You don't know what it's like. Please listen to Nina and the others. Whoever's behind this is far more evil than even I imagined, and they're desperate to get out of Hell. That means they're willing to do vile, ugly things in order to make that happen. I'd go myself, to keep you all out of harm's way, but I can't seem to summon the usual portal. I don't know what's happened. I can't even manage to cast spells that were once easy, though not very impressive. I'm no good to you if I can be detected, but please know this much: I would go if I could."

"It's okay, Frank," Casey reassured him with a generous smile. "I think Darnell and I have a handle on it. You guys just sit back and wait for word from us, okay?"

Tessa would never be able to sit still, but what choice did she have? It wasn't like she had the directions to Hell bookmarked on Google Maps. If her going with them would only put the baby in danger, then she'd do what she was told.

But she didn't like it. Who would fight harder than she and Mick for the baby?

Casey gripped her arm. "I know what you're thinking, Tessa. No one would fight to save your baby harder than you. But that's not true in our cases. We're dedicated to this cause—to helping people. I promise you, we'd take the hit if it came down to it."

Fear swelled up inside her, raging though her veins. "I can't let you sacrifice yourselves like this because of my mistake! You have families, children and husbands—"

"Who all knew what they were getting into when we started OOPS," Marty reminded her in a gentle tone. "If we all don't look out for each other, who will, Tessa? It's not like you can call the FBI and tell them your egg's been kidnapped. We're all we have, and we fight to keep each other safe in a world where humans outnumber us by the millions. We do this because we want to. So please, listen to Casey and Darnell. Trust us."

Wanda gave Casey a quick hug. "Keep that phone with you at all times, you hear me? Text me the second you get in. Darnell, you, too. I love you."

"They have cell phone service in Hell?" Mick said, as astonished as she was.

Darnell grinned. "Yeah. It's a little slow, though. Now don't you go worryin', okay? We'll see what we can see, and form a plan of attack."

It was then that Tessa felt the rumble. The distinct shift in her body, a vibration that ran bone deep, shocking her to her core. Instinctively, she knew what it was. Whether it was her maternal connection or some otherworldly event, she knew.

Not now. Please, please, please, not now.

Mick was at her side in an instant. "Tessa? What's happening?"

She licked her dry lips, the words hard to form. Clinging to his arm, she gripped it tight. "The egg. It's hatching."

CHAPTER 15

Everyone fought a gasp, but there was no hiding their concern as Tessa looked into the faces she'd become so familiar with. They were afraid, and that meant she should be afraid, too.

Casey blew a kiss to the group, grabbed Darnell's hand, and said, "Love you all!" before they disappeared in puffs of misty smoke and a glittery afterglow.

Tessa couldn't breathe from the fear, from the wretched, ugly, clawing-at-her-guts fear.

Nina came up behind her. "It's gonna be okay, kiddo. Casey and Darnell are badass. Just breathe."

But she couldn't. There was no breathing when your child's life was at stake. She needed air. Pulling away from Nina, she grabbed her coat from the hook on the coatrack and threw it on, bursting from the crooked cottage door out into the freezing air.

She began to run the second she hit the edge of the path leading to the road, heedless of the ice as she slipped and stumbled, ignoring the throb in her chest and the burn of her thighs.

Snow began to fall, clouding over the clear skies she'd awakened to, mirroring her emotions, slapping at her face in cold bites.

Without even realizing it, her jacket fell away, tore right off her, and she was suddenly above the trees, pushing her way through fluffy clouds, soaring.

As her wings began to flap, she forced herself to concentrate on them, move them in her mind, visualize the up-and-down motion needed to catch the air beneath them.

"Tessa!" someone called. "Wait!"

She couldn't wait. She couldn't think of anything but running from this pain, getting away as fast as she could from this helplessness.

The air shifted, carrying with it a slapping noise. Her eyes sought the ruckus, widening when she found Mick beside her, soaring closer, holding out his hand.

His eyes were pained, and she knew then that he was suffering as much as she was. This wasn't just her agony alone. Mick hurt, too.

Tessa grabbed his hand, clinging to it until they fought the force of the wind separating them and managed to pull their bodies together.

Mick lifted her arms, putting them around his neck until his lips were at her ear, and he was doing the flying for both of them. "I know this hurts," he whispered against the wind and cold, so raw, so real it tore her heart. "I hurt, too. Let's hurt together, not separately anymore. Please, Tessa. I need you right now, and you need me, too."

Tears flooded her eyes, tears that turned to stinging icicles she had to blink away. Wrapping her legs around his waist, she hung on to Mick, feeling his heart beat against hers, hearing his breathing, letting him navigate.

They flew like that for a time, silently, absorbing each other's pain until Mick circled back and swooped downward, landing just shy of her front door.

Their wings deflated together in fits of flapping and crunching until they stood in front of each other in shredded clothing.

Mick shook the ice from his hair as the snow battered his face, so vulnerable and full of sadness.

"I feel helpless," she said, voicing her emotion.

"I do, too."

"I don't know what I'll do if something goes wrong . . ."

"Don't go there, Tessa. Don't allow yourself to," he admonished, his jaw clenching.

"But so many things have gone wrong. My parents, Noah." Her voice cracked.

Mick gripped her shoulders, staring down at her in the darkening gloom of the day. "I said, don't go there."

"Why won't you ever let me talk about how I feel? What is it that keeps you from talking about how you feel? What is it about saying 'I am fill-in-the-blank today' that's so hard? Do we need flash cards? Maybe colors for your moods? What?"

He let go of her, turning his back to her and jamming his hands into the pockets of his wet jeans. "I thought we agreed to let this sit?"

But she wasn't having this anymore. Enough hiding, running away, shutting her out. She was sick to death of his avoidance.

"When better than now, Mick? Because this is our biggest problem—this right here. When you're faced with something that hurts, you shut me out. You shut everyone out. I'm not going to raise a child with you if you can't teach them to openly express themselves. It's unhealthy. So spit it the hell out! What's the problem? What happened after Noah died that made you shut down?"

He whirled around, his large body looming over hers. "What do you mean you won't raise a child with me if I don't do what you want?"

"I mean exactly what I said. You have to set an example. Shutting off your feelings like you're shutting off one of your stupid fire hoses isn't going to work for me."

"You can't take my rights away, Tessa."

She crossed her arms over her chest, her teeth chattering when she said, "What are you going to do—take me to dragon court and sue me for custody?"

Now he was really mad; if his eyes could shoot fireballs the way his mouth did, they'd be shooting them at her. "Okay, if you wanna know, let me lay it on the line for you. The night Noah died? Remember that? We were both heading into that big fire over in Burlington. The five-alarm. Remember?"

She took a deep breath. She remembered every detail of that night, from the sounds of the bleating sirens to the knock on her door where Mick stood, his face covered in soot, his eyes worn, his body sagging. "What about it?"

"Just before Noah and I went into that fire, I told him I was in love with you and I was going to tell you as much, and then he told me something. Something that changed everything between us. And then he died, Tessa. He goddamn well *died*."

She was only astonished for a moment before she realized that she'd let him off the hook again if she kept allowing herself to be blown away by the fact that Mick had loved her for so long. *"What?"* she yelled up into his face. "What did he tell you?"

Mick's lips thinned, his face ugly and hard when he snapped, "He told me he didn't want me to date you. He said I was no good for you, that's what!"

The wind in her lungs evaporated, making her stumble backward. She fought to catch her breath. Why would Noah say something like that? He'd loved Mick as much as she had. There had to be a reasonable explanation. "Noah would never, ever say something like that without a reason. He loved you, Mick. He loved you like a brother. Sometimes I think he loved you more than he even loved me!" Hysteria began to rise, not just in her words but in her soul.

Mick scoffed. "Really? Well, I wouldn't have known it by the way he sounded that night. No explanation—we didn't have time for them—just his disapproval. I saw it all over his face, Tessa. And that's why I kept you at arm's length. That's why I reacted the way I did when we found out about the baby. Is that what you wanted to hear? That Noah would probably rather let you date Satan than me?"

There was no time to react, no time to hash things out because Nina flew out the cottage door, her face paler than Tessa had ever seen it. "Inside. *Now!*" she shouted, not bothering to wait for them.

Mick and Tessa exchanged stricken looks before rushing inside to find everyone up and about. Marty was pacing. Wanda was doing that nervous nip to the tip of her nail. Both Carl and Arch were on the couch, Arch soothing Carl, and Frank was huddled in a corner, his eyes closed tight.

"What happened?" Mick asked. Tessa heard the fear in his question. Knew something was terribly wrong.

Wanda's head popped up, her eyes shiny with tears she fought not to shed. "Casey and Darnell were captured," she said quietly, only a slight tremor in her voice.

Her worst fear come true. Tessa reached for the back of the couch, gripping it tight. "By who? How?"

Marty held up her phone and pointed to the screen. "Nine-one-one! They've found us out. Only a matter of time before we're caught. Hiding now, can't hide much longer. Get help!"

Tessa's stomach rolled, horror, terror, anxiety forming a pit in her belly. "So what do we do? How do we get into Hell to help them?" She couldn't even stop to consider how unbelievable that question really was.

Wanda sucked in a hard breath, her next words tight. "We're trying to find some of Darnell's contacts, but it's like everyone's on lockdown. No one is answering us." In a rare act of frustration, she lobbed the phone onto the couch.

Mick grabbed Wanda's hand and squeezed it while Marty wrapped an arm around her waist. "I'm sorry, Wanda. If there's something I can do, just say the word. I don't know enough about your world to understand what's involved, but I'm in."

Frank, Tessa thought, narrowing her eyes. Frank was the answer. He was their only in to Hell, and by God, he was going to find that portal. "Frank!" She fought not to yell. The minion scared easily—too easily, which lent credibility to his story that he'd been caught up in an accident and fallen to Hell rather than sent there for misdeeds.

He uncovered his head, his eyes and nose a distinct red. "I'm sorry. I'm so sorry. If I could take this back, I would. I swear, I would!"

She rounded the couch and knelt beside him, sitting him upright and stroking his arm. "It's okay, Frank. I know you didn't do this on purpose. But you have to pay attention to me now. Please. We need a vehicle to Hell. You're our only chance."

He shook his head, the hair on it flapping, he shook it so hard. "I don't know how to get back. I've tried more than a dozen times so I can go back and fix this, and the portal won't open!"

"Define the portal, Frank. Does a hole just appear out of nowhere and you jump in?" *Of course it does, Tessa. Stupidhead.*

Frank sat up then, gripping Tessa's arm. "Yes! Used to be I just thought it up, but not anymore. Don't you think I'd go if I could? I know I appear meek and cowardly to you. My whole life was spent being laughed at with the misconception that I'm weak because of my appearance. I may be weak physically, but not morally. I was a good person. I might not have been a superhero, but I wasn't morally bankrupt like Skeeter."

"Bet this Skeeter was the motherfucker who pushed you out of the line," Nina added, her laptop now open.

"What?" Frank said, aghast.

Nina showed the laptop screen to Frank with the article on his death. "I didn't want to tell you, because it wasn't gonna make you feel any better, but Skeeter died that night, too. I looked it up on the Internet. You fell on his worthless ass, which made his gun go off. The bullet ricocheted off a vase and hit Skeeter—took his ass right out. What comes around and all that euphemistic jazz, eh, Frank? Though I bet you'll be glad to know, not one of your fancy clients believed you had anything to do with it."

Frank's lips grew tight. "Oh, that smarmy so-and-so!"

Nina leaned into him, her eyes intense. "Is that the best you got, Frank? 'Smarmy so-and-so'? Dude, curse his ass out! Not only did he make you help him rip off your clients, but he knocked your ass out of a line to the great beyond. Dude, that shit's wrong on all counts. If I were you, I'd be pissed. I'd want revenge."

Frank's breathing became rapid, his eyes round like dimes. "You don't really think he was the one who knocked me out of line, do you? What a horrible thing to do!"

Nina poked him in the arm. "Yeah, I do. He died that night, too. If only nice people go upstairs, who else would knock you off your cloud?"

Frank popped up, taking Tessa with him, holding her hand so tight it was cutting off her circulation. "Oh, that bastard. That dirty thug! I should have known he'd be no good. All my clients' daughters loved him. In fact, he spent more time flirting with them at their pools than he ever did hauling mulch and caring for those precious roses!"

Nina jumped up now, too, her eyes shiny, full of antagonism. "And he's got your special seat on some cloud up there, Frank. Just lollygaggin' around, watching your ass sweat and do shit that goes against your nature just to keep your soul," she jeered.

Tessa didn't know where Nina was going with this or why, but she was afraid to interfere. It involved a plan—she just didn't know what it was.

But Wanda jumped between them. "Nina! Stop harassing this

man and focus on our problem. Casey and Darnell are trapped. We need to find a way to get them out."

Nina gave Wanda the eyeball—her dagger of death, used especially to warn you to duck. "I'm just tellin' it like I see it, Wanda. Frank here got the shitty end of the stick. All because of Skeeter. Skeeter stole his life and his fucking afterlife. Frank could be up there, swinging on a cloud, maybe tendin' to the big guy's roses. Bet he has some, too, Frank. Like, as far as the eye can see. But no. Not gonna happen because this dude Skeeter stole that shit right out from under you, didn't he, *Frank*?"

Frank's face was so red now, if he weren't already dead, Tessa worried that he'd die of a heart attack. He squeezed her hand harder, digging his nails into it, his jowls quivering.

"Nina!" Mick bellowed a warning. "Stop! Please. Jesus. The poor guy's been through enough without you rubbing salt in his wounds. This isn't getting us anywhere right now. The focus should be on getting into Hell."

Nina threw up her hands, letting them slap to her lithe thighs. "Fine. You're probably right, King Kong. Let's just forget about how Frank's life was stolen from him and that he gets to rot in the fiery depths of Hell because that's just the way the cookie crumbles. When they come drag his ass back there, that's what Frank can say. Darn you, Skeeter, you smarmy so-and-so," she taunted.

Frank began to tremble, his anger palpable, his brow beaded with sweat. He let out a scream so primal, so raw, so full of frustration, Nina clapped her hands over her ears.

It literally made the windows shake.

But that wasn't all his scream did.

It opened back up that portal he'd been talking about.

Transporting both him and Tessa down a black, dark hole.

Okay. So no Google Maps required.

No one moved. No one spoke.

For all of five seconds.

"Fuck!" Mick yelled. "Tell me what just happened isn't what I think it is, Nina!"

Nina was in his face in a blur of limbs and color. "If you'd have just shut your big ass mouth, everything would've been fine. I had a plan, Gigantor. I gave you the eyeball, you ignored it."

But he was angry, angry and worried, and Nina screaming at him just wasn't going to cut it. "*A plan?* What kind of plan involves Tessa disappearing?"

"The plan where we get Frank all riled up. Works for you and Tessa and your wings, figured it'd work for Frank and his portal, too. And look, Sasquatch, it fucking worked!" She swiped a finger under his nose. "If you'd have just stayed the hell out of it, I would have latched onto Frank like he was a chicken wing dipped in ranch and he and I would be in Hell right now. Not him and hardly-able-to-stand-up-with-those-freakin'-wings-of-hers Tessa. You jackass! I gave you the eye!"

Now Mick gave her the eye. "The eye? How the hell am I supposed to know girl code? Men don't work like that. We just say it."

"You know what, Bigfoot, that's why you have all this trouble with your girl. You don't look for the signs, stupid-ass. And you don't just say it. You hide it away until it damn well festers and starts oozing puss. Then, when it's good and infected, and you're madder than a hornet because it hurts, you spew your frustration and screw everything up." She tugged her ear. "Vampire hearing, remember? We all heard you out there. This is exactly why I hate almost everyone beyond the age of ten. Now shut the fuck up and let me figure out how we're going to get into Hell. Because you squashed my ride as sure as you stomped all over it with those size sixteens."

Frustration, rage, fear all coiled deep in his chest, looking for a way out. He fought the urge, fought the feel of his wings wanting out. But he couldn't fight his roar of fury—he blew like a top, howling, spraying Tessa's kitchen, balls of fire erupting from his throat.

It was over in a matter of seconds. Nothing left but the smoke and cinders.

Tessa's wall oven, distorted from the heat of the flames, fell out of the wall and to the floor with a loud clatter.

Marty and Wanda came to stand on either side of him, their arms crossed over their chests.

Arch popped his lips as Carl shook his head. "I fear, Sir Mick, upon Tessa's return, Hell will be the least of your worries."

"I have to get to her, Arch. I have to get to her and the baby." Misery crowded his heart, anguish that he'd never see Tessa or the egg again taking over.

"I know, sir. We shall find a way. Of this, I assure you. We've not failed yet. I won't allow us to now. Until then, as I ponder, I shall clean this mess. Ladies, help is most appreciated. It will keep our minds busy as we devise a plan."

Everyone filed into Tessa's kitchen, stepping over the dishes that had exploded from the cabinets, picking up the fridge door that had blown clear off.

Tessa was going to kill him.

He prayed with everything in him that she'd be able to do just that.

Because it meant she'd be back here—with him.

Where she belonged. Where she'd always belonged and he'd just been too damn stupid to tell her.

Jesus. Please let her and the baby be all right.

I'm begging. Whatever you want, it's yours.

Just say the word.

CHAPTER 16

Tessa slammed into the ground, a puff of ashes swirling around her, making her cough until her throat was raw. Frank landed on top of her with a heavy thud. She grunted at the impact, her head hitting something sharp.

Frank rolled off her to his back, moaning as he tried to sit up, his sweet round face tight with visible pain.

Jesus, it was hot here. Yet another reason she loved living in Vermont. She hated the heat and despised being sweaty. Pulling herself to her knees, she scanned the landscape on all fours, catching her breath. "So is this it, Frank? Are we here?" She shouldn't have bothered to ask—she didn't really need to. She felt the egg, felt the connection to it, the warm, thready tendrils of life coursing through her veins.

The egg was here somewhere.

And by God, she was going to hunt down whoever wanted it

and incinerate them into a pile of ashes with her scary fire-breathing. She didn't know if you could really freak anyone out in Hell—because really, it was, after all, Hell—but she was damn well going to try.

"This is the outskirts, yes," Frank said with a grunt as he rose to his feet, this time offering her his hand and yanking her upward. "You have to pay very close attention to me from here on out. I have to find out where Casey and Darnell are. That won't be easy. I've been gone for too long. They'll consider me a traitor at this point. So we have to hide in the shadows and eavesdrop. Please, don't do anything rash. I'd rather be thrown in the bowels and lashed day in, day out than see you hurt."

Tessa nodded, her smile intentionally warm. "Thank you, Frank. Thank you for helping me. I know you're afraid, but I'll protect you as best I can."

"We'll need all the help we can get, Tessa. I'm a weak minion, but there are others like me who are here under unfortunate circumstances. I don't know if their declarations of innocence are true, but I hope to glean some information from them."

"But how can you trust anyone? Look what they did to you."

He pulled her close to his side. "Let's deal with that when the time comes. For now, stay close, and whatever you do, don't give in to your fears."

"Right. Nina told me the demons will try to prey on my worst nightmares. No giving in. Swear it. So where are we going?" A stab of anxiety drilled at her, at what they were facing, but she fought it off.

"We're just outside the gates. The trick is to get inside without being noticed, and not let anyone out in the process."

"There really are gates to Hell?"

"Yes, and they're heavily guarded. This is the wastelands where lost souls roam endlessly until they choose an allegiance to Satan. It's dismal, arid, and sure to make you lose your mind. Which is the point, of course. You either give in out of sheer desperation or you wander endlessly, always alone."

As Frank tugged her along, she forced herself to look straight ahead, ignoring the faces peeking out from behind blackened shrubs and trees, their mouths slack, their eyes black orbs in their heads.

The street, like torn cobblestone, rippled beneath their feet, making their journey that much more difficult. As she walked, she focused on visualizing the egg and Mick. The only two bright spots that kept her from dwelling on what she was about to do.

There was an incessant throb, like a heartbeat, pulsing in her ears, growing stronger as they went, beating, swelling, pushing until she thought she'd go mad.

Frank gave her hand a yank, squeezing it hard. "Block it out, Tessa. Think of something else. Something happy—something that brings you great joy."

She stopped short, wanting to rip her eardrums out. If it didn't stop, it would drive her right out of her mind. "What is it? Jesus Christ, it's like an incessant drone," she spat.

"Heartbeats. It's the heartbeats of the souls lost here. Ignore them, Tessa. You'll have to be strong."

Tessa closed her eyes and fought the wave of anguish and misery. So many heartbeats . . .

Frank yanked her hand, jerking her to him again. "Tessa! Stop now. You can't give in."

Right. No giving in. They needed a distraction, something to occupy their minds. "Sing with me, Frank. Do you like music?"

"Broadway show tunes."

Tessa sucked in a deep breath. "You're in luck, I know 'em all. You choose."

"*Cats*?"

"Really, Frank? 'Memories'? Has to be one of the most depressing songs on the planet. How about *The Sound of Music*?"

He winked. "Good choice. I'll start." He cleared his throat. " 'Doe, a deer, a female deer,' " he sang, pointing to her.

" 'Ray, the guy who cleans my gun!' "

Frank stopped, letting his shoulders sag in disappointment. "Really, Tessa? 'Ray, the guy who cleans my gun'?"

Tessa winced. "Wrong?" She stunk at song lyrics.

"Yes, it's wrong. It's 'Ray, a drop of golden sun.' "

"Sorry. Give me another chance. Let's start again."

He tugged her along. " 'Me, a name I call myself.' "

Oh, she knew this one. "Uh, 'Fa, a thong made out of thumbs'?"

" 'A thong made out of thumbs,' " he repeated, disappointment in his tone. "Does that make any sense to you, Tessa? Any at all? Who makes a thong out of thumbs?"

"Serial killers? And are you one of those sticklers about this sort of thing, Frank? Because you're sucking the fun right out of this."

He shook his head with a scowl. "You've desecrated Rodgers and Hammerstein, you know that, don't you? Nothing will ever be the same."

She giggled. "Wanna try something else?"

"Not on your life. Besides, we're coming close to the gates." Frank pointed up ahead to where the lines of a black wrought-iron gate were just becoming visible.

Tessa pulled at her sweater, which was clinging to her body like a second skin due to perspiration. "I hope they have AC inside. I'm dying here. No pun intended."

Frank pulled a handkerchief from his pocket and handed it to her to wipe her brow. "We need to discuss how we're going to get inside, Tessa. We need a plan. A solid one at that."

The ground beneath them shifted again, a soft rumble that only became louder as rocks from clear out of nowhere began to pelt them. "What the hell?" she shouted to Frank, zigzagging with him to avoid the boulders rolling from the landscape, gaining speed as they came closer to the gates.

"They sense something's out of place, Tessa—this is their version of the welcoming committee!" Frank yelled before pulling her so hard to the right, the bones in her arm cracked and popped.

Tessa caught sight of a carved-out nook in the center of a burned tree and yanked Frank toward it, her chest heaving from the physical labor it took not only to breathe in the humid air but to fight the strange pressure in her chest. Pulling up short, she kept Frank close and hid inside the small enclosure. "Okay, so a plan. How to get inside the gates of Hell. Thoughts?"

Frank's breath wheezed from his lungs. "Some sort of deception? Wait, what if I just give myself up and when I do, I create a ruckus—a distraction. Then you sneak in."

"Um, no. No way I'm giving you up. We're in this together. Where I go, you go. Period. Got that? Better plan, please."

The ground stilled momentarily, making her wonder if they'd found a way to stay out of Hell's radar for the moment.

Until a set of ugly, jagged talons reached around the opening of the enclosure and snatched at her, the beast's scream a wail of desperation, its claws ripping her sweater, gashing her arm. Searing pain shot along her arm as blood gushed from the wound.

Tessa bit her lip, fighting a scream not just of agony but of rage.

Frank's eyes went wide, but he remained silent, pressing his hand to Tessa's mouth to keep her from screaming. He shook his head, sending signals with his eyes that she should stay quiet, and took the handkerchief from her hand to wrap around her arm.

The talons dragged their way back out, leaving deep gouges in the burnt trunk of the tree, but the heartbeat had begun again, the unmerciful pound and throb, worming its way into Tessa's head.

She pushed Frank's hand from her mouth, clinging to it, trembling, fighting despair. *"What now?"* she mouthed to him.

He pressed a pudgy finger covered in her blood to his lips, rising on his haunches in order to peer outside the opening. He sank back, gasping for breath. "They know we're here, Tessa. Think! Think fast. We have to get inside those gates soon!"

Her heart began to match the rhythm of the ceaseless drone, filling the hot air. "Then we need to move, Frank." Grabbing his hand, ignoring the aching sting of her torn arm, she helped him back out of the tree, her feet aching from fighting the ever-shifting landscape.

They both looked forward at the daunting task ahead, sweat pouring from their bodies, hands entwined tight. "I can do this,

Frank. *We* can do this," she said just seconds before he was torn from her grasp and hurled high into the air.

MICK paced the small length of floor between the entryway and Tessa's bedroom, his chest so tight he didn't think he'd ever breathe again.

He shouldn't have told her about what Noah had said. He should have shut his goddamn mouth and let it be until they could talk about it rationally, without the fear that their baby was going to be taken from them.

Fuck. Their last words might be the only words he ever said to her again, and it was more than he could bear.

"Stop," Nina demanded, stepping in front of him.

"Stop what?"

"Stop thinking about what happened outside. No way I'm going to let the kid or Tessa die. So fucking stop now."

"And how are you going to prevent it, Nina? Are you going to strong-arm your way into Hell? Will your bad language and threats get us there?" he shouted, then hated himself for being such an asshole.

They'd been nothing but damn good to him and Tessa, and he was pissing all over it by insulting their efforts. He put his hand on Nina's shoulder and gripped it. "I'm sorry. That was shitty."

"Yeah, it was," she said, gazing up at him, her beautiful coal eyes glittering. "But shitty I can live with. Giving up? Not on your fucking life. We don't quit. We don't goddamn quit. Ever. So shut down that train of thought now."

Mick closed his eyes and took a deep breath. "It's the waiting. All this damn waiting."

The couch exploded then in a loud bang, the legs breaking and flying in a million different directions. Material ripped and split wide open, sending foam upward in large chunks of puffy white.

"What the fuck?" Nina yelled, spinning around.

Mick put his hand in front of Nina, glancing over the couch as Marty and Wanda came out of the bedroom, their eyes wild.

A groan came from beneath the cushions, making Mick narrow his eyes and take another step in front of the women to shield them from possible harm.

Stupid as that was, because they didn't need no man, as Nina put it. In mere seconds, they were tearing up the ruined cushions to find out what was beneath them.

"Darnell!" Marty yelped, throwing her arms around his neck.

Wanda was instantly at his side, running her hands over his face. "Oh, my God, Darnell, what happened?"

He gasped for air, his breathing labored and harsh, his clothes torn and singed. His face had slashes of crimson running along one cheek. "We gotta help her. We gotta help Casey," he wheezed, coughing.

Mick watched Wanda fight for composure, saw her clench her fists. "Where is she, Darnell? How did you get away?"

Leaning forward over his knees, he shook his scruffy head. "I dunno. I had her, right in my hands. We was runnin' like the devil himself was behind us. We looked everywhere, couldn't find that egg anywhere. But I lost my grip on her. She got torn away. You don't know what they'll . . ." He jammed his fist into his mouth.

Mick's mouth was dry, his throat so tight he thought it might explode, but he had to know. "Tessa. Did you see Tessa?" Mick knew his question sounded full of desperation, but he didn't care. He needed to get to Tessa.

Darnell's head popped up; his weary eyes held fear. "Miss Tessa?"

Nina clamped a hand on Darnell's shoulder, her tone as somber as he'd ever heard it. "Frank got his mojo back just in time to drag Tessa back there with him. She's down there with him now."

Darnell was on his feet in a matter of seconds, wobbling, but his eyes screamed determination. "Then I gotta go!"

Marty flipped a finger upward. "Not without us, demon."

Arch stood in the doorway of Tessa's bedroom with Carl right beside him. "Miss Wanda? How can I help?"

Nina strode over to them and wrapped her arms around their necks. "You watch my boy, Arch. Promise me, you'll watch my boy and Charlie."

Arch gazed up at her while Carl ran his stiff, duct-taped fingers along her cheek. "Always, Miss Nina. *Always*."

In a blur, she was back beside Darnell, cracking her knuckles as each woman latched onto the demon. "Ready when you are, big guy."

"Hold on. You're not going without me," Mick protested. Not a chance. No way he was leaving one less possible chance they could find Tessa and the baby out of this equation.

Nina flipped her hand upward in his direction. "You stay the fuck put. One less novice running around down there is one less fucking headache for us."

The. Fuck.

"Go, Darnell!" Nina ordered on a shout.

As Darnell began to shimmer, Mick made a choice. One he knew he was going to pay for if he lived and these women got their hands on him. There was no other alternative in his mind.

With a howl, he lunged at the group, sailing over the remnants of the couch and latching onto Nina's back, hanging on for all he was worth.

He might die, but if Tessa and the baby weren't here with him anyway, then he didn't care.

He didn't want to live without them, and he'd die if he had to, trying to find them.

"FRANK!" Tessa screamed so loud she was sure all of Hell was awake now.

Frank soared through the gray and black sky, his coat whipping behind him as a demon's claws held him hostage, sinking into his flesh.

Like a slinky, the demon had cropped up out of the ground, pitching forward and snapping back, dangling Frank in front of her like a carrot.

And still, the maddening drum of the heartbeats played, eating at her soul, working their way into her heart, gnawing at her hope until she thought she'd scream.

"Run, Tessa! Run!" Frank screamed.

No. No. No! They were in this together. *Think of Mick. Think of the baby. Think of all the things you'll miss if you give in. Save Frank, Tessa. SaveFranksaveFranksaveFrank!*

This reminded her of all the times Mick and Noah had shut

her out. How they'd lured her in, letting her believe she was part of the gang, only to ditch her later on.

They had been just kids at the time, but she remembered how helpless she'd felt. How angry that helplessness had made her. And if she could just summon those two bastards' faces, giggling and punching each other in the shoulder because they'd sucked her into their game again, she could do this.

So she closed her eyes, she mumbled the words to "Do-Re-Mi," as inaccurate as they were, drowning out Frank's screams and the pulse of the hearts. Mick's and Noah's faces flashed before her mind's eye, their bright, young faces taunting her.

And, letting the events of these last few days wash over her, she lost it.

Her mouth opened wide and her wings ripped from her back, unfurling in billowy waves. Her eyes pinpointed Frank and her rage whooshed from her mouth in a stream of fire, aimed directly at the faceless demon.

Rolling her head on her neck, Tessa ran, spraying anything within the stream of fire's way, howling, picking up speed until she was in the air.

Frank's screams whizzed past her ears, filled with horror.

Her eyes caught him, rolling, twisting in the air, limbs flailing. Swooping downward, she aimed for the inky dot he'd become in the cruel landscape, plowing through the air until she felt the hard thump of him on her back.

His hands wrapped around her wings, his breathing ragged.

"Hang on, Frank!" she roared against the acrid smoke billowing from her mouth.

More demons appeared, their mouths open in perpetual screams, their bodies slick like oil, screaming their rage at her.

"Use your fire, Tessa!" Frank bellowed, crawling to her back, wrapping his trembling arms around her neck.

She opened her mouth again, spraying anything in her path, fighting the stench of burning flesh and her own singed hair. Then she saw it.

The gates.

If she was gauging them accurately, she could fly right over them. "How high do the gates go, Frank?"

Acrid air shifted under them, creating turbulence, but Frank held on. "Oh, Tessa!" he said with weak excitement. "You can soar right over the top of them!"

The pull in her chest began once more, the rumble of the egg calling to her, and then a coo. A soft, barely audible coo sang in her ears.

Without thinking, without breathing, without any plan at all, Tessa roared over the top of the gates, spiked and jagged-edged, like a jetliner.

The baby was coming. She couldn't think of anything else but her helpless baby alone somewhere without her.

And the motherfucker who'd taken her child was going to pay.

So hard.

CHAPTER 17

Mick gripped Nina's jacket, his hands clenched so tight his bones ached as they flew through a black hole of nothing.

They fell, literally, into Hell with a hard blow to the ground in a tangle of limbs, perfume, shoes, and demon.

Nina was the first to rouse, shoving at Mick's shoulder. "Get the fuck off me, Gigantor! You weigh as much as a damn bus."

Mick moaned, rolling to his side, scrunching his eyes shut to keep the drip of perspiration from stinging them.

Wanda and Marty shot to their feet, the clack of their heels a desolate echo.

Darnell dragged him upward, grabbing Mick's face in his hands. "Dude! Are you crazy?"

He shook his head. "No. Is it crazy to want to save the woman I've loved all my life and our baby? If that's crazy, fuck all of you.

I'll figure it out myself," he said with a tight jaw, shrugging Darnell off and taking his first good look around.

Jesus. Jesus Christ. They were in Hell.

Hell. And it was everything horrible he'd learned as a child times a million. Ugly, tormented, desperate, with miles and miles of barren wasteland.

Nina planted a hand on his shoulder—a firm one that wouldn't let him move. "Don't be an asshole, Sasquatch. You're here now, and we work as a team. Got that? No rogue freeballin'. So stay close. You have wings and some fire, but that ain't a whole lot of power in your arsenal. Keep something in mind, too. If I gotta, I'll haul your ass over my shoulder and make you look like a GD sissy. So don't be stupid."

God, she had a way of taking your manhood and stomping on it until it squealed. Even if she was right.

Wanda's face was stricken—she was clearly trying to hold it together, but her facade was cracking. "Where to now, Darnell? Where are we?"

"It ain't far, but y'all gotta stay close. I know some underground tunnels we can use and, Nina, I'm gonna need you to reach out to Casey with your mind mojo. We need to find her."

Nina's nod was brisk as she set off after Darnell with Marty and Wanda right behind her.

Mick took hold of Wanda's arm, squeezing it, offering quiet support. He focused on remembering that Casey was Wanda's sister, and she didn't want to lose Casey any more than he wanted to lose Tessa and the baby.

Wanda patted his arm before smoothing her hair back, righting her shoulders, and plunging her way down the road of Hell, filled with potholes and rubble.

The heat pounded him, forcing him to pull off his sweater and discard it, leaving him in his T-shirt as they walked.

His throat was drier than it had ever been in any fire, sweat poured from him in salty tracks, but he felt Tessa. He felt the baby. They were close.

As they made their way toward a series of black holes against a stark backdrop, Darnell asked, "Anything, Nina?"

Nina shook her head, her expression grimmer than usual. "It's so damn fuzzy. Every time I can almost see her face, it fades away. I can almost hear her, too. She keeps saying the same thing over and over."

Wanda grabbed the back of her hoodie. "What? What is she saying?" The worry in her tone tore at Mick. All of this sacrifice without a single word of recrimination made him so grateful.

Nina grabbed Wanda's hand and held it. "I can't make it out yet, Wanda. But I will. Promise I will."

As they approached the holes, Darnell stopped, turning to face them. His face, almost always smiling, held nothing but darkness. "It ain't pretty in here, but it's the only way I know to get to where we gotta be. I want y'all to know, the stuff you'll see, I want no part of, but it's so damn ugly, it hurts a soul I ain't even got no more. Makes me ashamed I'm really one of 'em. Look straight ahead. Don't make eye contact. Stay close. You hear?"

No one spoke, but they all nodded, following the demon into the first hole.

The moment they entered, Mick felt what Darnell meant.

Palpable fear, thick and hungry to feed. Need, lust, an overwhelming stench assaulted him all in one fell swoop.

But he focused, prayed, thought about nothing but Tessa's face and the egg.

Golden, shiny, ready to hatch their future.

FRANK slumped against a wall, a wall that was moving with life, slurping and gurgling until Tessa thought she might vomit. She knelt down beside him, his face so pale he was almost as white as Nina. "Frank! Oh, God, Frank. Tell me you self-heal, please." She pushed a clump of his stringy hair from his face.

His gasps for breath were shallow now, but he gripped her hand. "You must find the baby and Casey and Darnell. Go!"

"Oh, no, pardner. We're a team. Where I go, you go. I need you, Frank. I need you to be my guide. So we'll rest for a minute, okay?"

"Tessa, I'm injured. I don't know if I can heal myself now," he gritted out, sweat beading on his upper lip from the effort.

"You can. *You will*," she muttered fiercely. "Never give up. Just concentrate. Besides, who'll sing to the baby if you don't? You don't want me to mess up a good lullaby, do you?"

His flesh was torn in so many places she didn't think there were enough Band-Aids in the world to patch him up. *Please, God. Please let Frank be all right.* Pulling him near her, their sweat sour in her nose, she rocked him. "Sing with me, Frank. Let's do *The Lion King*, okay? I love that movie. My favorite is 'The Circle of Life.'" Taking a deep breath, she began, "'Pennsyyylllvaniaaa!'"

Frank's laughter was weak. "'Pennsylvania'? Oh, dear. If I

survive this, we'll have to consider a hearing test. It's 'Nants ingonyama bagithi Baba.' "

Tessa frowned, just happy he was alert enough to correct her. "Impressive. Okay, so what you said. You go next."

" 'From the day we arrive on the planet and blinking, step into the sun,' " he whispered, hoarse and raw.

" 'It's the circle of liiiife, it's a wheel of something!' " she sang back, tears forming in her eyes and splashing to her torn jeans.

Frank struggled to push away from her. "You missed an entire verse."

"Yeah, but look at you," she said on a smile, pointing to his fading wounds. "It would seem someone likes my singing. So, hah!"

He held up his hands, once bloodied with scratches and gouges in his skin, now clearing at a rapid pace.

"See, your magic isn't totally gone. Wanna sing till it comes back entirely?"

Frank scowled, though his eyes were amused. "Not if you're singing."

They both stilled for a moment, Tessa assessing their surroundings, forcing herself to think of anything but the slimy walls burbling behind her back. "Where are we?"

"We're close to where the most dangerous souls who are locked up are kept, Tessa. I don't know how you managed to get us here, but you did it."

"So whoever wants the baby is somewhere around here?" She fought the utter terror those words brought.

"Yes. I've never been in these chambers, but I've heard them described. You have to be exceptionally careful, Tessa. These are the most tortured souls, the most reckless humanity had to offer, the scourge of society. The very bottom of the barrel."

Breathe, Tessa. Breathe. "Okay. So this is where I go poke around and you sit still and keep healing."

Frank shook his head. "Not a chance. Where you go, I go," he said rolling to his knees and rising.

A quaking began under their feet, the floors slithering in ribbons of bloodred beneath them.

She gripped Frank's arm, her hands aching. "The egg. I feel the baby!" she whisper-yelled. "We're close, Frank."

As though tied to an invisible rope, she followed the pull, the vibration, letting it lead her, passing chamber after chamber, open door after open door, the halls bereft of anyone, containing only the gloom of isolation.

Frank stopped short, tripping and falling into her. He held his finger to his lips and pointed to his right.

Relief welled in her, making her bones feel like butter. Casey! Oh, thank God, it was Casey. Sitting on a chair in a dark room with two torches on either side of her. The walls were damp, rivulets of water sluicing down along the cement, and covered in thick moss.

Sitting?

Why the hell was she sitting when there were babies to be saved?

Tessa pushed Frank behind her, peering around the corner. Oh, no, no. She'd been fooled before by the "I'm your mother and father" demon shapeshifter posers once. Twice? Not this time, Tricky Dick.

Frank sniffed the air, his nostrils flaring. "That's really her. I can smell her."

Tessa breathed a sigh of relief, rushing in, ignoring the fact that Casey was shaking her head, bouncing the chair up and down by pushing her feet against the floor.

"Casey!" She fought not to yell. "Are you all right?" Tessa put her hands on Casey's shoulders. Nothing was keeping her in the chair. She wasn't tied to it, and her mouth had nothing to prevent her from speaking. Yet she remained mute.

"It must be a spell of silence," Frank offered, coming up behind her. "Let me try to break it."

Casey bounced up and down again, her brown hair falling about her shoulders in a tangle as she shook her head.

But Frank closed his eyes and made a fist, popping it open with a sudden burst of movement, and whatever held her in the chair suddenly let loose.

"Get out!" Casey yelled the moment her lips were capable of moving, jumping up from the chair. "Run, Tessa!"

Tessa took a step back, afraid they'd made a big mistake. Maybe this wasn't really Casey?

Casey grabbed her arms, her eyes glowing red. "Listen to me carefully. Get out, Tessa! Take the baby and run!" She pointed to a basket on a small shelf, surrounded by snakes.

Lots of slithering, slimy, gooey snakes. One of her worst phobias.

Tessa swallowed her fear, darted toward the basket, forced herself to reach past the snakes, hissing and spitting, fought a scream, and peeked inside the basket to be sure the baby was safe. There was a hairline fracture of a crack in the shell, meaning it wouldn't be long now. The pulsing heartbeat quickened, picking up its pace, throbbing, calling to her.

Frank motioned Tessa toward the door only feet away. Yet Casey stayed rooted to the spot she'd been in. Another spell? "Casey, hurry! Let's go!" she yelled.

Casey shook her head. "No, Tessa. I'm finishing this, and I'm finishing it for good! Get out. Take the baby and run. Mick's here. So is everyone else. Find them, Tessa, and get out!"

Mick was here. Instantly, her heart began to crash against her ribs. But she couldn't leave Casey . . . What did she need to finish? "What are you talking about? You have to come with us, Casey!"

"Tessa!" she roared, lobbing a fireball from her hand in the direction of the snakes. "Get the fuck out now!"

Tessa's eyes widened, but she clung to the basket. What was happening? What was Casey finishing?

The sudden slam of a door and the clink of locks being pushed into place made her stomach fall to her feet with dread.

Yeah. That couldn't be good.

Casey stood in front of Tessa, putting a protective arm in front of her. "You stay away from them, or so help me, I'll—"

"You'll what, husband-stealer?" someone said in a cultured voice, interrupting Casey. "What exactly do you think you can do to stop me, whore?"

Whoa, whoa, whoa. Whore? Someone was calling conservatively dressed, mild-mannered Casey a whore?

Tessa pivoted on her ragged sneaker, the canvas catching on the rough floor and making her stumble into Frank.

One of the most beautiful women she'd ever seen slinked

toward her; every step she took was poetry in motion, fluid, graceful. Her gobs of blond hair fell past her perfect breasts in swishy, beachy waves, gleaming beneath the torches' lights, matching the glitter of her blue, blue eyes.

The white gown she wore flowed about her feet, showing just a hint of creamy thigh at the slit in the skirt. "So you must be the new mother? Congratulations, darling!"

"Who are you?"

She sighed, her slender shoulders sagging. "Honestly, all this notoriety and I can't get any credit, can I, Casey?"

Tessa gripped the handle of the basket as the egg began to roll, another crack in the shell clearly visible. "I'm new to this, uh . . . scene. So out of deference to my newness, I'd appreciate a heads-up."

The woman smiled down at her, her lips full and red like plump cherries. She walked a long finger with a nail tipped in red that matched her lips along the handle of the basket. "I'm your worst nightmare, darling. And such a coincidence, too. Is this another one of your accidents, Casey?"

Tessa's eyes frantically sought Casey's, but she wasn't providing answers. "So, still pretty new to this. While I realize you're probably not up to explaining yourself, humor me, please? What's this about?"

The woman folded her arms under her insanely pert breasts. "This is about your child, of course. I want it. That means you can't have it anymore. Also, I'm a little miffed at you. You tricked me." Her beautiful face went sad, her lips forming a pout. "My feelings were crushed when I found out the egg my demons stole wasn't real."

Tessa waved her free hand. "I get that part. I know all about unleashing the souls from Hell and freeing yourself. The whole brimstone-and-dragon-scales thing. I mean, what's Casey got to do with it?"

The woman moved toward Casey, wrapping an arm around her shoulders, something Casey strangely didn't fend off. "Casey stole my husband. Right out from under my nose, didn't you, darling?"

Casey didn't respond, scaring Tessa. "Okay, so you're still mad about it, right? The wound is still fresh. Why don't we talk this out? Maybe we can resolve your differences. And here's something else to think about. Who wants a man that cheats? He's a pig, right? Why cry over spilled milk?"

The woman snatched Casey up and threw her away as though she were throwing away a piece of tissue. Casey slammed against the wall, the crack of her head making Frank wince as he inched his way behind this giant of a woman to run to Casey's aide. "Oh, I don't care about the man anymore, sugarplum. He's water under the bridge. That Casey ended up here in an attempt to save you is just some delicious irony of frosting on my cake. It's like killing two birds with one stone. I free myself from Hell and kill the woman who put me here to begin with, which means I don't have to hunt her down. Thank goodness, too. The chase is tedious."

Sweet baby Jesus, how were they going to get out of here? "So in the spirit of killing, should we exchange names? I'm Tessa Preston. You are?"

"Hildegard."

Oh, she'd heard Darnell talking about Hildegard. She was a mean, mean, vengeful vampire who'd turned Casey's husband into her lifemate by biting him while he slept. Worse, she'd bitten his daughter, too.

Oh, hard feelings were surely abound.

"Hildegard," Tessa repeated. "No last name?"

She smiled, serene and gorgeous. "Baby Snatcher?"

"Do you hyphenate that? I could see that as an attractive option when looking at it as a signature on checks and thank-you cards."

Hildegard moved toward Tessa, her pale skin eerie and perfect, her mouth hard and determined. She held out her hand, uncurling her fingers. "Give me the baby, Tessa."

Tessa began backing away. Swallowing hard, she licked her lips nervously. "I just can't do that, Hildegard. I know it'll free you from Hell, but, and this is a biggie, I hear it's not just you who'll be freed. I heard a rumor that it'll unleash some really bad demons. What then? I'm responsible for the world being turned upside down? I don't know about you, but who wants that on their shoulders? It's great street cred—"

"Give. Me. The. *Baby!*" she screamed, blowing the loose tendrils of Tessa's hair not plastered to her head with sweat away from her face.

"No," she said, surprising even herself with how calmly she spoke the word.

The egg began to roll back and forth, back and forth as she clung to the basket.

"What did you say?" Hildegard appeared astonished by her refusal.

"I said no. Absolutely not." *No fear. No fear. No fear.*

"No one tells me no, Tessa. *No one.*"

A thought breezed through her mind at that moment as she stared up at this Nordic goddess, and Tessa wondered just who Hildegard thought she was to come and snatch up a baby just because she wanted to break out of her prison—a jail cell she was in due to her bad behavior. So what was this sense of entitlement about? Serving a sentence had reasoning behind it—even if it was in Hell.

So boo-hoo.

Tessa squared her shoulders, lifting her chin. "Well, I just did. I think if more people had told you no, you wouldn't be where you are right now. So no. And no again."

Hildegard took another step toward her, making Tessa's heart crash, but not in the way she'd have expected. It wasn't out of fear—it was out of anger. Ugly, kill-a-bitch-without-looking-back anger. "I'd back up, Hildegard. Now, I'm asking nicely. But I won't be quite as accommodating if you come one step closer."

"Do you have any idea who I am? I'm a centuries-old vampire. Who are you?"

Tessa fought the bubbling rage in her stomach, forcing its way into her throat, and just before it spilled from her mouth she answered, "I'm a mother."

And for the first time, the phrase "All Hell broke loose" held real meaning.

CHAPTER 18

Mick heard the blast from along the corridor seconds before they were all flying in every direction, crashing into walls that were writhing with a life of their own.

Nina was on her feet first, lunging upward, her image a blur as she sped down the hallway to the door the blast had come from.

She began to ram the door with her shoulder to no avail, her grunts harsh and frustrated. "Tessa! Answer me, goddamn it!

There were screams, loud, piercing screams, coming from behind the door. Tessa's screams, shredding Mick's soul. "Move!" he roared, making a run for the door, slamming into it only to bounce back as though a linebacker had thrown him into a wall made of rubber.

"It's gotta be some kinda spell keeping it locked!" Darnell yelled over that unmerciful heartbeat pounding the air.

Wanda's face was grim and rife with anxiety, but she looked

at both women, her eyes fierce with determination. "On three. One, two, three!"

All three of them went at the door, screaming like the warriors they were, clothes torn and burned, shoes broken and battered, hair singed and mussed.

They bounced back, too, smacking into the ground.

And the screams, they went on and on until Mick thought he'd lose his mind.

So basically, that's what happened next.

He lost it. Full-on, rage-fueled lost it. "Get out of the way!" he bellowed to Darnell and the women.

His mouth opened wide as he ran at the door, his roar deep and ugly, echoing throughout the cavernous hallway, and fire spewed from his mouth directly at the door.

As though he were using a blowtorch to open a safe, he decimated the door, cutting away at it until it was nothing but ashes.

Everyone rushed past him then, screaming, pushing, working as one entity to get inside the door. Mick followed, his long legs eating up the distance.

He skidded to a halt just behind the girls and Darnell. What he saw made his chest so tight it ached.

Frank hung on a rusty hook, out cold, his feet dangling in the air, his body limp and soaking wet.

Tessa was clinging to a basket, her face chalk white, her body violently shaking as snakes wound up around her legs, circled her arms, caressed her cheek.

She hated snakes. Had one of the biggest phobias he'd ever encountered.

Their eyes met, hers filled with sheer terror. "Run!" she whispered, her fear so evident, so palpable, he tasted it on his tongue. *"Run!"*

Darnell was the first to react, snatching at the snakes as Tessa shook. "You have to run," she said from clenched teeth. "She has the egg and it's hatching. Casey's chasing her. Run before everything explodes!"

Nina yanked Frank off the hook, throwing him over her shoulder. "Who has the egg, Tessa? Who the fuck is it?"

"Hildegard," she said on a terrified shudder, a tear slipping from her eye.

Nina was moving before Tessa said another word, plowing out the door in her fast-forward motion, screaming Casey's name.

Wanda followed close behind Nina with an order for Darnell to stay with them as Marty flung the last of the snakes off Tessa and Mick used his fire to incinerate them.

Pulling her into his arms, he clung to her, pushed her soaking-wet hair from her face. "Where, Tessa? Where did they go?"

She fought for breath, her fingers digging into his skin. "I don't know. They just disappeared. But I can feel the baby, Mick. I can find the baby!"

Darnell scooped her up, throwing her around his waist and latching onto her legs. "The gates! She'll be headin' for the gates, lookin' to get out! We gotta stop 'em! You hold on, Tessa, We'll never make it if you don't let me carry you."

Marty pointed to her back. "Get on, Mick!"

He began to back up, but Marty jerked his arm. "Get on my back, Neanderthal! You don't have the kind of speed I have, and we need to get to everyone else to help!"

The mere thought of climbing onto this petite woman's back

left him unable to move until she roared in his face, "Get the fuck on, Mick, or I'm going to knock your scales right the fuck off your back!"

He fought every chauvinistic, knuckle-dragging notion he'd ever had and jumped on, wrapping his arms around Marty's neck and watching Darnell take the lead.

Tessa banged against the demon's back like a wooden sign in the wind until she was nothing more than a fuzzy image as Darnell headed back the way they'd come.

And Mick prayed. He prayed the baby was still safe. That somehow Casey had gotten to it.

And if she hadn't, he was going to hunt Satan down in this maze of hopelessness and make a deal with the devil himself.

A stream of blond hair became visible just as Darnell came to the gates, flying through the air like a vanilla-colored flag.

Tessa fell from Darnell's back, dropping to the ground and hitting her knees with a yelp, but she was up and back on her feet within seconds, running as fast as her legs could carry her to catch up to Wanda.

The long stretch of road leading toward the gates rolled upward, then slammed back down, making it almost impossible to keep her footing.

"Casey! Nina!" Wanda screamed amidst the fireballs hurtling her way, her cry dry and hoarse.

Nina was but inches from Hildegard's back and, reaching out, she snatched her hair, wrapping it around her fist until she almost had her in a choke hold. "I'll kill you, you fucking bitch!"

Hildegard's laughter thundered in Tessa's ears, mocking them as she clung to the egg, bending at the waist and twisting around so Nina lost her grip on her hair just before she shot upward into the air.

Hildegard rose high above the smoke, and that was when Tessa saw it. A foot, the teeniest, tiniest foot, pink and perfect, poking through the egg.

Panic seized her just before she stumbled, falling to the ground and bouncing against the pathway that had turned hard like concrete.

Mick fell against her, sliding into her with a hard jolt, knocking them into a dizzying spin. He clung to her, digging his heels into the ground, rolling and pulling her up with him.

Nina flew into the air, her face a mask of fury as she torpedoed toward Hildegard, aiming for her midsection and smashing into her, making her lose her grip on the egg.

The egg sailed across the bleak sky as fireballs pelted the air, narrowly missing it.

Nina roared her anger as Darnell yelled, "Everybody spread out!"

Marty, Wanda, and Casey fanned out, trying to anticipate where the egg would move next, but the back draft of arid wind blew it around like a beach ball.

Mick grabbed Tessa by the waist and began to run, picking up speed, grunting in her ear until she heard his wings unfurl. He spread them wide, pumping against the current. "Grab the egg, Tessa!" he yelled as they flew so close to it she almost had it in her grip.

Tessa strained, screaming out her frustration when they just missed it, the shiny surface slick against her fingertips.

Pieces of eggshell began to fall beneath them, small bits of gold swirling to the ground. She fought her terror, clinging to Mick as he circled back around.

And the vibration continued, seeping into her pores, tearing her focus to shreds.

"Look out!" Wanda screamed from below just as Nina lost her grip on Hildegard, taking a blow so hard to her head from the woman that Tessa cried out.

Nina hurtled downward while Hildegard rose upward, shooting through the air like a beautiful cannonball, her gaze on the egg, which was still bouncing about like a helium balloon.

Darnell and Casey lobbed fireballs upward with angry bellows, and Frank was suddenly on his feet, running under them, sending up weak fizzles of electricity. Wanda and Marty dragged Nina to her feet, and through it all, Tessa kept one eye on the baby, all her energy focused on reaching the egg before the vampire. "Faster!" she yelled up at Mick.

The hot wind washed over her, her eyes watering, her body aching, but moments before Hildegard threw a lithe arm out to capture the egg, Tessa spewed a roar, fire flying from her mouth and knocking the vampire out of the way.

The egg sailed almost over their heads, but Mick drove upward, his soaked shirt pressed to her back, his breathing heavy. Her fingers reached upward toward those precious toes, stretching, straining, latching on to the heel of the baby's foot and pulling it toward her.

Tessa pulled it to her chest, tucking it close, running her fingers over the small foot as Mick zoomed toward safety.

"Go over the gates!" Nina bellowed, running beneath them, waving her arms. "Get the fuck out!"

Seconds before they almost hit the top of the gates, Hildegard proved she wasn't so easily conquered.

She blindsided them, jarring the egg in Tessa's hands, almost sending it flying back into the air. The vampire began to ram them, her beautiful body slamming into Mick's side over and over.

"Go long!" Mick yelled to Nina, who was back in action, whipping toward them. His voice was full of pain, his grunts increasing.

Nina changed direction, backing up, her eyes fiery, her face a mask of concentrated fury.

"On three, throw the egg to Nina, Tessa! Just like when we used to play football with Noah," Mick said in her ear.

Tessa gulped, caressing the hand that had pushed its way through the shell, fighting a sob at letting the baby go. But Nina would protect it. She had to believe it was the safest place for the baby.

Mick squeezed her waist to encourage her. "One, two, three!"

Tessa raised her arm, launching the baby through the air toward Nina, watching as if in slow motion as the egg hurtled across the distance between them.

And landed directly in Hildegard's hands.

Nina's howl of anger rocketed through the sky as she barreled toward Hildegard.

Tessa screamed her frustration, howling her anguish at Hildegard's smug smile.

But a blinding flash of light zigzagged between Hildegard and

Nina, so bright, so painful that Tessa could barely see. She threw a hand up to cover her eyes, wincing at the pain throbbing in her skull.

Then there was the voice, all around them, like an ethereal surround sound. "Catch the egg, Nina!"

Both she and Mick floundered, his wings stuttering, her mouth falling open.

"Catch it!" the voice sang.

She knew that voice. She knew it better than her own.

Noah?

THERE was a sudden stillness as the air seemed to evaporate. Colors faded, then brightened; a pleasant hum rang out as Tessa and Mick floated to the ground with Nina not far behind them.

Hildegard dropped like a rock, her gorgeous body plopping from midair to land in a graceful heap amidst the rubble, her hair splayed out behind her like a golden fan.

Mick fell to his knees, his face a mask of pain, his chest expanding, pulling air into his lungs. Tessa ran to him, throwing her arms around him as Casey and Darnell secured Hildegard and Marty and Wanda ran for Nina and the egg.

"I love you," she whispered, pulling Mick's ravaged body to hers. "I've loved you forever. I don't care what Noah said to you. I don't know what it meant, but I love you and there's no one I want to be with but you. Do you hear me?"

"I didn't mean it," someone said from behind.

Tessa gasped. No. This was another trick. She refused to be sucked in.

"Tessa? This isn't a trick. It's really me."

Mick's eyes rose as she turned around, both of them rising to their feet.

She stared directly into the eyes of her brother, seeking, searching for the demon behind those eyes. Surely it couldn't really be Noah.

He rocked back on his brown loafers. The same loafers he'd always worn and Mick had made fun of him for owning. Noah pointed upward, his eyes so warm and inviting. "That light that blinded the vampire? Me."

Tears began to flow, streaming down her cheeks. He sounded just like Noah. That rich, chocolaty voice that had always soothed her when she was a kid. "How?" she managed.

He folded his hands in front of him and smiled. "Let's just say a little birdy told me you needed my help, and we'll leave it at that."

Tessa's heart filled then, brimming with an emotion she had no name for. "You saved the baby?"

He smiled his crooked smile. "You all did, T. I just helped."

Mick finally spoke, the grumble of his voice low and husky. "You're up there?" he asked, the words coming out like a croak—like he'd worried it had been any different.

The peace on Noah's face was like nothing Tessa had ever seen before. "I am, Mick, and it's beautiful. So unbelievable, man. I can't wait till you get there. Mom and Dad are there, too. They miss you, Tessa. They miss Mick, too. I miss you—*both* of you."

Without hesitation, Tessa walked into his arms, her sobs cracked and hoarse. "I'm so glad to see you, Noah. I miss you so much. I miss you so, so much." He smelled just like Noah. If this wasn't Noah, if this was some cruel trick, she didn't want to know right now.

For now, she just wanted to hug her brother.

"I know you miss us, T. That's why I'm here. You have to move forward now. Without me and Mom and Dad. You've isolated yourself, and it worries us."

She knew what he said was true. She knew she'd hidden from her loss, maybe even as much as Mick had. She'd buried herself in work and cans of soup while Mick had buried himself in anger. "How did you know?"

He shrugged, his wide shoulders lifting and dropping. "I see sometimes. Mom and Dad see and tell me. So you have to promise me, with the baby and all of these new friends you've made, you'll move on, Tessa. You'll form new bonds, hold on to these new friendships you've made. Not just for you, but for the baby, too. *Please.*"

The thought of letting go of her grief felt like letting go of the only attachment she had to her family, like leaving behind a favorite blanket, worn from love.

"Your grief interferes with remembering all the good stuff, Tessa. I promise you, if you stop letting your sadness eat you up and leave you so empty, all the good times we had as a family, all those memories, will fill you back up again."

Tessa gulped back another sob, knowing these were probably some of the last words he'd speak to her until they met again someday. She nodded against his chest, squeezing her eyes to fend off more tears. "I'll try."

Noah set her from him, brushing a strand of hair from her eyes. "You'd have done it a lot sooner if I hadn't said what I said to Mick the night I died, and that's the other reason I'm here. To apologize."

Mick stayed silent, but she heard him breathing, knew he was struggling.

Noah approached Mick with slow steps. "I didn't mean what I said that night, Mick. It was a heat-of-the-moment thing that I can't ever take back, but I didn't mean it."

Mick, torn, ragged, looked into Noah's eyes, and for the first time, she saw the pain, the raw, agonizing pain he'd suffered because of Noah's words. "Why, Noah? Why would you say something like that to me? We were like brothers."

Noah's face was filled with remorse. "Jealousy is an ugly thing, man."

Mick stood still, not a single muscle moving. "I don't understand."

Noah's sigh reverberated around her head. "Because I loved you, too, Mick. Just like Tessa. I've loved you since we were kids," Noah said, his voice hushed and barely audible.

Tessa looked up then, wiping the tears from her eyes, unable to keep her surprise off her face. How could she not have known something like this about her own brother? Pieces of their life began to flit through her mind; explanations for some of the things she'd found odd began to add up. Things she'd never let her thoughts linger on because what he was confessing had never even occurred to her.

He'd hidden all these years, and Tessa's heart broke for him. He'd never truly lived his life.

Noah's shoulders slumped. "I tried to tell you a million times. I just could never come out of the closet. I was a coward, and in that cowardice, I said something rash. Something stupid I couldn't ever take back. I knew you loved T, Mick. I've always known, I guess. But the thought of you with her while I had to watch . . . it hurt. So I said something shitty, and I totally planned on explaining it to you, but I died before I could. So for the last three years, I've watched the two of you fight and be angry because of something I said, because you were trying to honor the last stupid thing I said to you. And now I'm here to make it right."

Mick swallowed hard, using his forearm to wipe the sweat from his brow. "I didn't know. I didn't know. If I had known . . ."

Noah's smile was gentle when he placed a hand on Mick's shoulder. "You would've what? Not loved Tessa? That's crazy. Look, buddy, this was on me. I could've told you, but it wasn't just about me telling you I was gay. I knew you'd handle that fine. But how would you have handled how I felt about you? We had an amazing friendship for a million years. I didn't want to blow it all to hell. But I was getting frustrated with my life—with my damn secret—and the night you told me how you felt about Tessa was the last straw. No fault of yours, that's just where my head was. But I'm here to tell you I was wrong. I was wrong for keeping you two from being together because of my baggage. No one is better for T than you, Mick. No one."

Tessa fought another sob for her brother—for his pain.

"You wanna know how I know no one is better for you, T?" he asked.

She nodded, still unable to process his words. "Sure."

"I heard a little something about dragons and their true mates. According to my sources, when a male dragon finds his mate, he throws off some kind of magical hormone. That's how you turned into a dragon, too, Tessa. Because you're Mick's mate, and whatever magic he had when he turned, he aimed it all at you because you're his one true mate."

Everything clicked then, the last piece of the puzzle falling into place.

Mick pulled Noah into a hard hug that made Tessa's heart clench so tight it hurt. "I'm sorry, Noah. I miss the hell out of you, and I'm sorry."

Noah slapped him on the back. "Don't be sorry. Just be happy, and promise you'll take good care of my baby sister and the little one."

"Always," Mick whispered as Tessa grabbed his hand. "You can always count on that."

Marty and Wanda came up behind them, putting their hands on both Tessa's and Mick's shoulders. "We have to get out of here before the egg hatches," Wanda said gently. "I'm afraid to take a chance that if we stay much longer, we'll only have more trouble."

Noah held up a hand. "I've got this part of it covered, if you don't mind. I'll handle her." He pointed to Hildegard, who'd now awakened and was spitting-mad. "She won't trouble any of you ever again." He snapped his fingers, and Hildegard was gone—just like that.

And there it was again, Noah slipping away from her, leaving, and the empty ache returned full force. If Darnell and Casey could live on earth as demons, why couldn't Noah live on earth as an angel—or whatever he was? "Come back with us," she pleaded in a voice full of more unshed tears. "You're going to be an uncle. You don't want to miss that, do you?"

Noah ruffled her hair, his eyes bright. "No, I sure don't. But I can't, T. I have to go now. I've been here longer than I should anyway. We'll see each other again someday. Promise."

Tessa grabbed his hand, more tears falling to her torn shoes. "Please, *please* stay, Noah. I don't know if I can stand—"

"Yes, *you can*," Noah said on a smile. "You can do this, T. You will. You have to, for the baby and Mick. I know you'll be well taken care of. Won't she?" He looked to the women and Darnell.

Nina answered him, and when she did, Tessa's ears picked up on something she'd never thought the vampire was capable of. *Tenderness.* "I'll make sure your sister always has us. We're a big paranormal mess, we're chaos times eleventy-billion, but we all love each other. Tessa and Mick and mini-dragon won't lack for family support." She paused a moment, making Tessa turn to look at her and find her pale face full of emotion. "She won't lack for some crazy, effed-up love. She'll have more than she'll know what to do with," Nina said hoarsely. "Swear it."

Noah smiled, handsome, perfect, beaming warmth and love. "Thank you, Nina." And then he looked over her head at the others and Mick. *"Thank you, all."*

He began to fade, then shimmer, much the way Frank had back at the store, his image becoming pale and filmy as he let go of Tessa's hand. "I love you, T, and you, too, Mick. Be happy. Be really happy," Noah said, the words becoming a whisper, whooshing through her ears.

And then he was gone.

CHAPTER 19

Tessa almost fell to her knees, but it wasn't in loss or even sorrow. It was in gratitude that she'd had those final moments with Noah. Moments she'd needed to heal.

Nina clamped a hand on her shoulder, pulling her back against her lean body and giving her a tight hug. "You're a badass, kiddo. Just thought you should know."

Mick pulled her into his arms, his sigh of relief seeping into her bones. "I'm sorry, T. I never had a clue about any of it. I loved him, so I wanted to honor his last words. I didn't want to do something he seemed so dead set against."

Tessa reached up, cupping Mick's face, her eyes searching his. "Please don't be sorry. I get it now. I understand, and Noah was wrong to want to keep us apart. But it's over. Let's just start this whole thing over, okay? You, me, the baby dragon. Begin again."

Mick pressed his lips to hers, making her knees weak with his kiss. When he pulled away, he brushed the hair from her eyes. “Then let me start over by saying I love you, Tessa Preston. I’ve loved you for as long as I can remember.”

She threw her arms around his neck. “I love you, too. Always,” she whispered. “From the moment you yanked my pigtails on the bus.”

Marty gave Wanda her shirtsleeve to wipe her eyes, pulling Mick and Tessa into a hug with Casey and Darnell, who invited Frank to join them.

“We have to go, honey. Now. Right now. You don’t want the baby to hatch here, do you? In Hell?” Marty asked. “Let’s get moving. We have a long trek back to the portal.”

The baby. She was determined to do this right, just like Noah had asked. “Then we’d better move.”

Nina handed Tessa the egg, where now not just a foot and a hand had pushed its way out, but another set of five toes. She smiled up at Mick, excitement and fear mingling into a ball of joy.

As they all began to consider the long journey back, Tessa suddenly remembered Frank. “Frank!” She spun around to find him hanging back at the opening of the gates.

Tessa looked to Darnell and Casey. What happened from here? Was he allowed to come back with them? Did his obligation to Hell mean they had to leave him? Nope. Wasn’t gonna happen. Where she went, he went. For good.

Darnell, his clothes plastered to his big body, sweat pouring from his face, grinned. “He’s good to go, if he wants to an’ all. I’ll help. So will Casey. Can’t fix what’s been done, but we can teach ya how to fly low, Frank.”

Frank looked unsure, tentative, his eyes watering.

Tessa handed the baby to Mick, holding out her hand to Frank, her smile inviting and warm. She hitched her jaw toward the gates. "C'mon, minion. Where I go, you go."

Frank took her hand with a quiet, happy smile.

"So, to help the time pass more quickly while we head back to the portal, let's sing, huh, Frank?"

Frank groaned like she'd just asked him if he wanted to eat newborn kittens for lunch. "Must we?"

She rolled her eyes at him. "Look, so I messed up some words a couple of times. Don't be such a stick in the mud. Now, c'mon. Sing with me, Frank! 'Pennsyyylllvaniaaa!' " she yelled to the tune of everyone's chuckles as they headed out of the gates and back toward home.

Home.

Yeah.

EVERYONE had gathered around the incubator back at Tessa's cottage, the egg safely returned to it as they waited, its rocking motion driving them all out of their minds.

Nina paced restlessly alongside Mick.

Darnell sat with Carl and Frank at the semi-restored breakfast bar that had been temporarily patched, his arm around their shoulders, their eyes heavy from lack of sleep.

Marty and Wanda busily knitted booties, their fingers moving at the speed of light as they peered over at the incubator from time to time from their places on the couch that Arch had replaced while they were gone.

Arch sat on the floor, putting together the last of the baby items Katie, Jeannie, Phoebe, Mara, and their husbands had brought over and set up, having had enough faith to believe they'd all return.

And Tessa waited, stroking the baby's toes, bonding with it, gasping with delight when three fingers poked through the shell after four hours of doing absolutely nothing.

Nina stopped her pacing and stood over Tessa's shoulder, running her finger along the shell with a smile, tickling the bottom of the baby's heel. "C'mon now, baby dragon. Auntie Nina needs some love. How can I buy stuff for you if I don't know what you are? So what's it gonna be, peaches, tea sets or baseball bats?"

The egg responded to Nina in the way all animals and small, helpless creatures did. It cooed softly, rolling toward her cool palm.

Tessa giggled. "I think we're in it for the long haul, huh, Auntie Nina?" Turning, she looked up into Nina's eyes. "Have I said thank you?"

Nina nodded, her eyes avoiding Tessa's. "Yeah, yeah. You scraped and bowed and all that crap almost the entire way back to the portal. Unless you were busy breaking my damn eardrums with that fresh hell you call singing."

Tessa put a hand on her arm, locking eyes with Nina's. "Don't joke, Nina. Not now. This is too important. This baby wouldn't have made it without you. *We* wouldn't have made it without you. I know you don't like hearing that. I know it makes you uncomfortable to hear someone praise you. But I don't care. *Thank you.* Thank you for literally going to Hell and back to help us. I won't ever forget it. Not ever."

Nina's beautiful face didn't change, but her eyes, they smiled. "You bet," she murmured.

Gulping back more tears, Tessa turned back around to the incubator. "As for this little one, it's clear we're in no rush, and Katie did say it could take up to twenty-four hours—or not. So we wait."

"Which means the new parents must rest for the oncoming deluge of nighttime feedings and diaper changes," Arch scolded with a smile, screwdriver in hand. "Now, off with you both to rest. Should my precious decide to come out and play with us, I shall wake you both posthaste."

Mick wrapped his arms around Tessa's waist, strong, secure. She leaned back into them and sighed, at peace. "He's right, you know. I feel like we've been up for a week straight. Let's grab a nap," he said.

She twisted in his arms to face him, her body molding to his, so happy she didn't have to hide how she felt anymore. "I could use a nap," she teased against his ear as he carried her toward her bedroom.

"You two keep the roller coaster of love down in there. I won't have you scarring my peaches before the poor thing learns how to defend itself," Nina warned on a chuckle.

Both Mick and Tessa chuckled, too, as they slipped into her bedroom and closed the door. Mick dropped to her bed, also miraculously clean and smelling of fresh laundry detergent. He patted the spot beside him, which she gratefully took.

"We're going to be parents," he said, winking at her.

Tessa nodded. "We are. Which means we need to think about names. I was thinking, boy or girl, we call it . . ."

Mick looked at her, taking her hand in his. "On three?"

Tessa nodded with a grin.

Mick counted out, "One, two, three . . ."

"Noah," they both said in unison.

Tessa's smile got wider. "Yeah. I think he'd like that."

Mick nodded his dark head. "I think so, too."

"Know what else I was thinking?" she asked, rising from the bed to stand in front of him.

"What's that?"

"I was thinking that as new parents, it's our duty to do what parents do—because I hear they don't get to do it often."

"Sleep?" he teased, pulling her toward him by the front of her T-shirt.

"Exactly. So help me get out of these clothes so I can get into my jammies, would you?" she asked, cradling the top of his head to her chest when he lifted her T-shirt and nibbled at her belly.

Mick nipped the bare skin, pushing her shirt above her breasts. "You don't sleep naked? I figured you as a naked sleeper."

She lifted her arms over her head as he pulled her shirt over it, leaving her breasts exposed, her nipples tight and needy for his tongue. "Did you? Not true. It's cold here, buddy. Is that going to be a problem for our sex life?"

Mick's hands went around her waist, his tongue slashing at the undersides of her breasts, creating a hot pool of lust between her thighs. "Nope. When I'm done with you, you'll never want to wear a nightgown again."

Her head fell back on her shoulders when Mick wrapped his lips around her nipple, circling it with his tongue, tasting it, tugging it to a sharp peak. "So what you're saying is, you'll keep me warm at night?"

He took her hand and put it between his legs, rubbing the

palm of it along the ridge of his hard shaft. "I think I've got warm covered."

"Remember you said that when my feet are ice-cold, Malone." Tessa's fingers reached for his belt, unhooking it before popping the button on his jeans.

Mick lifted up from the bed, sliding his underwear and jeans off while she rid herself of her sweats.

Then it was just them. Naked. In the moonlight streaming in from the window. Together. And she couldn't believe he was actually hers. Mick Malone was hers—forever.

She walked into his arms, sliding her hands over his chest, running them over his belly until she found his cock, thick and hot. Tessa stroked him as she knelt in front of him and spread his muscled thighs wide.

She didn't bother to tease and torment—she needed him, needed him to make love to her, fill her, touch her everywhere. She swooped her head downward, sliding her mouth along his length until he was completely in her mouth and his hiss of satisfaction rang out.

Trailing her tongue along the silky surface of his cock, she took him in long passes, licking, nipping, kneading his thighs until Mick's fingers were in her hair, pulling her away and tugging her upward.

Their lips met on a sigh, a sigh of completion, a sigh of years' worth of pent-up longing. Her moan was soft when Mick parted her flesh and dragged his fingers over her clit, making the aching bud swell with need.

Sliding up his body, Tessa drew him downward to her core, and Mick went willingly, letting his tongue slip inside her and swipe her desperate flesh. She rocked against him, cupping the back of his head, savoring the white-hot press of his tongue against her, moaning softly as she felt the sharp sting of orgasm.

It wasn't like it had been in the barn, with both of them so nervous. This time it was slow and sweet, a lazy river of completion.

Mick held her thighs until she slumped against him, her legs weak. He slid back to his position on the bed, kissing her skin along the way until he was seated in front of her again.

Their eyes met, their hands entwined, their breathing shallow and choppy. He was so insanely beautiful. So sculpted and hard, so much man, her heart tightened. "I love you, Mick Malone," she said before seating herself on his cock, biting her lip to keep from crying out at the pleasure he brought when he entered her.

Thrusting upward, enveloping her in his embrace, he whispered, "I love you back, Tessa Preston."

And they rocked, finding their rhythm, learning more about each other, discovering, becoming one.

Mick's mouth went to her throat, nipping at the tender flesh as he thrust upward, easy, slow, and the spiral of desperate need turned to a simmer, a reflection of her emotions.

His hands smoothed over her hips, stroking, rocking inside her as her hands kneaded his back, soothing the tense muscles until she felt him stiffen, felt the pulse of him inside her.

She brought his mouth to hers, capturing it and slipping her tongue inside. She wanted them to be connected on all levels when they came.

As their climax collided, rose up, synced, Tessa fought tears, scrunching her eyes shut from the perfection.

Mick groaned into her mouth, still rocking, still holding her close.

Falling back on the mattress, she grabbed the top of the blanket from the head of the bed and pulled it over them, snuggling into Mick's chest and closing her eyes with a sigh of bliss.

Safe, happy, and most of all, never without Mick again.

A light rap on the door five hours later had them scrambling to find their clothes.

"Hey, lovebirds, hurry it up in there. I think peaches is about ready," Nina whispered.

Tessa's heart began to throb with excitement, pounding so hard in her chest it was hard to focus on getting her clothes on.

Mick grabbed her up in a hug, scooping her off the floor. "You ready, Mom?"

She grinned, pressing a quick kiss to his lips. "Are you, Dad?"

He grinned back. "I don't think we have a choice," he said, sliding her to the floor and swatting her butt.

Tessa grabbed his hand and pulled the door open to find everyone gathered around the incubator. Her breath caught in her chest. These were the people who'd made this moment possible.

They were the people she'd turn to for advice, for help, for a shoulder to cry on. At this very moment, as they all waited to see the baby, it occurred to her that this was her family now. They were as invested in her as she was in them. This was where they all should be. Right here. With her and Mick.

But before she joined them, Tessa sent up a silent prayer to Noah. *Thank you. I love you. Always.*

A crack of the shell whispered in her ear, making her pulse race again. Nina pulled both her and Mick toward the incubator as everyone parted to let them see.

The egg rolled, restless and moving quicker than it had been last night. The cooing from within the shell became stronger while more of the shell fell away.

No one spoke. No one moved. Everyone's hands were clasped together in a circle when Tessa glanced at their faces over the incubator. Nina, her eyes shiny. Wanda, her hair perfect again, her eyes wet. Marty, clinging to Wanda's hand, joy in her expression.

Carl and Frank, hovering, anticipation on their faces, Carl's crooked grin in place. Frank's watery blue eyes extra watery.

Darnell, in the middle of it all, holding Nina's hand in his big paw and pressing it to his chin, with Arch on the other side of her, his arm entwined in hers.

And Joe-Joe, at Nina's feet, curled around her ankles.

This—this was how everyone should be born. Into a room full of love and support—into a room full of acceptance.

And then the final pieces of the shell began to fall away, and the miracle bloomed from within the confines of the golden egg. Arms pushed through, chubby, perfectly pink arms. A tuft of hair was next, dark as night like Mick's, silky under the incubator's light.

When the last piece of shell broke, a gummy mouth appeared first, open wide and screaming, and everyone cheered. "It's a girl!" Nina said, throwing her arms around Arch and Darnell.

Tears began to fall from artfully made-up eyes, and smiles wreathed even the hardest of faces.

Mick pulled her close when Tessa reached inside the incubator, brushing the shells from their daughter, Noa. She couldn't find words for this kind of instant love, for the sweet feel of Noa's skin, soft and peachy. She couldn't move past the lump in her throat at the perfection of her daughter's hand, reaching for hers and squeezing it for the first time.

She was at an utter loss for anything but the sweet squeeze of her heart, the intense, almost overwhelming joy of this moment.

Nina draped a blanket over Mick's chest as Arch scooped tiny Noa out of the incubator and handed her to him.

When she finally looked up at Mick, her heart swelled again. He cradled Noa in his arms, close to his heart, his eyes wet. He looked at Tessa and shook his head as Nina pressed her chin against the top of his shoulder and smiled down at the baby. "I . . ." His jaw tightened, and she knew that words were just as hard for him. "Thank you," he whispered, hoarse and thick.

Tessa stood on tiptoe, reaching for Nina's hand and pressing a kiss to Mick's lips, tears splashing down her face. "No. Thank *you*."

Noa squirmed against her father's chest, her tiny legs kicking outward, strong and healthy.

And then Noa let out a howl. One that had everyone laughing and hugging, Mick and Tessa included.

It went something like this: "Rawrrr!"

EPILOGUE

Seven Months and Thirteen Days Later—Nine Utterly Implausible Paranormal Accidents, Two Brand-New Dragons, a Baby Dragon, Three Doting, Constantly Interfering Aunties and Their Whacky Family Members, a Manservant Grandfather, One Not-So-Bad-After-All Minion Who Sounds Like Winnie-the-Pooh and Loves Living on the Fringes of Hell While Singing Broadway Show Tunes, and a Vegetarian Zombie-Slash-Babysitter Extraordinaire attended a barbecue on an unusually warm fall day in honor of the prettiest baby dragon ever . . .

Mick handed Noa over to Nina the moment the vampire laid eyes on the baby, not even bothering to deny her. He smiled when his daughter threw her chubby, awkward arms around Auntie Nina's neck and planted a gummy kiss on her nose, sucking it into her mouth like she did everything she could get her hands on.

"Oh, my goodness, it's my peaches!" Nina cooed, nuzzling

Noa's neck. "Who loves this baby girl? Who?" she asked, pulling something from her pocket.

Tessa smiled, knowing what Nina had. Yet another toy Noa didn't need but would end up with anyway because Auntie Nina spoiled her rotten.

Noa bounced gleefully in Nina's arms, tugging on her hair, her toothless smile wide with adoration for her aunt the vampire.

Tessa loved when everyone gathered here in their backyard like this. They tried to do it at least twice a month, and in the process, she'd met Katie's grandmother Teeny; Greg's mother, Svetlanna; and Nina's grandmother Lou.

Add in Katie's assistants from her veterinary practice, Kaih and Ingrid; Phoebe's assistant, Mark; Jeannie's girlfriends, Betsy and Charlene; Guido the Witch Doctor and his new fiancée, Astrid, and it was a full house.

She loved sitting under the big oak trees and spreading blankets under them, watching everyone just be together while music played and laughter grew rich in the air.

She loved cooking, for everyone who could eat, that is, and swapping recipes with Arch and Jeannie. Loved the laughter that ensued—loved when Nina and Sloan fought over touch football and Keegan and Heath had to break them up while Sam, Clay, Shaw, Harry, and Greg snickered behind Sloan's back.

She loved that Darnell and Frank had become such good friends and Darnell was teaching Frank how to live his life as a good minion without getting caught. She loved that both of them came to read to Noa once a week without fail—sometimes sharing a meal, sometimes just swinging on the hammock Mick had installed over the summer.

She loved that Carl babysat for them, taking Noa on long walks in the backyard so she and Mick could have an adult night out. She loved that she and Mick had learned to fly together.

Whoever said that the Mile High Club was overrated sorely underestimated dragons' nookie—in flight.

She loved that they were teaching Noa to fly, too. Her wings had popped out the first week after her birth, and everyone said they were the spitting image of Tessa's. She didn't love that it was a helluva lot harder to keep track of a baby who could fly—especially seeing as Noa wasn't even walking yet—but she wouldn't change it.

She loved that Arch insisted Noa know him as her grandfather, and was teaching her how to cook before she could even walk. She loved that every single husband of every single woman in the group had come to help Mick put the addition onto her small cottage.

She loved it even more that with so many paranormal men in the mix, it had only taken seven hours and twenty-two minutes, by Wanda's stopwatch, before Noa had her own bedroom and Mick and Tessa had a bathroom fit for a king.

She loved that Marty, Nina, Wanda, Katie, Phoebe, and Mara insisted that their offspring, Fletcher, Mimi, Charlie, Hollis, Alistair, and Daniel, along with Penny, Skyped together with Noa no less frequently than once week.

Sometimes, even Casey and Clay's perpetual teenager, Naomi, joined in, haughty adolescent disdain and all. Their chats had strengthened Tessa's sense of family, strengthened the decision to give Noa people in her life who weren't just like her, but people she could always trust, people who would love her no matter what.

It was always chaos, but Tessa loved it all with every breath she took.

Nina held up a book made of thick material that squeaked when she pressed the middle of it and handed it to Noa. "This is for you, fairy princess. It's all about how my snugglebunny came to be. On this day, seven months and thirteen days ago, your mommy plunked you right out into my hands. Go, Team Noa!"

Noa nabbed the book in her chubby hands, jamming it in her mouth to gum it, making everyone laugh.

Nina laughed, too, sweeping Noa away, taking her to where Carl and Joe-Joe and the other children sat by the swings.

Tessa sighed with happiness. Their lives were so blessed. The day had turned out perfectly. She turned her face up toward the waning late-September sun. "Who woulda thunk it, huh, Malone?"

Mick gathered her in his arms, fitting her to him as he had so many nights since they'd become an official couple. "Thunk what?"

"That all of this would come from swallowing some dragon scales? That you and I would have a baby and be getting married next month. That we'd meet all these people who've become such a huge part of our world?"

Mick kissed the tip of her nose, his grin happy and warm. "Would you have had it any other way?"

Standing on tiptoe, she kissed his lips. Lips she loved on the man she'd always loved. "And miss all this crazy with you? All this wonderful, amazing crazy? Not in a million years, Gigantor."

Not in a million.